I0760773

PRAISE FOR
REDEMPTION

"*Children of the Gods* is a must-read for fans of fantasy, romance, mythology, YA or anyone looking for a great read. Five stars!"

—**KAT ROSS**,
BEST-SELLING AUTHOR *of*
THE FOURTH ELEMENT SERIES

"I've loved following Elyse and her friends as they've grown and fought, loved and lost. This last book brought the series to a wonderful close."

—**MERADETH HOUSTON**,
BEST-SELLING AUTHOR *of*
THE COINCIDENCE MAKERS

"The Children of the Gods trilogy is highly recommended and has earned the Literary Classics Seal of Approval."

—**LITERARY CLASSICS BOOK AWARDS**

REDEMPTION

CHILDREN OF THE GODS
BOOK 3

JESSICA THERRIEN

FROM THE TINY ACORN...
GROWS THE MIGHTY OAK

Redemption
Children of the Gods, Book 3
Second Edition

Acorn Publishing
WWW.ACORNPUBLISHINGLLC.COM

Cover design by Damonza

ISBN-13: 978-1-952112-47-8

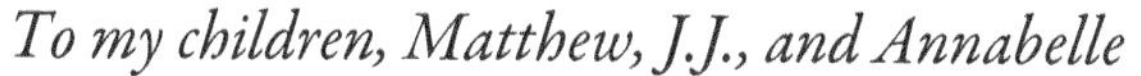

To my children, Matthew, J.J., and Annabelle

I love you more than all the planets, and all the moons,
and all the stars...

PROLOGUE

OUR SECRET WAS OUT. AS I LAY AWAKE BESIDE William the night after my escape, it was the first time I allowed that thought to sink in. Of the hundreds of Descendants who sought refuge in these caves months earlier, only my friends and family had waited for me to return. The rest were out there, and the world was watching.

A part of me felt relief. It was out of my hands. Those who'd trusted and followed me were free, and in a different way, so was I. No more prophecy weighing me down. Still, as the twinkling lights that lit the cave at night dimmed and withdrew into darkness, I couldn't find peace enough to sleep.

After all I'd been through, the fighting, the death, the seclusion, I'd survived. We'd won. But I still felt like I'd lost the one thing I'd always counted on—William. I stared through the pitch black to where he slept next to me, warm and real. He was alive. He was mine. For that I was grateful, but my heart felt empty. He didn't remember.

He'd always told me he'd lose me to this war. I never imagined I'd be the one to lose him.

The moment I killed Christoph, the Council shifted generations. Dr. Nickel's power fell to his daughter, Edith. Now she was the one who could mimic the ability of any Descendant she came into contact with. The cave's stars belonged to her tonight. At first I was hopeful she could give her brother his memories back, but at her young age, she hadn't been in contact with many abilities, mind-wipers included.

A piece of me had been convinced I'd get William back, the man I married, the man who loved me before I knew him. Now our love was one-sided.

I stared at him through the darkness. He used to know me intimately. Knew my fears. My secrets. Now all of our wordless moments were lost. I wondered if he'd ever get any of it back, the tangled legs and warm skin of so many nights together.

WE MOVED OUT OF THE CAVES THE NEXT DAY. With so few of us left, there was no reason to stay. Dr. Nickel arranged for a house in a small town called Sattley nestled deep in the Sierras. It was private and surrounded by pine trees that reminded me of home. As the weeks passed, it inherited a nickname: The Compound. It was large enough to house all fourteen of us. The Nickels, Mac and Anna, and William and I had our own rooms on the top floor, while Nics, Sam, Paul, and Rachel shared rooms on the bottom floor across from Edith, Chloe, Kara and Alex.

In the mornings the kitchen warmed with the smell of breakfast, and at night the cool evening air carried the fresh smell of freedom through the open windows.

Things were too normal. Too calm. It had me on edge.

"Yes!" Sam jumped to his feet in the middle of the living room. "Did you see that?" He slapped William on the shoulder as he passed, forgetting his best friend wasn't who he used to be. They shared an awkward moment before William continued on into the kitchen.

"Okay, so you beat me." I struggled over my pregnant stomach to pick up my cat's eye shooter from the floor and moved to the leather sofa. "I'm terrible at Marbles." I smiled, pretending I wasn't dwelling on what was happening in the real world.

William stepped in front of me with a bowl of stew.

"Is that for me?" My mouth watered at the smell of garlic and beef broth.

"No. It's for the baby," he teased. He sat next to me and put the bowl on the coffee table. "*This* is for you." He lifted a napkin off a plate like a magician revealing his trick. Voila—two chocolate chip cookies. "Mrs. Nick—" He stopped himself. "Mom just baked them."

Mrs. Nickel smiled at me as she closed the oven door.

She'd been extra doting since she'd found out her first grandchild was on the way.

"I see how it is," Sam complained. "The pregnant girl gets all the good stuff. I wish I could get pregnant." He winked at me.

"Ha!" Nics laughed. "I'd pay to see that."

I rubbed my gigantic watermelon-sized stomach. "Believe me. If I could trade places with you, I would. You want to carry this belly around for a while?"

Sam chewed on his lower lip. "Yeah, not really."

"There's plenty more," Mrs. Nickel said, placing a plate on the coffee table. "Save some for Paul and Rachel." The two of them were gone more often than not these days, taking advantage of their freedom to fly wherever they liked.

Sam grabbed a cookie and took a bite. "Okay, who's next?" he asked, turning his fingers into guns and shooting them at Nics.

"Only if you want to get crushed," she said from her seat on the floor.

Chloe scooted closer to the yarn circle taped to the oatmeal-colored carpet. "I'll go."

I opened my mouth to egg her on, but stopped as I heard laughter down the hall that wasn't there before.

"At least take this with you." William reached for the bowl of stew as I pushed myself off the couch.

The door at the end of the hall closed with force, but I didn't care. I needed to know how things were out there. I turned the knob and stepped into the room.

Alex pulled his lips from Kara's as soon as he saw me. The two of them straightened up and tried not to smile.

"You could knock," Kara said, giving me a look.

"You can hear my thoughts." I glanced away. "You knew I was coming."

She turned back to Alex, who brushed a thick black curl away from her apple cheeks, and shrugged. "I was... distracted."

"So what happened?" I asked.

"What do you think happened? Same thing every time, Elyse," Alex answered. His hair, a shade darker than Kara's, made his eyes seem too blue. "Why don't you just watch the news?"

"They won't let me," I said, my voice raised with irritation.

"It's on all the time," William said from behind me. "We needed a break." He raised his eyebrows. "*She* needed a break."

Alex nodded, his constant smirk pulling into his cheek. He reached into his back pocket and pulled out a rolled-up magazine. "Those crazy humans can't get enough." He threw it at me, and I caught it against my chest. "The paparazzi do get a little annoying." He kicked his shoes off and stretched out on his bed, hands behind his head like he was sunbathing in bliss.

I unrolled the magazine and shook my head. A smug picture of Alex posing on top of the Golden Gate Bridge took up most of the cover, and around the edges were other Descendants flaunting their skills. In the four months since Christoph's death, there were those who'd made names for themselves. They had fans, appeared on talk shows. They'd become celebrities overnight, and Alex was one of them.

I threw the glossy roll of pages back at him. "This isn't a game, Alex. It's too soon for this."

"Come on, Elyse. We finally have freedom. What did you expect?" Kara said, loosening the laces on her army boots. "Besides," Alex's cocky tone seeped into her voice, "they love us."

"I'm just saying that we should be preparing for their reaction, not posing for pictures."

"What if this is their reaction?" Alex jumped in.

I crossed my arms. "I know you don't honestly believe that."

"No, we don't," Kara added, "but we're going to enjoy it while it lasts. You should too."

I turned to leave, too frustrated to continue the conversation. They were being reckless, and they knew it. Or maybe I was just being pregnant. Either way I needed to get out of this house.

I stopped before I went through the door, my fingers lingering on the wooden frame. "Did you find anything?" I asked without looking back.

Soon after my escape we'd returned and buried Alex's father, but that still hadn't given him closure. He claimed these adventures were just for fun, but I knew he was searching for her. His sister.

"No," he answered.

I let my fingers fall and heard William shut the door behind me.

Nobody looked up from the marble game as I passed through the living room and walked out the front door. They were used to my fits of paranoia by now. I headed for the shed. I knew Mac would be there. At least he was on my side.

I pushed the door open with force. "Alex is on the cover of Starz posing on top of the Golden Gate Bridge."

Mac grunted with disapproval. "I'd say they're gonna get themselves killed, but I might end up doing the job." He turned back to the twelve-inch TV above the mini fridge, accidentally knocking a can of nails to the ground. He was a giant in this shed. So was I. Both of us stared at the pointed metal pieces and silently agreed to leave them.

I hoisted my awkward body onto the stool beside him.

"You forgot your food," William said appearing in the open doorway.

"Thanks." I took the bowl and stared down at my belly. "There's a lot in my stomach already. I'm not sure this is going to fit."

I took a bite and he laughed. "So you *do* still have your sense of humor." He stepped inside the shed. "Don't worry. I won't tell anyone."

"Yeah, we wouldn't want anyone to think the pregnant lady was acting normal, right? Then they might actually take me seriously."

"Imagine that," Mac mocked, his eyes still glued to the local news. I watched with him as a cocky Alex-type grew webs between his fingers for a crowd.

"It's not me. It's them," I said through another bite. "Right?" I raised my eyebrows as I waited for an answer.

William squinted like he was trying to see through me. "This isn't some pregnancy trap type question is it?"

I laughed. "Yes, it is. And the correct answer is, *Right, Ellie. You're absolutely right.*"

He pulled up the empty stool so he could sit next to me. "Do you really want to know what my memory-less head thinks?"

I licked the salt from my lips and answered with a sigh. "Yes."

"Okay." He swiveled a little on the stool. "I think you're stuck in the past. The war is over, Ellie. You killed Christoph, broke up the Council, and Descendants and humans are living together in peace. There's nothing else for you to do."

I stirred my stew in vicious circles as I tried to keep myself from bubbling over. "I see what you're saying. It's just...what if something happens? What if the world gets scared? What if this gets out of hand?"

He nodded at the bowl, and I took another bite. "First of all, that's not your problem anymore." For the briefest moment I saw the old William shine through, the one who wanted to keep all of this war away from me. "And second of all, yeah, it probably will get out of hand. But until it does we just need to live our lives."

CHAPTER ONE

I LURCHED AWAKE, AND AN UNNATURAL MOAN forced its way through my lips. The pain wasn't gradual. It didn't wait for me to be ready.

"What?" William breathed from next to me. He sat up, looking at me through the moonlight.

I braced myself against the mattress and lay back down, curling into a ball. I couldn't talk.

He kicked the blankets off and came around to my side of the bed. "Are you okay? Is it time?" He crouched down to eye level and placed his warm palm to my pregnant stomach. I pushed it away without thinking.

"I'm sorry," I breathed. I didn't want it there. I didn't want to be touched. "I..." I couldn't explain. I couldn't think. Pain. All my brain had room for was pain. I clutched the sheets, forcing all my muscles to stiffen so I wouldn't move, as if that would make it stop. It didn't. Nothing did. Not any position.

"I'm going to get someone," William said, standing to leave.

I grabbed his hand. "Don't." I didn't want an audience for this. If the baby was coming, I wanted to shut myself up in the dark and find my own way through. I dealt with things better alone. "Just you." Every word I uttered seemed to take all of my strength.

"I don't know what to do." His voice was thick with doubt, breathy and tense. "I can use my ability. It would—"

"No," I interrupted. "I want to feel it." I sucked breath through my teeth. Some part of me felt like this was a challenge, like it was some right of passage into womanhood. I was stronger than this. I would beat it just like I beat Christoph.

"Okay." William brushed my hair from my face. "Is there *anything* I can do? What should I do?"

"Don't talk."

He nodded, taking hold of my hand as I clenched my jaw so hard I thought my teeth might shatter. It wasn't supposed to be like this. Anna's labor had been gradual. This was so sudden. I wasn't ready for it to be unbearable so quickly. I let my features twist as another wave of pain came, one right after the other, the next always more severe than the last. Maybe Descendant births were different. Maybe it would be over soon.

—

"I can't do this," I said in tears, hours later in the dead of night.

William took my face in his hands. His golden hair fell into his eyes as he held me in stillness. "Yes you can. I know you can." There it was. That glimpse of the old him. That piece that had been missing. His lips touched mine. A moment of what had been between us. "You're strong, Elyse. Just breathe."

I shook my head. "I *can't* breathe."

As I blinked the tears away I expected my vision to clear, but the room was fading, and my entire body broke into a cold sweat. The pain was more than I could take. It would kill me. I was sure of it. Colors around me began to bleed into each other, and just before everything pulled away I got one last glimpse of William. He moved his mouth, but I couldn't hear the words.

When my surroundings shifted I realized what was happening. The pain that had clouded my head was gone, and I knew this was one last vision, the final images my daughter would give me before our connection was broken. Before she alone became the oracle of our generation.

I found myself in a dimly lit apartment. It was loud. The kind of loud that makes you stop and look up. The sound of engines roaring. Everything was vivid. More so than my visions had been in the past. I could smell the smoky air. The ceiling rained dust as an explosion rocked the building from the outside.

"Get down. Over here," William said, pulling me to the floor.

I pushed my back against a wall and William stood

over me, using his body as a shield from the falling debris.

"It's okay," I said to him, but my words were more to calm my own heart. "We survive this. I've seen it." I tensed as another blast shook the floor.

William looked down, his hair brushing against the tight muscles in his cheeks. "I'm not taking any chances."

I covered my face as the walls shuddered. The air felt thick and chalky, hard to breathe.

The sound of Edith's voice made me look up. "Hello?" I'd never seen a girl become a woman in so little a time. Only months ago she was William's little sister, amber hair, freckles, braiding my ponytail as we sat on the floor. Now she was anyone we needed her to be, and today, we needed her to get us out of here.

The room blurred like watercolors seeping together, the vision shifting to a new time and place, and within seconds silence replaced the chaos of sound around me.

I was no longer in the room, no longer with William. I stepped over rubble, and bits of glass cracked against the pavement under my feet. On one side of me buildings were toppled and leaning into each other for support, their windows punched through like missing teeth. Crushed cars rested under metal beams and pieces of walls that used to be structures. Bodies of the dead lay abandoned in the streets, left behind by those who'd survived. The wreckage smoldered, as if the city was trying to breathe around the destruction. I inhaled the thick air and choked out a cry. To my right everything was leveled. I could see over the gray water of the bay. The cables of the Golden Gate snapped and twisted in the distance, the red metal protruding from the sea like the skeleton of a serpent. I put my hand to my mouth, trying not to let the anger and grief pour out of me.

My chest felt tight, sick with regret as some other part of me recognized what I was witnessing, like realizing the mind is dreaming while still asleep. This was a vision, which meant this was coming. I closed my eyes and dropped to my knees. I'd done this. I'd started it all. I reached for my belly without thought, but it was flat. Instead of my child, I was left with an aching hollow feeling. She was gone. Alive somewhere, but lost.

My hands pressed into the asphalt, and the stinging in my throat began to give way to tears.

"Sarah!" I called out, feeling empty without her.

The emptiness, the silence, it was final.

I clung to the vision as it pulled away, releasing me. Despite its devastation, it was my only escape. I woke with a gasp, shocked by the pain, which had not let up in my mental absence. It was too severe. Immediately I was pushed beyond coping, to a place where I couldn't talk or breathe.

"Ellie?" My best friend's voice lifted me out of it.

Only my eyes moved as I looked across the bed at her, my body trembling and wrapped in drenched sheets. "Help me, Anna," I whimpered.

She put a hand to my arm for comfort and smiled as

if apologizing. "That's what we all say."

I cried out, muffling the sound with a pillow.

William held his hands to his head, holding his hair out of his face. "She's okay, right?"

"No. Not really," Anna answered. "She's in labor. It's not fun." She knelt down beside the bed. "Ellie, look at me." I did, breathing hard. "Remember Chloe? Remember how wonderful it was? This is pain for a purpose. This is for your baby. Right?"

I nodded, trying to slow my shaking lips. Pain for a purpose.

William slid into the bed next to me, taking my hand in his. "If you feel like punching something or squeezing my hand until it breaks...I'm here. I can take it."

Even without his memory it was in his nature to try and lighten the mood when things were tense, but I wasn't capable of laughing. Instead I looked at him, seriously considering the offer. He tightened his grip on my hand as the next wave came, and I rolled into him, burying my face into his chest.

"Make it stop," I moaned, and he did the only thing he could do.

"Okay," he whispered. Heat grew between our palms the way it always had, proof of our connection, and as it began to spread up my arm I felt relief. Not completely but enough to sooth the worst of it. I let the euphoria of his ability take me, carry me away to a place where he was more important than pain, than life, than breathing.

As my eyes lifted, he leaned in to press his mouth to mine. "I couldn't help it."

"Thank you," I whispered against his lips.

—

WHEN SARAH WAS BORN I PULLED HER INTO MY chest, staring into those baby eyes like I'd known her soul for all eternity. "I love you, sweet girl," I said. Tears spilled over my cheeks in amazement. She was perfect. "Thank you for helping me. For saving me." My heart ached and throbbed with love, like it was bleeding life into me for the first time. How had I ever felt whole without her?

She looked nothing like me, but I recognized her daddy's golden hair in the blonde peach fuzz against her soft head. She had his long beautiful eyelashes, his chin, his nose. Her lips, stenciled pink against delicate powder-white skin pouted while she slept. Each feature exactly the way it should be in its tiny form. I'd never seen anything so miraculous as a living, breathing piece of myself suddenly real and in front of me. She was my proof, evidence that there was more to this life than I could ever understand, a gift from something higher that knew what it was all for. Her face pressed against my chest as I held her, and every muscle relaxed as I became a blanket of motherly warmth. She was my peace. My reason. My life.

William and Anna stayed with me until light began

to warm the windows with a soft glow. The sound of morning voices made their way through the walls, and the smell of breakfast followed.

"Should we go out there?" I asked, cradling Sarah as she slept.

"Only when you're ready," William answered.

"I *am* starving."

"I'll get you some food," Anna said. "You just rest."

As Anna opened the bedroom door, someone turned up the TV.

Breaking news this morning regarding the new race of Descendants that have emerged...

The voice faded as the door clicked shut behind her. I turned to William, still trying to listen, but I couldn't make out the words.

"Do you want me to go see what it is?" he asked.

I nodded.

Another fragmented sentence slipped through the door as he left.

The public's reaction has been divided since the mysterious bombing of the Statue of Liberty several months ago. People are being cautious...

I waited. Until it had been too long. Until I couldn't take it anymore. I pressed myself out of bed, carefully laying my sleeping baby in her bassinet, and stepped into the living room.

Only Chloe looked up. Her eyes said it all. I focused on the TV and joined in the grave quiet that had settled over the rest of them, Mr. and Mrs. Nickel, Mac, Nics, Sam, Paul and Rachel. We all watched as if the reporter was speaking directly to us.

We've been told they're primarily living in five communities in the U.S. Though some may be in other countries around the world. President McKinney has requested that all Descendants report to city hall buildings in New York, San Francisco, Chicago, Dallas, or Los Angeles in order to be properly registered. In his speech earlier today he made the point that it was only fair that all citizens of the United States be treated equally. Over the years Descendants have evaded our systems through what can only be explained as fraud. Though none will be charged with any crimes, they will need to be issued new social security numbers and sign up for any other necessary forms of identification.

"Thank you, Cathy," the news anchor said. "For more information on where to report, please visit our website."

Sam muted the TV. "So do we go, or not?"

"No way," Nics said from the couch.

Eyes began to lift in my direction. I opened my mouth to say something, but all I could think about was my baby and the vision I'd seen during her birth. Maybe this was the beginning of it all. This was what we'd fought for, integration of our races, but my gut was telling me to be cautious.

"We wait a few days," I answered. "See what the reaction is before we jump in head first."

"Good answer," Mac said from the kitchen as he cooked, his brawny back still to me. "This isn't over."

CHAPTER TWO

FOR THAT FIRST WEEK, SARAH WAS THE PERFECT distraction. She filled the house with smiles and kept us all entertained. For everyone else, having her here was a blessing. For me, it was terrifying. Every night I wrestled with sleep, my body wracked with nerves. The shakes came the minute the sun went down, and I was left with a crushing pain in my chest that came over me as I watched her rest. I was afraid to close my eyes, afraid I'd lose her if I couldn't witness every breath. Something in me, call it mother's intuition, knew she wasn't safe.

Like every morning, I held Sarah close to me as I stared at the television, light glaring off its black surface. I kept if off for a reason—it only made me worry. Mac was right. This wasn't over. What I'd seen in my last vision was worse than anything we'd encountered so far. I just didn't know how it tied in with everything else, when it would happen, or why.

As Sarah's baby eyes blinked up at me, I wished I could see through them, know what she knew. What would happen next? Could I change things?

"Okay now, bear with me," Chloe said from the kitchen as she opened the oven. It was just the two of us this morning. Everyone else had decided to keep up their training efforts with Mac, just in case. "This quiche is kind of an experiment."

She laughed, but the word *experiment* made me think of Christoph. It made my stomach pull in and feel sick. Who knew what he'd left behind after I'd killed him? He'd experimented on so many, humans and Descendants. I'd been a part of it. My mind relived the moments I'd tried to forget. Inescapable darkness and needles. I started to sweat as I thought about it. Baby girl kicked and squirmed, pulling me out of it, just like she had when it was happening. I smiled down at her, and that alone made me remember.

"Chloe," I said, sudden eagerness in my voice. "Can you watch her? She's being really good. I just fed her."

She laughed. "She's always good. I think she's only *really* cried maybe once."

"Okay, so will you?" I asked, standing as she came into the living room. "Just sit on the couch and don't move. Okay?"

"Yeah," she answered, her voice breathy and confused. "Where are you going, though? What's going on?"

"Just don't move. Sit here and be careful. Don't...just

hold her," I said a little nervous.

"I got it," she said with raised eyebrows.

I opened the front door. "If she needs me, I'll be in the shed. I'll be right back."

The shed was filled with weapons of all kinds. Even with everyone at training, handguns and rifles covered the work surface to my right. Knives, long and short, hung on the walls like pieces of art. I was used to seeing Mac here, but as expected, his stool was empty and the small boxy TV that usually lit the space with an eerie glow was turned off. I breathed in the smell of metal and wood as I stepped forward toward the mini fridge on the floor in the back. My fingernails tapped the insides of my palms with each step. I hadn't thought about what was inside for months. I hadn't known what to do with it. Now I did. At least I hoped I did.

I knelt down in front of the icebox, opened the door, and curled my fingers around the tinfoil wrapped cylinder. It was cold. Real. I peeled back the foil revealing the syringe beneath, and my eyes closed at the sight of it, remembering the torture Christoph had put me through. The feel of the needle penetrating my pregnant belly was too easy to recall, and bile rose up in my throat. I swallowed down the feeling and forced myself to remove the foil completely. As I held it up in the dim light, it shone a translucent yellow. It was all that was left of my amniotic fluid, what Christoph believed was the key to the oracle ability.

The way I saw it, it was now or never. I needed to know what was next, how to stop whatever was coming, and *I* had to be the one who used the fluid. Everyone Christoph had used it on had died. There had been countless failed injections, each life another for me to carry on my shoulders. But it would be different with me. It had to be. It came from my body.

I removed the sterile cap and flexed my arm, straightening my elbow to look for a vein. As I pressed the tip of the needle to my skin, something stopped me. I hesitated, resisting the impulsive urge to do what needed to be done.

I had a daughter now. No more foolish secrets. No more behind people's backs. I couldn't take these kinds of risks. Not without telling William. Even if he would try and stop me, he deserved to know.

"You're kidding, right?" William sat in the rocking chair across the room and looked up at me from under his eyelashes. He held the syringe in his hand as I bounced with the baby on the edge of the bed. "We have a daughter. What would happen to her if something went wrong?" He stood and turned away from me. "I can't even believe you're asking me this."

"That's *why* I think I should do it," I urged. "She's the one who showed me. She made sure I got the fluid before we left Christoph. This has to be the reason."

"How do you know for sure it was the reason?" He walked closer, watching the baby as he moved. "Did you see yourself being injected with it?"

"No," I admitted, "but what I saw during her birth, I can't just let that go."

He knelt down in front of me. "You have to." His eyes were pleading. "This isn't our fight anymore."

I shook my head in disagreement. "How can you say that?" Just this time, couldn't his love for me mean his support? "It will always be our fight, *because* we have a daughter. If we're not going to protect her from what's coming, nobody will."

He brushed a finger to her cheek, knowing at the very least I was right about that. "So what? I either let you risk your own life, or we both risk hers?"

"That's the way I see it."

He let out a heavy breath, the muscles in his square jaw tight as pulled wire.

"I shouldn't have to make this kind of choice."

"It's not a choice, William. You know that."

His eyes became narrow in his silence. I'd never seen anger so visible on his face.

"I was going to do it without telling you, but I didn't," I admitted, letting go of that secret.

"Is that supposed to make this easier?" he asked.

I looked away. This wasn't how I expected things to go.

"Why are you even asking for my permission if you aren't going to listen to me anyway?"

"I'm not asking for your permission. I'm trying to get

you to see things my way. I want your support."

"Well, I guess I don't see it your way. I don't see why Sarah's in danger if San Francisco is bombed. It's one city, and we're not even there. We're sixty miles from any city, and I can count the number of humans in this town on two hands. I don't even think anyone living here even knows we're Decendants."

"It's hard to explain. There was something else. There's more to this. I need to find out who did it, when, why."

"Why *you*?" He walked toward our bedroom window, facing away from me.

"Because, William." I stood to follow him. "It's *my* fault. I'll never be able to live with myself if I could have done something to save all those people. And if the bomb was meant for Descendants...well, I owe them because I did this."

He turned to face me. "Is that more important than your own daughter?"

"Nothing is more important than her, but I'm not afraid. I know this is what I'm supposed to do."

His face softened, and I could see him surrendering. "I don't think it's smart." He leaned down and kissed Sarah's forehead.

"It is if it means I can know what's coming. If it means I can protect her."

I stayed silent as he considered my point of view.

"When do you want to do it?" he asked without

looking at me.

I stared down at my daughter, the knot in my stomach softening.

"In the morning."

CHAPTER THREE

I DIDN'T WANT A LOT OF PEOPLE INVOLVED. MAC and Anna were the only two who followed William and I into the shed. We pushed toolboxes and weapons aside, but there still wasn't much breathing room. The air was stuffy. Shards of light seeped in through the planked walls inviting dust to dance through the beams. To anyone else the shed was a junk shack, but the familiar workshop smell conjured up memories of my father. If I *was* going to die today, this was as good a place as any.

"Put the blanket here on the floor," I said to Anna.

She motioned for Mac to hand her the broom in the corner.

"It's fine." I shook my head. "Just close the door."

Before she had the chance, Edith appeared in the doorway.

Anna shrugged off my look of disapproval. "You think I would really let you do this without a backup plan?"

I should have been expecting someone to insist she take part. She had made friends with Aaron, a descendant of Clotho, back in the Lenaia caves. If things really went wrong, if I did die, Edith would be able to bring me back. The thought should have comforted me, but instead I felt frustrated. I couldn't have her interfering before I saw what I needed to see.

"If you're going to be here, you have to do what I tell you," I said to her.

She pulled at the ends of her amber hair. "I know," she answered, stepping toward her brother. I looked to William, knowing her loyalty would be with him. He'd be the one to decide how far this went. His green eyes were unyielding.

Anna unrolled the wool blanket she'd been carrying under her arm and placed it on the floor.

Without a second thought I lay in the center of it. "Let's get this over with."

My hands trembled. Not for fear of death. It was the fear of knowing what was to come that shook me. The idea that even if I saw the future, I may not be able to stop it.

William knelt next to me and threaded his fingers between mine, the heat of our palms a familiar comfort.

"Thank you for not fighting me on this," I said.

His features were tense, but he tried to smile.

He leaned forward, stopping just before our lips met.

"Please come back," he whispered. I stared into his eyes, so close I could see where the green bled into brown.

"I will," I promised, but we both knew that when I did, nothing would be the same. He pushed his soft lips into mine and held them there too long.

Anna sat still and quiet to my right, silently supporting me, but I could feel her nerves. She put a hand to my arm as Mac's rough fingers pinpointed the vein above my collarbone.

"Last chance, kid," Mac said as he shifted his heavy knees on the floor next to me. His thick fingers were steady as he held the syringe, and the muscles in my neck tightened. I swallowed and nodded for him to go ahead. "Good luck."

My eyelids pressed together as the needle bit into my skin. Before I could open them, my head split down the center, like the swift thrust of a blade, piercing from chin to brow. An awful sound escaped my lips but was stifled by a sharp light that seemed to press from behind my eyes until it broke me into a thousand pieces. Until there was no longer a mouth to make sound, only a memory of a part of me that used to exist.

In place of the pain there was another existence, one of the mind, one that felt like reliving memories. A drifting consciousness that I could only assume was the future. A line of people curled around a building. Inside, signs read *No Abilities During Registration*. Surrounding the snake of unsure Descendants, police wore clear plastic shields over their faces as if that would protect them or at least separate the air they breathed from those around them. They wore thick black body armor and carried guns.

At the front, a young girl reached her arm out in front of her. It trembled as a woman in a white coat grasped her hand and held a metal device against the soft part of her wrist.

"Ability?" the woman asked without looking up.

"I can take away sound." The girl's words were little more than a whisper.

"Bloodline?"

"Harpocrates."

The young Descendant cried out as the machine punched her skinny arm like a time clock. She pulled it back when she was able and held it to her chest. Her eyes flickered toward the pain and found a barcode tattooed and something imbedded under the thin skin.

"Line 3," the woman instructed. "Next!"

Then everything shattered like a wall of falling beads until something new was in front of me. Only there was no me. Images collapsed into a second of time. They flickered. One after the other like a vintage cartoon. More destruction. More death. Screaming. Starving. Blood. City after city turned to rubble. Until there was nothing. Until each one was only the corpse of a city and America was gone.

I found myself on a once busy street amidst the fallen

traffic lights and upturned cars. My body somehow returned to me. A calmness had settled over the destruct-tion, like the enemy waiting for the smoke to clear. I stepped forward, heart beating in my throat. The sun painted everything in gold, dancing off of metal and glass like the sea at dusk, making beauty out of devastation. It blinded me with its light so that everything was gleaming and silhouetted in shadow.

I stood still as a figure stepped through the wreckage, through the sun's luster, into view. Her white hair blew in the breeze. Her aged cheeks wrinkled into a smile.

"Oracle," I whispered. "I thought you were dead."

"I am," she answered. "And if you stay, you will be too. You need to go back. You've been here too long."

"Where's here?"

"You only need to know one thing," she answered. "You need to lose to win." Her eyes turned down with regret, and I thought I saw them linger on my flat stomach. "I'm sorry."

I hugged my skinny frame, wrapping my hands around my belly, as if that would protect my daughter. She couldn't mean Sarah. I wouldn't lose her.

I opened my mouth to ask what she meant. Lose what? Lose how? But nothing came. Instead I felt my heart slow. Too slow. Things began to fade to black, like getting up too fast. I resisted it, forcing my eyes to focus, though my chest felt heavy, though my knees could buckle.

Lose what? I tried to form the words, but my lips felt sewn shut. The black throbbed against my eyes in rhythm with the slow beat of my heart. Pain seared inside my head. I felt myself breaking apart. My vision pulsed. Harder, until tears tickled my cheeks.

"Go." I didn't hear her say it, but I recognized the way her lips moved around the word.

A tear hit the top of my hand. Then another. They dripped quickly from my chin onto my shirt, my shoes. Not clear. Not watery. Thick. A bright blood red.

I gasped awake, unaware I wasn't breathing.

"Ellie!" My head was in Anna's lap. William's stacked palms were still pressing on my chest. I felt the weight of them over my heart.

He brought a palm to my face. "Are you okay?"

I nodded, still confused, but when he pulled his hand away it was covered in blood. I felt it now, the wetness on my face. The red tears I'd dreamt about.

"I need help over here." Mac's low growl sounded distressed.

Edith's young and delicate frame lay limp on the ground next to me. Blood trailed from her nose, a deeper red than mine, like black velvet.

"What happened?" I asked, but I didn't wait for an answer, and no one offered one.

Instead, I pushed myself to my knees, ignoring the throbbing in my eyes. Ignoring the way the room spun as I moved. *What did I do?* I pressed the buttons on my healing bracelet, and flinched as the blades punctured my skin to draw blood. It had been a while since I'd had to use it. Mac held Edith's lips open as the blood dripped over her tongue. My head went fuzzy, but I didn't care. William took my free hand, and the warmth spread quickly over my fingers, up my palm, up my arm. Things seemed brighter, and my head cleared just as Edith's eyes blinked open.

She wiped the blood from her nose as she sat up, and we were all silent.

"What happened?" I repeated.

"You died." Edith's child-like face had lost a little more of its innocence. Her forehead was tight and serious. "I used Aaron's ability to bring you back."

I remembered the night Aaron saved Rachel. If it hadn't been for his ability she wouldn't be here now. Neither would I.

"Are you okay?" I asked. I hadn't meant for anyone to get hurt.

She nodded.

"Haven't practiced that one yet have we, kiddo?" Mac grabbed her shoulder, testing her strength. "Sometimes those stronger abilities need a little more training. She's going to be one tough cookie pretty soon, though."

"Thank you," I said, taking her small hand.

Everyone was quiet around me, waiting, hoping it was all worth it.

"What did you see?" William asked.

I relived the whole experience. Every bleak moment until the end trying to find purpose in what I saw, going over every detail as if I'd missed some hidden clue, but none of it gave me the peace of mind I was looking for. I didn't see a clear path to follow or any way to stop it, and not one of them offered any advice. Their troubled eyes weren't helping me think.

I needed to be alone.

I left the shed and sat at the base of a pine tree amidst the dry weeds trying to come to terms with what I knew had to happen. One thing had never been clearer—Sarah wasn't safe. My throat stung at the thought, and tight sobs formed in my chest. Every instinct in me fought the idea, but something deeper had already made the decision. The same part of me that would always fight to survive also fought to protect her. She was a part of me, the most important part.

William approached slowly, still unsure of my boundaries. I stared ahead into the trees as he sat next to me.

"Sarah's crying. I tried, but..."

I bit my lip, forcing down the throbbing guilt. "It's because she knows."

"About what you saw?"

"No." A sob rose into my throat, and I felt my face twist and ready itself for tears. When I was alone I could be strong, but facing the truth out loud made it too real. "She knows what I decided. I have to finish this, and I can't do it with her around. She won't be safe."

I turned to William, desperate for him to understand. He took my hands. "What do you mean?" he asked quietly. "She's ours. *We* have to keep her safe..."

"What if we can't?"

His brow wrinkled with a mix of sorrow and apprehension as he let my hands slip back into my lap. "Of course we—"

"The oracle said I had to lose to win." My dark hair covered my face as I studied the tiny blades of dry grass around my ankles. "What if she meant Sarah? I can't lose her."

"I won't let that happen, Ellie." My nickname rolled sweetly off his lips for the first time in months.

"There's still a fight to be won. If I can stop this from happening...I have to. I'm the only one who knows what's coming."

He straightened up and dragged a hand through his golden hair. "What are you saying?"

"Sarah can't stay here. Not with all of us. She needs to be protected..." suddenly this life I was mapping out for her seemed too familiar. It was my life. My childhood. A girl without her mother. "She'll be safer alone, with Anna and Mac." I knew what this decision might mean. My shoulders tightened in preparation for his reaction. "You don't have to stay with me. I can do this alone."

He didn't speak, but I could see the frustration in the tight pulse of his jaw muscle.

"Is this how it was before? You always called the shots?"

"It's the right thing to do, William."

I'd never felt our love so divided. At any moment our hearts would collide.

"Not for me." He stood, pacing in front of me with his hand on his neck. "Look. I've tried to be the person everyone wants me to be. I've tried to be the perfect husband. Haven't I been there for you?" He didn't wait for an answer. "But I can't do this." I stayed quiet, dreading his next words.

I couldn't look at him. He stopped in front of me and fell to his knees. "Elyse. I don't mean that I don't have feelings for you." He tilted my chin up so our eyes connected. "I do." He took a breath, putting space between the good and the bad. "I just love her. More than anything else..."

I nodded, letting the final blow hit me in the chest.

"More than me," I finished for him.

I couldn't blame him. I loved her more than him, too, and she needed him. One of us, at least. Still, I felt myself collapse under the pain of losing them both.

"You should probably pack then," I whispered.

"Elyse—"

"It's okay," I interrupted. My cheeks stung as I thought about saying goodbye. "It's for the best."

I'D NEVER LOOKED SO DEEPLY INTO SOMEONE AS I DID when I held her for that last aching moment. Before I let go. I could see eternity in her silvery blue eyes. They owned me. Her powder soft cheeks warmed my lips as I kissed her face, praying she'd forgive me. I never imagined I could love someone like I loved her. Her body pressed against me was an extension of my own. To give her up would leave nothing but promises where my heart should be. Still, I stood up from my seat on the bed, regretting each step as I walked toward the door of my bedroom.

These last seconds alone were ours. They ticked away like they were nothing. I stopped with my hand on the doorknob and a knot in my throat. *They won't love her like I do.* The thought made my eyes brim with tears. It didn't matter. It was *because* I loved her that I had to do this.

Outside Mac, Anna, and Chloe were waiting with Edith. Their bags were packed. William was at my side as I clutched Sarah to my chest.

"You're sure you want to do this?" he whispered into my ear.

I couldn't look away from her. "Of course I don't *want* to. I have to."

Mac cleared his throat, forcing me to glance up. He stood so stiff I could see the worry in his bones, but he hadn't disagreed with me yet.

"We'll be fine," Anna said to me. I tried to keep my

eyes on her, but they drifted toward Sarah, and my heart tightened in my chest. It was desperate to keep her, like it wouldn't beat when she was gone.

I nodded, afraid if I tried to speak, nothing but sobs would come out.

Chloe took my hand. "We love you. We'll take care of her."

The hollowness that formed inside me when my mother died crept up like a dark secret I'd always wanted to forget. It was a darkness that never strayed too far. Was I doing the same to her? Now all of my mother's sacrifices made sense. I'd blamed her for my solitude, my loneliness, my life back then. Now I understood. I was doing this for my daughter. No sacrifice would be too great.

I looked up at the sky and blinked the tears into thin sheets of strength over my eyes. William took her from me, and my skin went cold without her body there to warm it.

"Please go," I said. If I waited any longer I would break.

CHAPTER FOUR

I CALLED EVERYONE INTO THE LIVING ROOM. RACHEL and Nics were in their pajamas snuggled up on the couch. Dr. Nickel, who was at the table discussing abilities with Edith over breakfast, stood up and stepped closer. Alex and Kara appeared by the front door in the clothes they had been wearing yesterday.

"Here's the situation," I announced. Getting down to business was the only way to hold myself together. I stood in front of them as a hollow body masked by black leggings and a hoodie. Everyone I loved had left with a piece of me. "During Sarah's birth I had one last vision. Mac was right. This isn't over." Curious faces watched as I explained everything I knew about the devastation to come. When I was finished, my empty heart skipped in the uncomfortable silence. "Sarah will be with William until we figure out what to do."

"Do you know what to do?" Alex asked. For once he

was curious, not defiant. Black tufts of his windblown hair had yet to settle, and he combed a hand through it.

"I don't have much to go on." I repeated the oracle's words. "*We have to lose to win.* That's all she said. I'm not sure what that means yet."

We. I'd chosen the word without thought, but doubt began to circle like a vulture. Maybe *I* was the only one destined to lose something.

"Well, we can't let them blow up cities," Rachel insisted. She stood up from the couch, adamantly. "If we know it's coming, we have to try and warn people."

She'd changed over the months. The superficial bubbly girl I'd met back in San Francisco had become someone new that night she died in the Lenaia caves. The bullet we'd lifted from her chest had left her more focused, determined. These days her cheeks shined with a passionate glow.

"I agree." I rested a hand on the back of my neck, then pulled it away. William's mannerisms had rubbed off on me, even in his absence. "I just don't think it's going to be that easy. They're not going to evacuate the country's most populated cities because we tell them to."

"She's got a point," Dr. Nickel added, crossing his arms in resignation. "Do we know who the threat is? Do humans or Descendants initiate the attacks?"

I picked at my thumbnail. "I'm not sure."

"It's unwise to act too soon," he continued. "We don't know who or what we're up against."

Sam turned his palms up unsatisfied. "We can't just do nothing."

"Maybe we can go directly to the people." Paul looked up from his folded hands. "Rachel and I were in LA yesterday and people were protesting. The whole 110 freeway was shut down with Pro-Descendant camps on one side and anti-us on the other. I don't imagine they have it cleared up. We could tell them the cities aren't safe. Word of mouth might do some good."

"Or it could spread panic," Kara countered. I could see her looking into the minds of those around her, drawing conclusions based on other people's thoughts. "We can't act until we have more information. As soon as things begin to escalate we can make a move. There's no sense in acting when we don't have a target. We'll just be drawing attention to ourselves."

I could see both points, but I didn't like the idea of waiting around for things to go wrong.

"Doing something is better than nothing," I agreed with Paul. Kara shook her head, and I tried to ignore the conflict in my gut. "Alex, keep us updated. If you notice anything else out of the ordinary while you're hopping from city to city, let us know and we'll go from there. In the meantime, get us to LA."

—

THE FREEWAY WAS A CAMPGROUND. A VILLAGE OF tarps and blankets spanned both sides of the once traffic-jammed Interstate like a technicolor quilt.

The sea of people terrified me. Mobs could be unruly and inhuman. Talk to the wrong person, and things were bound to get out of hand.

"How do we know which side supports us?" I asked, craning my neck to see past a group of tall men playing hacky sack.

Nics nudged me and nodded to a cardboard sign traced over multiple times in black ink. It read: *Descendants are people too. Down with the human race.*

My shoulders relaxed knowing we weren't surrounded by the opposing crowd, though too much enthusiasm could get us in just as much trouble.

An older man with a greying beard played a broken guitar behind us, singing lyrics to the sky with his eyes closed. *God bless the new gods. Let me be sacrificed for them.*

Sam cleared his throat and whispered under his breath to Paul and Rachel. "Anyone else feeling a little iffy about admitting to these people that we're Descendants?"

"I'd say about half of them are nuts," Kara added, looking over her shoulder as Alex trailed behind.

I led the way through the crowd, trying to decide the best possible group to start with. Snoring bodies hid in makeshift tents undisturbed as I kicked beer bottles aside, not bothering to step around the litter. This wasn't the warm welcome I'd been naïve enough to imagine.

We can always go back, Kara slipped into my thoughts.

I shook my head, still determined to make something good of the mess around us.

"Everyone take a buddy and find someone who's not crazy," I said, stopping to face my friends. "Don't give yourselves away if you can help it. Maybe say you heard something from a reliable source. I don't know." I glanced around orienting myself to the surroundings. "Meet back at this light post in fifteen minutes."

I pulled Nics by the hand, and Sam followed without question.

As I waded through the crowd, picketers began to circle near the center of the freeway. A line of police in riot gear formed the only barrier between the two sides. I slowed my pace as voices began to escalate. Jeers and taunts were shouted over the heads of the police blockade.

"This is crazy," I said as Nics passed me. I couldn't decide whether to stop and watch or get the hell away from it all. I let my gaze linger even as I slowly moved farther from the teeming train of people who marched with signs. A part of me admired them for their unwavering support, even if some were crazy.

Up ahead, Sam and Nics pushed past a wall of tattered umbrellas. I could make out a brown folding table with a megaphone resting on the corner as I followed.

Two teenage girls sat behind the table, and the one with braces stood as I approached. She smiled, flashing a mouthful of pink rubber bands and silver brackets. "Would you like a button?"

I took the circular pin from her hand and held it in my palm. One word stood out black and clean against its glossy white surface—*Freedom.*

"Thanks," I said, returning her smile. "We were wondering if you could help spread a message."

Her ponytail bounced as she nodded. "We've been doing that all day." She reached for the megaphone and raised a fist into the air. "Freedom is a right. Not a privilege."

I shook my head. "No...I mean, yes, you're right, but our message is different. The cities aren't safe. We've heard things from a reliable source and—"

Her eyebrows lowered into a glare. "Nice try." She raised a hand to her hips. "I know you're from the other side. We're not leaving."

"We're not from the other side," Sam chimed in. "She's telling the truth."

The girl rolled her eyes and snatched the freedom pin from my hand.

"Hang on," Nics groaned with annoyance before she could turn away. "You want proof. Here's your proof." Nics checked her surroundings and vanished just long enough to make her point. "Should I make you invisible next or are you ready to believe us?"

"Oh, I...um," she stuttered, fumbling with her megaphone as her gaze darted back and forth between the three of us. Then realization struck and her eyes widened. "The cities aren't safe. We have to—"

"ALEX!" The shrill shriek of ten female voices at once echoed somewhere in the distant crowd.

Within seconds he was in front of me. "Ready?"

He disappeared again as the voices calling his name headed our way. Before I could even give Nics my *I'm confused* look another voice screeched his name and he reappeared again.

"Yeah, not so easy for me to stay discrete. People are recognizing me." Alex checked behind him then to his right as the screaming fans closed in. "Can we go now?"

He didn't wait for an answer.

Over the next few weeks we did our best to spread the word that the cities weren't safe. Whenever a protest erupted rallying for Descendant rights, we were there, but one small group at a time wasn't working the way I'd hoped.

The quiet moments were hardest. When Sam and Nics locked themselves in their room to fight or kiss. When Paul and Rachel took trips to new places. When Alex and Kara disappeared without a word. Every day that passed without my baby girl, without William, was one more day I could have been with them. I spent my free time trying to outrun my demons, finding distractions wherever I could. The floors were spotless, the sink free of dishes, the bathrooms scrubbed. Anything that took my mind off of what was missing seemed better than sitting still.

Sleep was nearly impossible. Each night I'd wake to the empty room, my neck damp with a cold sweat, my hands searching the darkness for something, for the pieces of my heart that were missing. I never tried to hide from the emptiness. I didn't close my eyes and push it away. Instead I let that sharp ache sit inside my chest until I felt the urge to run. To beat it.

Running was my way of pushing forward, of fighting my way toward her, toward the end. Like every night for the past week, I dressed in running shorts and quietly laced up my boots before sunset. I needed my feet to get used to moving in them again. The evening air combed through the pine needles and slid past my skin, fresh and cold, washing away the hurt. With my dart gun strapped to my left thigh and a gun to my right, training was the only way I knew how to deal with my loss.

When I was far enough away from the house, I took off into a sprint. It felt good. My body remembered how to move, but it wasn't as strong as it used to be. Pregnancy had taken its toll, and my burdens weighed me down. My muscles tensed as I pushed myself as fast as I knew I could go. My lungs burned and my sides ached with each step, but I welcomed this new pain. As my heart raced, it didn't get a chance to pulse with sorrow. Instead it had to work and struggle. I felt grateful for the cold air that stung my arms, my face, my bare thighs and calves. I breathed it in, working my lungs in a way they hadn't been worked in so long.

I aimed the gun at a nearby tree and fired. The bullet broke the bark with a loud crack. It's true what they say about taking your aggression out with your finger on a trigger. It released something, like shaking rust from my bones. I ran and fired. Again and again. Until I was out. I reached for my dart gun next, and tried to work my breath behind each shot, even as my lungs struggled to keep up with my quick pace. It was harder than I remembered. I slowed to a walk and the prickle of sweat crept over my skin. I missed the itchy sting of exertion. I promised myself I was going to train every day until my body came back.

I found myself sitting at the base of my favorite pine breathing in the smell of sap and dry needles. The earthy scent wrapped itself around me, close and familiar. I wanted to stay hidden in the hollow of my tree forever, but it wasn't long before someone came looking for me.

Sam found me and folded his long body up next to mine on the ground. He didn't say anything at first. We just sat and watched the light fade against the trees. I was glad he came, but something about his silence made my eyes sting.

His long arm reached for my shoulder, and he pulled me into a hug without asking. I didn't resist.

"I've been thinking," he said, keeping his arms around me. "I'm kind of in need of a new wingman."

I laughed against his chest, happy to have a friend.

"Yeah?"

"Maybe it's just me, but this new William hasn't been much of a buffer. It's like he lost his memories or something. I don't know."

I pulled away, letting his lightheartedness lift me out of the fog. "I kind of got that feeling too."

He tapped his Pumas against the soft dirt. "Seriously though, someone's got to be the middle man with me and Nics or eventually she's going to scold me to death."

I nodded. "Good luck with that."

"Good luck? No way, you're not getting out of this. I'm not joking about the wingman thing." He shook his sandy hair, dappled with streaks of grey that shouldn't be there. "First assignment. Protect me from her at the bonfire."

"Bonfire?"

"Yeah, Rachel wants to roast marshmallows." He raised his eyebrows. "I told her sugar wasn't going to make it all better, but she's insisting. And Nics is on her side, so neither of us really has a choice."

THE FIRE STRETCHED ITS ORANGE WINGS INTO THE night air, fighting the dark with sharp fangs of light. The flickering color made the faces around it glow. Kara sat on the dirt between Alex's legs and leaned her head into his chest. Nics jabbed the ruby embers with a stick, releasing wafts of sparks that floated up to Rachel and Paul.

The two of them danced above the flames in the undulating waves of heat.

Rachel descended as I approached with Sam. "You got her to come," she said with wind-blown hair.

"Who can say no to marshmallows?" I shrugged with a fake smile.

I grabbed a stick and sat next to Alex and Kara.

"*I* said no," Alex laughed. "Didn't work. She's got the whole night planned."

Sam took a spot next to me, but Nics was quick to give him a look that said he should be sitting next to her. My lips twitched into a smirk.

He shook his head at me as he passed. "Step it up, wingman."

"Okay," Rachel said to everyone with her hands on her hips. "We're going to do something really ridiculous but fun. We need to lighten things up a bit around here. No talking about plans or attacks or war." For tonight, I was glad she was slipping back to her normal cheery self. Her eyes singled each one of us out like she was challenging someone to protest. "We're playing truth or dare. No opting out. Everyone has to play."

Alex laughed. "Seriously? What are we, fifty? I'm not playing that."

"Oh don't be a wuss," Paul said, leaning over his knees. "Scared of a little truth or dare?"

"Fine." Alex rolled his eyes. "Why don't you go first?"

Paul shrugged. "Truth."

"Are you going to propose to Rachel?" A smirk crawled up Alex's cheek as Paul glared at him with closed lips.

No one spoke.

"Come on, Alex," I said with an edge to my voice. "He shouldn't have to answer that."

"Yeah," Rachel said busying herself with a package of graham crackers. "You don't have to—"

"I was planning on it," Paul interrupted her. Their eyes connected for a moment as if none of us were there.

"You were?" She broke the cracker with a sudden snap and cleared her throat. "When?"

"Nice try," he answered. "Half the surprise is already ruined. I'm not telling you anything else."

"You're such a jerk, Alex," Nics snapped, staring across the flames.

"He wanted to play," Alex taunted.

Rachel kept her lips tight, trying to hide her smile, but her eyes were so wide they could pop.

Paul bit the inside of his cheek and shook his head. "Can somebody else go?"

Kara's marshmallow caught fire sending pieces of flame into the black sky. "You have to pick someone." She peeled off the black layer of burnt sugar and blew on it before popping it into her mouth.

"Fine. Sam. Truth or dare?" Paul asked.

"Easy," he said, licking his fingers. "Dare."

"Kiss Nics."

Nics stopped poking the fire, and we all looked at her. Sam turned like he was actually going to do it. For some reason I expected him to laugh or tease her until she rolled her eyes, but his eyebrows rose in consideration and she got nervous.

"Um, excuse me, but don't I get a say in—"

His lips were on hers before she could finish. For a moment, Nics froze, and I could almost see her trying to decide how to react. I waited for her to pull back and slap him, for him to laugh it off as a joke. Instead, they were locked in the moment, despite the fact we were all staring in surprise, and when his hand reached for the back of her neck I saw her eyes soften.

She pulled away and shoved his shoulder, realizing we were all watching. "What the hell, Sam?" But it was too late. We'd all seen her enjoy it.

"Ha!" Paul clapped his hands together. "How long have you been waiting for him to do that, Nics, huh?"

"Oh shut up. It was a dare, all right?" She looked away embarrassed. "Somebody hand me a damn marshmallow."

"Pick someone else, Sam," Rachel said, nearly shaking from excitement.

"Okay." As he looked around I focused on making my marshmallow perfectly golden. "Nics," he said taking a bite of his s'more.

She cocked her head, causing her dreads to dangle

against her ear. "Why? Are you going to dare me to kiss you again?"

"Maybe." He shrugged.

She rolled her eyes and Rachel laughed through her teeth.

"Truth," Nics said.

"*Do* you want me to kiss you again?"

The corners of my lips pulled up.

"Maybe," she answered in a mocking tone.

Sam leaned in, and she shoved his chest. "Not here, jeez."

The bonfire was a good distraction. More than once I caught Sam watching me, trying to decipher whether or not my smiles were genuine. Sometimes they were, when I managed to forget what I was waiting for. Some sign that things had started.

Any day could be the end for millions of people. I had to think of something, a way to work faster.

I looked for Kara through the flickering flames, and she caught my gaze almost instantly.

I have an idea.

CHAPTER FIVE

I'D BEEN VIEWING ALEX'S FAME AS A BAD THING. UNTIL now, drawing attention to ourselves seemed too dangerous. Maybe it still was, but the people's attention was what I needed.

The five of us gathered around the TV as if it were Oscar night. Alex clutched a bowl of popcorn while Kara tucked herself into his side, snacking as we waited for the commercial break to end. Nics and Sam sat a little too close to each other on the couch and Paul and Rachel sprawled out amongst their bed of pillows on the floor.

"Shhh! It's on," Rachel hushed us with a wave of her hand.

BREAKING NEWS scrolled across the screen in big red letters as the national nightly news came back on the air along with dramatic music that sounded like a melodic morse code. An older gentleman with too-perfect grey hair addressed the American people with a serious voice.

"Earlier this evening we had the privilege of sitting down with one of the country's most well-known Descendants. It seems they have a message for us. One that isn't easy to ignore. Take a look."

The screen transitioned to a dimly lit living room with two formal armchairs facing each other. The newscaster sat in one and Alex in the other.

"Thank you for being with us, Alex," the older man said.

"Eh." Alex shrugged. "It's the least I can do before the end of the world."

My jaw dropped as Alex popped a crunchy kernel in his mouth and smiled.

"The end of the world?" I repeated. "What the hell, Alex? We're not trying to spread panic."

"Hey, you wanted people to get the message. This way they'll listen."

I turned back to the show, desperate to assess the damage.

The newscaster's brow sank in what seemed like mock concern. "What makes you say that?"

The Alex on TV leaned forward, clasping his hands and resting his elbows on his knees. "My friend sees things. She saw the cities blown to bits. We're thinking people need to get out while they can."

"Hmmm." For a moment the statuesque anchor broke character and threw a nervous glance off camera. "How certain are you? Do you have any sort of timeframe? I'm sure the American people have a lot of questions, one of which is how can we believe you?"

Before we could hear Alex's answer the screen flipped to a blocked multicolor pattern followed by a pitched warning tone—the emergency broadcast system.

We waited for it to clear, for a message to pass along the screen declaring it was only a test, but the tone continued and nothing changed.

"Jeez. Turn it off. That sound is annoying," Nics complained.

I shook my head. "I want to see what happens."

Alex clicked the mute button, and the five of us waited in silence a minute longer.

"You think it's just our TV or something?" Rachel wondered out loud.

"No. I don't," I answered.

"Check online," Alex said, nodding to Rachel. "We filmed it earlier so it should be on their website."

Rachel reached for the laptop on the coffee table and typed in the web address. I watched as her eyes searched the screen until she turned the computer my way. The video player was blacked out.

"This video is unavailable."

"Can they do that?" Paul scoffed in disbelief.

"I guess the network changed their mind," Sam said.

"It wasn't the network, Sam. They would've cut to a different program or story or something."

"Well, we got the message out in a way. He *did* say

the cities weren't safe," Nics reminded us.

"I guess we just wait and see what happens," Rachel concluded.

We didn't have to wait long. People had gotten the message. Within two weeks a visible migration of city dwellers packed up and fled. The internet and news media reported images of grid-locked freeways full of moving trucks and pickups loaded to the max. People had packed up their lives and ripped their families from their homes based on Alex's claim, on *my* claim.

Doubt played her games, toying with me whenever I was alone to think.

"Hey Rach," I said, peeking my head into her room.

"Yeah?" She finished toweling her wet hair and hung her damp towel on the hook by her bed.

"Feel like going to the store with me? Mrs. Nickel needs stew meat for dinner."

"Sure." She smiled. "I can't remember the last time I was in a car. It'll be fun."

We hopped in the family vehicle, a white Dodge Caravan. Dust swirled behind us as I drove down our dirt road toward the rugged two-lane highway that led to Sattley's local shop.

Nelson's Market was the only proof Sattley was an actually town. No other buildings marked its borders. Most houses were hidden in the depths of the evergreen forest, and the store itself looked more like someone's home than an establishment. The owners lived in the back and did their best to provide the many services needed by the town's residents. They were the post office, the butcher, the grocer. They sold fishing licenses, bait and poles. Saddles and dog food.

As the brown façade came into view I pressed my foot to the brake. Cars and trucks lined both sides of the road.

"Wow," Rachel said. "What's going on?"

"No idea," I answered, driving slowly past the small building.

With no place to park, I ended up adding our Dodge to the line of cars along the road.

Rachel gave me an unsure look as I locked the doors and headed back toward Nelson's. I tucked my hands in the back pockets of my jeans, refusing to let my hesitancy trump my curiosity as we walked in silence.

People milled about the storefront sipping homemade lemonade in Dixie cups while others packed ice chests and duffle bags full of odds and ends. The brass bell attached to the front door chimed as I entered. The sound of my boots against the old wood floor planks was lost to the din of conversations. A line had formed to the left where the owner's teenage daughter took deli orders behind a glass counter. Not a single face looked up, but the balding orange cat that hung around the checkstand arched his back into a stretch and rubbed his head against my leg.

"I'm going to get s'more stuff and hot chocolate. Meet

you in line," Rachel said, ducking past dusty fishing poles and bait into the next room.

"Okay." I headed to the back of the meat counter line and pretended to look at some handmade jewelry while I listened to people talk.

"Where are you guys coming from?" a man in a collared button up shirt asked the woman in front of me.

"Oh," she said, hugging her young son into her side. "We're from Sacramento. It's not a huge city, but we just wanted to be safe."

I held a pair of twisty silver earrings and pretended to eye my reflection in the distorted mirror display.

"You headed up north a ways or..." the man pried.

"No." She shook her head. "We're going to settle in here somewhere. Probably at the campground until my husband can find a place." She sighed. "Apparently a lot of other people have the same idea."

We moved forward in line, and I decided now was a good time for questions.

"Why here?" I asked, trying to seem nonchalant. I placed the earrings back and picked up a necklace. "I mean, there's not much around."

"Exactly," she said through a smile. Then she leaned in to whisper. "My husband heard that guy Alex lives around here. If he's here, this is the safest place for us."

I cleared my throat trying to mask my surprise. "Wow," I whispered back. "How did you hear that?"

"Oh, I don't know. Someone my husband works with.

Might not even be true." She shrugged off the comment to place her order and left me standing by the jewelry in shock.

After I had the stew meat, Rachel and I fast-walked to the car, our shoes crunching against the dirt shoulder of the road. I waited until we were in the car to explain.

"How do they know that?" her voice shot up in disbelief.

"I don't know, but I think we should send Alex someplace else to get whatever we need from now on. Just in case."

She nodded in agreement. "This is crazy. Look how many people are here." Her head turned as we left the last car behind us.

"I guess it's partially a good thing though, right?" Rachel asked. "People are leaving the cities. That's what we wanted."

"Yeah," I agreed. "It's what we wanted." At least I hoped it was.

As anxious as I was to interrogate Alex about the sudden influx of people in our town, he was nowhere to be found.

In typical Alex fashion, he showed up days later at my bedside in the middle of the night. "Wake up," he said through the dark.

My eyes snapped open with a start. "Huh?"

"They're rioting." He pulled the blankets off of me. "I think you should see this."

CHAPTER SIX

I FOLLOWED HIM THROUGH THE LIGHTLESS HALLS until we reached the living room. Kara sat on the couch watching the TV with the volume on low. Her wild black curls were more windswept than normal, and something dark was smeared across her face. Blood or dirt, I couldn't tell. Only then did I notice Alex looked the same.

"What happened?" I sat down next to Kara and stared at the flashes of smoke and people on the screen, flames and picket signs. One man took a sledgehammer to a row of police cars and another wave of men tried to tip them on their sides.

"We didn't see it coming," Kara said, still in disbelief. "We were out late in LA and—"

"You were in the city?" I asked.

"Oh relax. We can leave in less than a second if we need to," Alex brushed off my concern.

"Anyway," Kara continued. "Things started closing up around 3 a.m. so we thought we'd get a cup of coffee in New York, you know. It was morning there." She rubbed her eye as she remembered, clearly tired from lack of sleep. "At the coffee shop these two guys were talking about Descendants lining up at city hall for registration, and we thought we'd check it out."

Alex shook his head. "I had no idea there would be picketing. I should've guessed...I just...I put us right in the middle of it. Thank God for my ability. They would have torn us to pieces."

I turned back to the TV. Apparently not everyone was fleeing for the countryside. The mob was human, and they were violent. I didn't understand. A motherly looking woman with gentle features screamed at the camera and into our faces. "Say no to evil. Say no to playing God!"

"I always thought it would be us," I said as I sat next to Kara. "I thought we'd be the ones to get out of control."

She handed me the remote. "This is just the beginning. Who knows..."

I took it and switched channels, turning up the volume. Another angle of the riot showed a group surrounding something. I could see the hate in their eyes as they pressed in around it.

A reporter with long blonde hair spoke hurriedly into the camera.

*We're at the scene of one of the centers for Descendant registration where a confrontation started between some hostile citizens and those waiting to file with the government. Since the outbreak of the riot, most Descendant have scattered. The three that remain have become a target for violence, though we haven't confirmed their abilities. It's hard to get a good look...*The camera zoomed in, catching fragments of three scared faces. *Continued attempts by the police to break through the riot have been unsuccessful—*

The woman's voice cut out and the image froze on the screen. Technical difficulties. I flipped the channels trying to find the same story, but it was lost.

"Can you get them out?" I asked Alex, scared for the three who were trapped.

"I tried," he said shaking his head. "Almost got myself killed. One of their abilities must be to repel things. I couldn't break through and ended up being thrown in the crowd."

"Can you at least get us there?" I stood and looked around for my army boots. "Somewhere on the sidelines? If Kara can talk to them..."

Alex nodded as I laced my boots up over black leggings. I reached for their hands, and in moments we were gone.

When we appeared on the city street, the white abyss of the upper air gave way to daylight. The sun struggled against the smoke of burning cars and buildings and garbage. We pushed our way through throngs of angry bodies, swarming and buzzing.

If not for Kara, our words would have been lost to the running river of jeers that floated above and through the crowd.

There are too many people here, she said in our minds. *Get us closer.*

At first I couldn't tell where *closer* would be, but the people around us were facing one direction. Their shouts poured out in front of them.

Something was taking too long. I looked back, expecting Alex to move us somewhere we could see, but he was gone. Kara's eyes were wide, mouth open.

"Where'd he go?" I yelled the words into the crowd, forgetting to say them in my head.

He— She stared at me but didn't continue.

Tell me.

She didn't get the chance to. Something made the crowd erupt up ahead. I didn't have time to figure out why he left us. Instead, I grabbed Kara's hand and pressed my face through shoulders and elbows. The closer we got, the colder I became, as if someone had created an instant winter. I could see my breath by the time I found the opening. Against the brick wall of a building, three faces stared back at the mob—a man, a woman, and a young girl. They were surrounded. A powder white semi-circle of ice separated the three from the crowd, but it didn't keep their aggression at bay. They threw coke cans and shoes, whatever they could find. The girl with dust brown hair blocked each piece of debris with a pulse pushed from her hand. Another ability held those closest to them idle in the effort. A wall of indifferent strangers stared in their direction forgetting to take action.

I searched for Alex behind me. We needed to get them out of here.

He'll be right back, Kara said silently.

Right back? Where did he go? I can't believe he left us here!

Still no answer. I shook my head. He never stuck to the plan. Ever.

A shoulder shoved me from the right, and I stumbled into the man in front of me. I wasn't used to humans being the aggressors. Looking around I felt a knot form in my throat. Is this what I was fighting for? Suddenly I didn't know which side I was on, or if there were sides anymore. Boundaries had bled together, mixed like paint into a new color. One that wasn't so clear and clean and lovely to look at. This wasn't how I imagined it.

The voices rose. A wave pushed us forward. Someone stumbled onto the ice and that was all it took. They lunged toward the three.

"Wait," I yelled, but I knew it was useless.

Kara was already running, trying to beat the others. I didn't know what she intended to do, but I followed, though I was drowning in a sea of bodies. They crushed my feet, pulled and pushed, spit angry words. For a moment, I lost them. I lost Kara. A man with sweaty arms threw his body into mine, and I reacted out of frustration. My elbow to his sternum. Somehow, I found myself at the front. The three Descendants were huddled together, caged birds behind a tangled mesh of arms that stretched and grabbed like weeds trying to choke the life from them.

There was nothing I could do. The bodies around me rose like water above my head. I couldn't get a breath. A winter fog blinded me, and I shivered as frigid air penetrated the warm bodies of the mob, trying to freeze them out.

"Alaximandrios," I said through the mess of sound. Nothing. "Alaximandrios!" I shouted it loud enough that some faces turned, but waves of bodies kept crashing.

Finally he was there beside me, acting before I had to ask. He grabbed my hand, thrusting me into the white upper air for what seemed like a flash of light, then we were next to Kara who had managed to fight her way beside the three Descendants in trouble.

"Make sure you're all touching," he said, but I didn't know if they could hear him. Even if they could, we were too late.

The force field bubble protecting all of us began to weaken, and hands had found their way in. They had a foot and they pulled, sucking the youngest into their forest of arms.

"Grab her," I yelled to the woman. She reached out,

but the barrier was broken and her fingers slipped against the girl's. All I saw was her empty hand as we disappeared.

"Go back," I insisted as soon as we were in the living room, but Alex wasn't there to hear me. He was already gone.

We stared at each other. Me and Kara back at the man and woman. Nics broke the silence. She stood in the kitchen in her pajamas, the light of the refrigerator pouring onto her bare feet.

"What happened?" She didn't move. Instead she looked at the strangers waiting to see if they were a threat.

"There was a riot," I answered, moving to the couch. I sat on the edge and waited for Alex. Still nobody moved. "It's okay, Nics. They're with us. They're Descendants."

The man was short and lean with dark hair and a goatee. "I'm Robert," he said to Nics, mechanically reaching to shake her hand.

She closed the fridge with her hip, the milk jug still in her grasp. "Bloodline?"

"Boreas," he answered, dropping his hand. "This is Eva. She's of Bia."

I wasn't really listening. All I could think about was the girl and Alex. They should be back by now. Kara and I shared a look. I could hear time passing it was so quiet.

"Thank you for helping us," the woman said. She was taller than Robert, with carrot-red hair and peach lips.

When Alex appeared with the girl, I stood, but that was as far as I got. She was covered in blood. Scratched and beaten. I wanted to close my eyes and swallow down the disgust in my throat, but I didn't want to scare her. Instead I dropped to my knees in front of her. She was just a child, with dark stringy hair like mine, and wide saucer eyes too scared to blink.

"It's okay," I told her. "You're safe here." I forced my voice to be high and casual. I forced myself to smile at her bleeding nose, her swollen lips and red teeth. "And I can heal you."

She sniffed at the dripping blood and wiped her tears with the back of her hand, leaving red streaks on her arm. Everyone stood around me, still as Stonehenge.

"Come on," I said gently as I led her slowly to the bathroom. I blocked the mirror as she passed and sat her on the toilet. The small room helped her relax.

"You were really brave," I said, taking a towel from under the sink. I warmed it with water and knelt in front of her, wiping away the mask of blood streaked with tears. She stared at the shower curtain as I tried to unravel her from the pain.

"What's your name?" I asked, hoping to distract her.

"Jules," she answered, her voice scratchy and quiet.

"That's a pretty name," I said, folding the towel and resting it on my bent knee. "How old are you?"

My questions didn't seem to divert her attention.

"Forty-two." She watched with concern as I pressed

the buttons on my bracelet.

I bit my lip in anger as the blades sliced my skin. Would the mob have subjected a human eight-year-old to this brutality? I let the blood drip onto the towel, catching drops with my fingertips to heal her wounds. When I reached out she flinched, cowering backward.

"Will it hurt?" she asked.

I paused with my hand inches from her face, and my eyebrows pulled together like my mother's used to. "No, sweetie. I'm not going to hurt you." I wanted to promise her nobody would ever hurt her again, but I couldn't say the words. What if that was a promise I couldn't keep? I dabbed the blood over the scrape on her delicate cheek, her eye and chin. "See?"

She nodded, and I felt her scoot closer to me. "Do you want me to get your mommy?"

Her Bambi eyes flickered with a moment of hope, then faded with understanding. "That lady's not my mom."

"Oh," I whispered. I picked up the towel and wiped my blood from the healed skin on her face. "Where is your mom?"

She shifted her weight on top of the toilet and stared at the floor. "I don't know."

"What do you mean?"

Jules pinched the skin on her elbows as she spoke. "She went to register and told me to wait at the coffee shop next door, but she didn't come back."

"So when you heard the noise you went to look for

her?"

A silent nod.

I took her hand and wiped her red palm with the rag. "We'll find her, okay?"

As I cleaned her arms and neck, I felt the mother in me emerge. That empty, desperate person who needed to give all of my love to anyone who would take it.

I stood and tossed the towel in the sink. "Come on," I said, holding out my hand.

—

I WOKE UP EVERY HOUR THAT NIGHT TO CHECK ON Jules. My bare feet tested the sound of the cool planks of wood floor with each step. Every time I reached her she lay sound asleep. I watched her breath for a minute, wondering what my daughter would look like when she was her age. What she looked like now as she slept.

When I made my way back to my room, Alex was standing outside the door. I jumped when I saw him.

"Would you stop doing that to me?" I whispered. "It's creepy."

He followed me into my room and shut the door behind him. "I talked to Adrianna," he answered quietly. He flicked on the light and Kara was sitting on my bed.

I squinted. "What? When?"

"I'm pretty sure she started the riot." He cracked his knuckles as I sat next to Kara. "She was waiting in the crowd as soon as we appeared."

"That's why you took off?" I seethed with resentment. "You should have said something. You just left us there."

"He didn't want to lose her," Kara defended him.

I shook my head. "Why do you care about Adrianna?"

"She's a Council member—"

"Not anymore," I reminded him. "When Christoph died, their abilities fell to the next generation. Edith has Dr. Nickel's ability and her heir has hers. There is a new Council—"

"I know how it works!" he cut me off. He closed his eyes, regretting his temper. "Look, she was a Council member when Christoph took my sister. I thought she could help me find her."

I bit my tongue, understanding his side of things. "Can she?"

"Maybe," he answered. "She wants to meet with you."

"With me?" I stood up in surprise. "How will that help? Did you ask why?"

"Yeah," he answered, "but I'm not going to tell you. If I do, you won't come."

I crossed my arms. "Then I'm not going."

"He's right," Kara said, pushing herself off the bed. "If he tells you, you won't want to go, but you need to see this."

I had never completely trusted Alex, but I did trust Kara. "When does she want to meet?"

"Now," Kara answered.

"Now?" My voice shot up an octave.

"Yes," Alex said with irritation. "She just—" I could hear the desperation in his voice and wondered if Adrianna was using his sister as a bargaining chip.

Kara finished for him. "She's hoping for less interference because it's night and everyone with us is asleep. She doesn't want others involved in influencing your decision."

"That doesn't seem right." I shook my head. "I'm not going unless I know more."

"Elyse," Kara said with a seriousness in her voice I couldn't ignore. "The government is doing experiments on our people. Trust me. You need to go."

It was all I needed to hear.

CHAPTER SEVEN

WHEN ALEX TRANSPORTED US TO THE MEETING, THE intense glow of his upper air hardly faded against the brightness of the new space around us. The room was stark white. Sterile. I squinted, waiting for everything to adjust.

The soles of my boots shuffled against a shiny white linoleum floor as I backed farther into the corner behind me. Clear doors lined all four walls and each opened up to a small white box-like cell. The cells contained people, only none of them were conscious. Each was carefully strapped to a silver table. In the center of the room, scientists in white jackets milled about several feet in front of us.

When I realized what was happening, I reached for my dart gun, but someone stopped me.

"They can't see or hear you," Adrianna said from behind me. I recognized her voice without having to see her face. It was low and sinister, always wavering with the hint of distrust. "We're using the power of Kydoimos to cause confusion amongst the staff, and the power of Lelantos is keeping our presence hidden."

When I turned around Adrianna wasn't alone. I tried to speak, but my throat closed up. A group of four stood just behind her in the corner of the room, and at her side was a younger version of Christoph, a boy my age. He didn't look like he knew how to smile. Short straight blond hair fell toward his forehead. He kept his hands behind his back as he stared at me, and I wondered if it was a way of restraining himself. I was sure he wanted to kill me. I'd killed his father.

"This is my son," Adrianna said. For a moment I didn't believe her. Her thin frame and tiny waist didn't reflect motherhood the way my body did. She was too beautiful, with long brown curls and sweet liar's lips that hid deception behind a fake smile.

She was waiting for my reaction, just like I was waiting for his.

I clenched my teeth but didn't say anything as my mind connected the pieces. Adrianna and Christoph had a child. My nails bit into my palms. I shouldn't hate someone I didn't know, but I could see so much of his father in him, a smug reminder of my old enemy.

"I'm Grayson." Her son reached his hand forward, and I tensed involuntarily. I stared at him for a moment before I took his cold palm. He had his mother's eyes.

They were a flat hazel. I couldn't read them. Chameleon's eyes.

"Hi." The word scratched my throat as it came out. I cursed myself for seeming weak as I cleared it. "Hi," I said with more strength. I glanced back at the scientists shuffling about. There was no order to what they were doing. They seemed lost, but my stomach went sour. What had they been doing to our people moments ago? I wanted there to be some reasonable explanation.

"So what's the plan here?" Alex spoke up. "I thought you wanted to meet about what we discussed."

I didn't like the idea of a conversation between them that I hadn't been a part of.

"We are," Adrianna answered, "but I needed her to see this so she'd understand my reasoning. She's not going to agree easily."

"What?" I asked.

Kara said nothing, though I knew she was aware of the details, every subconscious thought floating in between their words. She watched me, and I could see uncertainty in the twitch of her lips.

"I want peace above all. You need to know that," Adrianna began. I wished I could believe her. "But a human can't be in control." She gestured to the rooms of our people encased in plastic cells like dolls on store shelves. "This is only the beginning of what they're capable of."

Why did she have to be right? I couldn't deny what

was in front of me. It was the evidence of my failure.

"I'm assuming you have a plan," I said, dancing around the edges of agreement.

"We do." She folded her hands together, hesitating. "One you're not going to like, but I don't have to tell you it's necessary. I know what you've seen." My eyes shifted between Kara and Alex, wondering how much of her plan they already knew. "The thing is, we need you on board. I have no way of knowing how far you were meant to carry out this prophecy, but if you're with us, we're more likely to succeed. You deserve to be in a position of power, though we plan to push forward regardless of whether or not you accept our plan."

"What is it?" I picked at my thumbnail as I watched the scientists wander.

She looked to her son, as if speaking for him. "We're going to assume control of the country and establish a new Council. Of course all original Council heirs will assume their rightful positions, Grayson included." She rested her delicate fingers on the tops of his shoulders. "However, you will have the opportunity to join us, bringing along any advisors you see fit."

A breathy laugh slipped through my teeth. "And you think they'll just *let* you take over?"

"No," she admitted. "We plan to use whatever means necessary, but we're hoping for a quick transition. A presidential assassination will send a message and allow us to assume control without much bloodshed."

At first, I didn't say anything. I was too shocked. Images of a broken country devastated beyond repair stole my words. Did she really think I was going to help in any plan to kill the president? I couldn't bring myself to believe that was the answer to finding peace. I started to shake my head, but caught too many eyes on me.

Careful, Kara warned.

Refusing outright could get me into trouble. I glanced at the cell doors to give myself a second more to think.

"All right," I said, trying to keep my face from giving away the lie. Maybe if I was involved I could stop it.

Adrianna nodded without smiling. "Good. We'll contact you through Alex when we're ready."

"Wait," Kara said. "What about these facilities? We have to shut this down."

Adrianna looked at me. "I'll let you make that call, Elyse. There will be consequences if we act before we have control."

I watched the white coats amble about aimlessly, shuffling supplies that made them look busy to the cameras but kept them from hurting anyone. As soon as we were gone, they would start up again. Testing our people. Poking and prodding them like aliens. My eyes settled on a young girl, her blonde hair draped over the silver edge of a table like a golden curtain. She was younger than I was. She was innocent. I couldn't walk away.

"I agree with Kara. We can't leave them here."

Even as I spoke the words I wasn't sure I was right. I didn't know what would cause the destruction I'd seen in my vision. Maybe this. But helping was the only ethical option.

"They're all yours." Adrianna looked at one of her companions, giving her approval.

Almost instantly the plastic cell walls started to crack into patterns. I was caught off guard and stared a little too long before I realized we were making our move. As the pieces rained into a clattered mess on the cement floor, I covered my ears and rushed to the first cell. The white coats stared in confusion, but it wouldn't be long before others started to realize what was going on. I was unstrapping the blonde girl's arms and legs when the first gun went off. I didn't know whose it was, ours or theirs, but I didn't stop. I pulled the IV from her arm, the taped wire from her chest, and dragged her to the ground.

Her unconscious body slumped, heavy and helpless into my lap. I pulled her to the corner of the cell as bullets clanked against the cement walls, and my forehead beaded with sweat. The room had become a haze of dust clouds and ear-splitting chaos.

I reached for the dart gun around my thigh and drew blood from the bracelet on my left wrist. It wouldn't be enough to stop the number of guns I heard, but I wasn't going down without a fight.

"Move. Move. Move," a voice shouted through the thick smoke.

A cough rose in my throat and I covered my mouth with my hand trying not to give away my position.

Every muscle tensed as a man in black pushed through a veil of cement dust toward me. I shot the dart without thought, hitting him in the leg, and he fell. I scrambled to my feet and pried the gun from his fingers, my heart beating in my ears.

"Alaximandrios," I whispered, and Alex was there. His right arm was covered in a sleeve of blood. "Take her." I pointed and both of them were gone. Even injured, Alex moved like a ghost.

My feet crunched bits of wall and glass as I thrust the gun in front of me. I couldn't see through the dust, so I stayed low with my back against the back wall of a cell. Bullets peppered the air, pinging against the overturned metal table in front of me. I cleared my throat trying to get some relief, but the air was another enemy of mine.

To your right, Ellie! Kara shouted in my cluttered mind.

I didn't know where she was, but I pointed the gun to my right and shot blind. *Stupid move.* But a shooter fell, and I ducked, inching closer to the table. My sweaty hands slipped against the tile as I crawled to the next cell, scooting toward the feet of the Descendant body laid out on the table above me. I pressed up to my knees, pulling clear tubing from his arms. As I reached for the taped wire, my knee slid. It wasn't sweat that made me slip. It was blood. On my palms, my pants, the souls of my shoes.

I saw it dripping from the table and from the young man's fingers. There was no saving a man who was already dead.

I turned and headed for the next table, but Alex and Kara appeared in front of me. Alex dangled three grenades from his fingertips. "Ready?" he asked.

My eyebrows raised in shock. "Ready for what? There are people in here."

"Not any of ours. I got them out."

I shook my head. "No."

A silver can leaking yellow smoke rattled around my feet, and time played against me.

Alex pulled the rings on the grenades, and for a moment none of it seemed real. He didn't flinch, not for a second, not until a bullet grazed my arm. I grabbed the searing pain and let out a loud cry through my teeth.

The white space of the upper air carried me away before the grenades blew. We stood on the roof of a tall building, the air around us cold and untouched by the rest of the city. The floor beneath my feet vibrated, and the explosion drew my eye. It erupted from the bottom floor of the facility like a blooming flower of flames before withering into a plume of black and grey ash.

I watched in horror as the smoke floated upward, rising like the face of death to look me in the eye.

He did what he had—

Don't. I stopped Kara's unspoken words before she could finish. There were men in there. They had lives and families. Now they were dead. *Just because they're human, doesn't make them disposable.*

"They were there to kill us," Kara said, too worked up to keep it inside.

I couldn't respond. I knew she was right, but I never thought I'd be on the side of killing humans. Besides, this was more than lives lost, this could be the beginning of the end. The first flame in a world ready to combust. It was a bad move.

The cold air turned musky with the smell of smoke as the dark cloud drifted closer.

I couldn't look at Alex. "Take me home," I said to the empty space in front of me. My fingers slipped against the skin of my arm, but I still held it, staunching the blood with my palm.

The white airless space washed away the filth of the city, and soon I was somewhere new. It wasn't home.

"Sorry," Alex said. "Home will have to wait." We were standing in a Victorian living room. The Descendants we rescued from the facility were strewn around us, a striking contrast to the Persian carpets, fringed red pillows, and carved wood framed paintings of Greek gods. A man standing on the other side of the room lit candles with just his fingers, giving extra light to the dim, windowless space. Adrianna spoke with her son privately in a shadowed corner.

Those who were still unconscious lined the furniture and floor like corpses. It took me a minute to recalibrate as they came to, their faces dazed and afraid. Those who had already awoken seemed even more terrified. Some were shot, others wounded and shaken.

I turned back to Alex, taking a second to gather my strength. "All right."

"Welcome, friends," Adrianna moved tall and proud toward the front of the marble mantle, like a queen basking in her power. "You've been through a lot, I'm sure. Food will be provided shortly, and we have a healer here to care for the wounded. I know you all have a lot of questions. I'll do my best to answer them in time, but for now, try and focus on recovering. Let me, or anyone else assisting, know if you need anything."

Adrianna made her way toward me, and I couldn't help wonder if the grenades had been her idea. She'd acted as if the choice to rescue these people was mine, as if I were the one responsible, yet here she was right in the middle of it all as if she'd planned the whole thing. She was a spider with long legs and a web of promises. A black widow who had eaten her mate. I didn't trust her for a second, even if she had helped me in the past.

Kara and Alex inched closer to me as she approached.

"Thank you for being here to heal. It's very helpful." Adrianna smiled at me. "Keep in mind, though, these people don't just need our help, they need us to make things right. We've seen what humans can do. What they *are* doing."

She glanced around the room as if for affect.

"Our intentions were good," she continued, "but those in control have chosen to act foolishly. We can't let them think we are theirs to manipulate. You're right, Elyse. The time of living illusively is over. We should be free, and the only way to do that is to take control of the situation. To facilitate things in a way the humans aren't capable of."

Alex and Kara both looked at me, as if waiting for my approval.

"I hope you agree," Adrianna said as she turned away.

"This isn't..." I stopped her before she could leave. Things weren't that simple. It could mean outright war, millions of deaths, but the room full of wounded weakened my resolve. I wasn't prepared for the crippled spirits of my people. "I never intended for this to happen..." I sighed, unable to deny the truth in her words. "We have to tread lightly. If we come on too strong the humans could get aggressive and that could backfire."

"What do you propose we do?" Adrianna turned back, crossing her arms over her chest, but I caught a glimpse of honest curiosity in her eyes. "If you have a better idea or a plan I'd be happy to hear it. We can't let this happen to our people."

I broke eye contact. She was right. I didn't have an answer or a plan, but I knew one thing. Humans weren't the enemy. Or so I thought. The pale faces and blood-soaked gowns of innocent Descendants said otherwise.

"I agree. We can't let this happen," I answered. "But maybe if we find a place for ourselves. If we show them how things can be..." Not even I believed the words coming out of my mouth. Not after what I'd seen. It wouldn't ever be that easy. "If we lead by example, we can make this a better world."

I met the gaze of an older man, graying into his fourth century of life. His face hung with hopelessness, and a knot formed in my stomach.

"Yes, we *can* make this a better world," she said after a moment, and I wondered if Alex and Kara picked up on the subtle smirk she'd been wearing while I was floundering. "We'll show them we don't want war. A simple transition of power is all we ask." Her voice was too kind. "If they refuse us, we'll use other means to ensure it's seen through. With as little bloodshed as possible, of course."

She placed a hand on my shoulder like a strict schoolteacher disciplining her student, and as she walked away I was left wondering if I'd agreed to something without realizing it.

I had no idea what time it was when I finally set about healing the wounded. They watched me with curiosity, trying to figure out where they knew me or if I was important. I wanted to tell them I was, for one reason. I knew what was coming. I'd seen it. But that secret gave away another, one I wasn't willing to share—Sarah.

Without William to amplify my strength, I had to

take breaks. I'd managed to heal my own wounds in the process, but I hadn't bothered to wash the blood from my hands. My stained red palms rested in my lap as I sat in a large cushioned chair taking deep relaxing breaths.

I opened my heavy lids and caught Kara watching me from across the room. She sat on the floor against the wall while others congregated into groups, reliving the moment they were taken from their families. Pieces of the conversations drifted between us.

"...carted off after registration..."

"...they grabbed me at home in the middle of the night..."

Her eyes dared me to listen, but I tuned them out. I didn't want to know.

Why?

Kara's voice in my head robbed me of my privacy. I closed my eyes and let my head rest against the back of my chair.

I don't want any of it to be true, I guess, I answered.

Well it is. Get over it.

My eyes snapped open to find her glaring at me over the top of her bent knees. I turned away, but that was no escape.

I know you want humans to be innocent in this, but they're not. We exposed our race, and there were consequences. Did you think there wouldn't be?

I knew...I just. I could hear myself start to grow defensive and settled my thoughts into an even tone. *I knew there would be conflict, I just thought we'd work together to overcome it. Not kill President McKinney. It proves them right. They should be afraid of us.*

Maybe we should be afraid of them, she countered.

I nodded, unable to disagree.

You need to figure out which side you're on here, Ellie.

CHAPTER EIGHT

WHEN I HAD FINISHED HEALING, ALEX AND KARA LEFT me alone in the living room of our house. I thought about stopping them before they disappeared, but I couldn't think of a reason they should stay. Only that I didn't want to be alone. They were gone before I could say a word, and I stared at the wall in front of me, feeling the solitude creep back in with each silent moment. When I turned around, Nics was sitting on the couch, elbows resting on her knees like she'd been waiting.

"Oh, hey," I said, trying to act as if I wasn't just drowning in my own emptiness.

She bit her lip and scowled at the floor. I tapped my hands on my thighs in an uncomfortable rhythm. Nics was always mad at someone for something. I just wasn't used to that someone being me.

"We saw the explosion on the news." Her eyes flickered toward the TV, which was on mute, but still flipping through images of the day's events. "Could have told us where you were. Edith, Dr. Nickel, and the others are out looking for you."

"Shoot." I pressed my lips together, mad at myself for not communicating. If I'd had more support, maybe things wouldn't have gotten so out of hand.

"I need to get something out," Nics said with an edge to her voice.

I shrugged, too broken to put up my defenses. "Okay."

"We're as much a part of this as you are. We've been waiting for this, too."

I didn't understand what she was getting at. "I know."

She crossed her arms and leaned forward. "Do you?"

I moved to sit beside her on the couch. I could see she wanted to open up, but that angry side of her was making it hard. "Christoph had us, Elyse," she continued. "Me, Sam, Paul, Rachel, Dr. Nickel. We were as good as dead until you came along. Who knows how long he would have kept us unconscious, or what he planned to do with us after he'd syphoned all the blood from our veins." Her eyebrows sank as she thought of it. "My point is that all of us have been here from the beginning. We're *still* here. We don't have to be, but we are. Because we're your friends." She looked up at me, making her final point. "Friends stick together, they don't do what you did. What if you were hurt or in trouble? We had no way to find you."

I swallowed down the knot in my throat. I didn't know whether to feel guilty or grateful, but I cracked open at the word "friends."

"You're not alone, Ellie," she said softly. Her large brown eyes were the most familiar thing I'd seen in days. The only eyes that truly saw me for what I was now—lost. "We have a reason to fight, too. So, no more disappearing without telling anyone where you're going or why. We're a team."

She had no idea how much I needed to hear that. "Okay," I said.

"And you have to get better at this cell phone thing." She handed me my old black flip-phone. "What's the point of having one if it's never with you?"

"I know. I'm sorry. I didn't think I'd need it." I dabbed the corners of my welling eyes, and tried to laugh away the tears.

Nics made a frustrated I-feel-guilty noise in her throat. "See, I told them I shouldn't be the one to wait here for you. I'm not good at keeping my thoughts to myself."

I wanted to be harder around the edges like her. "I think that's a good thing."

The screen door creaked open, and Sam entered mid-conversation. Rachel and Paul followed, but when they saw me, all their faces turned serious.

Rachel sighed a disapproving sigh. "We saw the explosion on the news." Her voice was high and full of blame. "We didn't know where you were or if you were there."

"What happened?" Sam asked.

Paul pulled Rachel onto his lap in the easy chair and Sam folded his legs Indian-style on the floor as I explained it all. Adrianna, the facility, the plan to kill McKinney and seize control of the country. It was a lot to take in even for me. So much had happened in the span of a few hours.

Rachel snorted out a laugh. "You aren't really going to help her *kill* the president, right?"

"No way." I enunciated each word with certainty, glad I wasn't the only one completely against her plan.

"Maybe we can stop her," Nics suggested.

I nodded. "That's what I was hoping."

"Do you know when or how they're going to do it?" Paul asked, hugging Rachel into his chest.

I wished I had more to go on, but the idea of having my friends on my side gave me confidence. "Not yet, but she wants me involved, so I'm sure she'll let me in on everything eventually. Then we can decide what to do." *We.* I hadn't realized such a simple word could change my perspective completely. I stacked the coasters on the coffee table, giving myself a distraction. "Sorry you had to go looking for me. It won't happen—"

"It actually worked out," Sam interrupted as if he just remembered something. "We found Jules's mom."

"What? How?" I asked.

"Edith took us to the sight of the riot to look for you. There was a lady there, and when she saw us appear she asked if we'd seen a little girl. She'd been waiting there, hoping Jules would come looking for her."

The corners of my mouth pulled into a smile. I couldn't remember the last time I'd had a reason to feel happy about something.

"What about the others?" I asked.

"They left this morning," Rachel answered. "They didn't say where they were headed, just thanks for the help."

It was strange to think Descendants were the ones in need of protection, but not all abilities were geared toward defending against attacks. Especially if they weren't trained. What was a descendant of Hegemone supposed to do? The ability to sprout trees and flowers from the earth would do nothing against physical assault. I'd always imagined it would be us helping the humans. Instead we were blowing up buildings with them inside in order to save our own.

I lay alone that night, hating myself for what I'd done, for what my fellow Descendants were planning. Crickets sang their lonely song outside my window, and the emptiness around me stripped me of my strength. No oracle to guide me. No visions. No William. No Anna. No baby girl.

I'd lost everything for what I'd always been told was my destiny. For a world where Descendants were free.

But this? The chaos and cruelty of a world unraveling and unwilling to change? It couldn't be how things were meant to unfold.

Warm tears snaked down my cheeks and bled into my pillow. In the dark silence I let them come, needing the hurt to seep out so I could leave it behind. My only hope of overcoming this was to move forward and trudge through the deep and treacherous waters toward the end.

I had to believe this new world could work. Even if I had to scrape my way through the blunt edges of hatred with thrashed skin and broken bone. I'd give every ounce of me to get there. To find peace. To have my family back.

—

We'll contact you through Alex when we're ready.

I woke up every morning with Adrianna's voice in my head. Every time I opened my eyes to the what-ifs and maybes of a new day, I wondered. Would today be the day? The day she came calling for me. The day the world would explode. The day I'd finally sink so deep I'd never be able to pull myself out.

Only it was never the day.

It was a hot sticky summer sunrise. Hotter than it should have been, which made it harder to run. No matter how many things I found myself running from, my guilt, my loneliness, Adrianna, I could never outrun the heat. It slipped beneath my t-shirt and shorts, dampening my back, the sun burning my skin into a rosy tan.

I had been running so often I'd beaten a trail into the wild, dry weeds. It bent around the edge of the forest and followed its perimeter, giving me the perfect vantage point of the cluttered highway. I stopped when I reached my halfway point and rested with my hands on my thighs. Sweat dripped from my temples as I reached to adjust my blow dart gun.

Alex had denied telling anyone about where we lived, but still, humans poured in, setting up their tents along the road like they were waiting for fireworks on the fourth of July. I watched as a man slammed the tailgate of his red truck and lugged a tarp toward their camp. No one had ventured this far yet, but I kept my guard up. My runs served more of a purpose than getting back into shape. I promised myself the moment I felt threatened we'd leave.

I pulled my leg into a stretch as I spied, balancing on one leg and pressing the back of my heel to my hip. The muscles in my thigh were becoming more defined. I was noticing the toned line above my knee when I heard dry foliage crack under footsteps behind me. Wind shuffled a pile of dry leaves, scattering them across the ground as I swung around, scanning the forest. A tall line of pine trees was all that stared back, but that didn't mean I was alone. I turned and pretended to move on, but my ears strained for whatever was out there. As I walked I slipped my fingers into my satchel of darts.

It's me. The voice that sounded in my head wasn't Kara's. I whipped my head around searching. *Don't shoot*, she said. I caught a glimpse of Edith's coppery hair before she emerged from behind a tree trunk.

My shoulders relaxed. "What are you doing out here?"

"Following you," she answered. Her timid eyes avoided me, and she crossed her little girl arms across her light pink t-shirt.

I bit back a smile at her defensiveness. "Why?"

She thought about her answer and shrugged. "I know something I shouldn't."

All the regretful feelings I'd had over the past months, all the wrong choices I'd ever made, they all betrayed me as they spilled into my mind for her to pick through. The secret guilt that I felt for all the reasons everything was my fault.

"It's not about you..." she said quietly. "Well, it is, but it's not something you know."

"Okay." I waited for more.

She dug her shoe into the dirt. "I shouldn't have been listening to his thoughts. William might be mad if I tell you, but I have to." Her voice was expectant, like she was waiting for me to give her permission. "Sometimes I go visit him. I know I'm not supposed to, but nobody knows. I stay hidden."

I didn't say anything. I knew I should, but I so desperately wanted to hear what he'd been thinking. The breeze chilled the sweat on my brow as I waited for her to tell me.

"He's been dreaming of you." She smiled.

I smiled back. "It's okay. I don't think he would be mad that you know that."

"It's more than that." Excitement overcame her nerves. "I recognized some of them. They're memories."

I became a statue, still with shock.

"How?" I walked toward her, afraid to believe it. What if she was wrong? I combed back the flyaway hair that had escaped my ponytail. "Does he know they're real?"

"He isn't sure." She tucked her hands in her back pockets. "He hasn't told anyone."

"You have to tell him," I said too forcefully, and her face instantly wrinkled with worry.

The brave girl I'd seen training, who risked her life for mine was gone. Suddenly she was William's little sister, more afraid of her big brother's disapproval than anything.

She played with the belt loop on her shorts. "What if he gets mad?"

I stepped closer and brushed her hair back out of her face, remembering she was just a girl.

"He won't. I promise." I smiled and freckles slipped into her dimpled cheeks as she smiled back. "He's going to be really, really happy. Just like me."

The day was a blur. I didn't have a clue what to do

with myself. Edith spent most of the afternoon training with her dad in the yard. I knew, because I checked every ten minutes. She had become one more thing to wait for.

"What's wrong with you?" Nics asked from the hallway.

I glanced away from the window. "Nothing. What?"

"You're acting antsy." She crossed her arms over her chest demanding an answer.

"Aren't you?" I asked, avoiding the real reason. "This Adrianna thing..."

"Yeah." She nodded, narrowing her eyes in suspicion. "Rachel and Paul called. They'll be back soon and want to bring us to some pro-Descendant political convention to try and get the word out to more people. Apparently there will be a live radio broadcast so maybe—"

"Mm-hmm," I said, half-listening in between glances out the window. Edith had to be done soon. She'd been training for hours.

"Seriously. What's going on with you?" Nics watched me as she grabbed a drinking glass from the kitchen. "You're distracted. The Adrianna thing isn't it."

I picked my thumbnail, embarrassed to be distracted by something so trivial in the scheme of things. At least Nics was my friend. I hoped she wouldn't judge. "Okay so it isn't," I admitted. "How'd you know?"

"You're smiling a lot," she said, filling the glass with water.

I bit the inside of my cheek, trying to tame my lips.

"Edith said William's remembering things…"

CHAPTER NINE

WILLIAM WAS SITTING ON THE EDGE OF MY BED. I could barely make him out in the darkness. The silhouette of his features, hidden by the dark hue of night, glowed under a stream of silver light that filtered in through the window. He didn't know my eyes were open, that I was watching him study the wall as he thought. The fabric of his t-shirt shifted against his skin with the cross of his arms like a whisper amidst the silence.

He straightened up when he saw me awake, combing the long golden hair out of his face, and I suddenly realized he must know the truth about his dreams. I turned the knob on the bedside lamp to the dimmest setting and sat up.

Both of us were speechless for a moment. My heart pulled at the edges, wanting him closer.

"Why are you here?" I asked quietly, needing to know my hopes were true.

He shifted toward me, and the muscles in his shoulders relaxed as his eyes traveled over my face. "To see you," he answered.

It hurt to resist being closer.

"Fate has a way of making sure we stay together, right?" he asked. He slid his hand across the bed and our fingers touched. The warmth beat in my fingertips, like his skin was breathing life back into me. "We're stuck with each other, whether we like it or not."

Suddenly I didn't feel the heartbeat in my chest. I didn't see the room around me or hear the cricket's serenade. Everything stopped, and I stared at him. The words were too familiar. They were exact, like a lyric from a song I'd forgotten. I knew where I'd heard them. We were in my room, just after he'd told me I was the new mother, explaining the warmth between our skin. I never thought the moment would be so precious. Before now it was just a snippet of something I'd kept from our past. A secret for me to hold in my mind's box of memories, because he'd forgotten.

"You remember?" My voice was so unsure it wavered into the form of a question.

His eyes seemed darker in the dim light, deep and evergreen like the pine trees.

"So it really happened." His fingers slid further into mine until our hands were laced together and the heat pulsed between our palms. I'd been vacant without that feeling.

I nodded. It was all I could do. I was afraid to blink. If I closed my eyes he could disappear and take this moment with him.

He turned his focus elsewhere, searching somewhere inside. "I've been dreaming about you."

"Edith told me." The words escaped my lips before I thought to keep them to myself, but he didn't seem to mind. "When did you..."

"They started the night we left." He stood, too excited to stay still. "I dreamt about that night in your room. Only I thought it was just a dream. You know? I thought my mind was just trying to cope by filling in the blanks with whatever it wanted." He knelt down in front of me, taking my hand and folding his fingers in between mine. The warmth grew between our palms. "But it was real."

I nodded my head, unable to keep from smiling. "It was real." I wanted there to be more. So many moments had been stolen from us. "Do you remember any other details? Anything else?"

His brow furrowed. "Uh...a night in the caves with lots of people. There was a show and dancing."

"Lenaia."

He stood again, pacing back and forth like he was solving a puzzle. His words were quick as if he could forget them any second.

"Then a café. I worked there."

"Yep. Where we met."

As he paced in front of me, my heart beat like birds' wings, taking off before I could catch a breath. The whole time I'd been waiting for him to kiss me, but not sure if he would. When he finally made his move I gasped with surprise. He came in so quickly, scooping my face up in his hands. His lips traveled to my neck and my skin prickled with goose bumps, each nerve asking for more. In the quiet room all I could hear was our breath. His hands slid against my waist, and the warmth was startling. I hadn't felt it in so long, not like this. It slipped into my hair, down my arm, against my hip. His hands everywhere.

I was lost to him. To myself. To the feeling. So deep it was taking me over and happening too fast. With every second that passed I wished for it back so that I could live each one again and again. I pulled away, trying to be present, hoping to make it last longer. Forever.

His chest heaved and I stared at his lips, which were flushed red from mine. They parted just slightly. "I..." My eyes shifted up.

"I was afraid of losing you," he interrupted, still spouting out pieces of memory. He tucked my hair behind my ear, and I could see him remembering moments of me. "I'm still afraid of losing you."

I lay my head on the pillow wondering which William would win out in the end, the one who believed in me, or the one who was too afraid to. "What dream gave you that memory?" I asked.

"A night in the coffee shop." He let his head sink

into the pillow next to me. "I was telling you about my dad..."

"It was our first kiss," I said, smiling at the ceiling.

"I dreamt the kiss. I didn't know it was our first." He turned on his side and propped himself up with this elbow.

"What?" I asked as his jaw muscle pulsed.

He sighed. "Maybe I'm remembering for a reason. I mean, now it's not just me who doesn't want to lose you. Sarah needs you. Maybe you're not supposed to be a part of this."

I sat up, suddenly on edge. "I have to," I said, afraid these new memories would bring out his protective nature. "I've seen too much. I can't stand by and do nothing, William."

He stared into the sheets and I could see him fighting the idea, but he looked up with an easy smile.

"I'll stay with you then."

I cocked my head, shocked by his response. "Really?"

He nodded, reminding me that after all we'd been through, he'd grown to trust me.

For a second, a part of me resisted. I opened my mouth to convince him it wasn't a good idea, but something else came out. "Okay," I said. I knew it was selfish. I shook my head, trying to take it back. "What about Sarah? You need to be with her. If something happens to me..."

"Exactly," he answered, sitting up. "If something happens to you, she'll always wonder why I wasn't there.

Why I didn't help you."

I wanted to agree. When he was around I felt at least halfway whole again. "You don't have to stay. I have people to protect me. Our friends, your dad, Alex, Kara—"

"None of them care about you the way I do."

I'd waited so long to hear him say that. It made my eyes well up.

He took my face in his hand so I would look at him. "The best thing I can do for her is to keep you safe, and I can't trust anyone else to do that for me."

Those words made me love him even more. All the feeling for him I'd been trying to push to the corners of my heart flooded back in, because he was not only here for me. He was here for her, too. For all of us.

"What is she like? Has she changed a lot?" I knew she hadn't grown much, but there were other things I was missing. She was learning, becoming familiar with her surroundings, and I wasn't there to see any of it.

"*I* think she's changed," he answered, laying down again. "Mac says I'm crazy because she really hasn't had time to reach any milestones, but I swear she's getting bigger."

"Really?" I focused on the empty corner where her bassinet used to be. "I can't imagine Mac with a baby."

"He carries her around like a little tiny bird in his giant ogre hands. It's pretty funny." The image made me laugh, and I had to dab the wet corners of my eyes. "And he does this baby voice. Wait'll you hear it. It's more like a growl, but a cute growl."

"What else?" I asked, lying next to him.

"She knows me. She's really comfortable in my arms. At night, before I go to bed, she likes to sleep on my chest."

I scooted closer and lay my head where her head would be. He wrapped his arm around my shoulder hugging me to him. I listened to his heart, knowing it comforted her in my absence. It comforted me, too.

"I've thought about changing my mind so many times," I confessed. "Just to be with her when we're not out trying to convince the world about the future..."

He stayed quiet, his chest moving up and down as he breathed.

"But there are camps of people flocking to the town," I continued. "It's not safe."

"You could visit," he offered in a quiet voice. His warm hand brushed my upper arm.

I let myself indulge in the idea, imagining holding her again.

"I'm afraid to. If I see her, I don't know if I'll be able to leave again." *You have to lose to win.* The oracle's words were a constant reminder of my greatest fear. That emptiness I felt on the mangled street of San Francisco wasn't worth the risk. "I know she's safe there."

When I lifted myself up, his face was inches away. I couldn't look anywhere but into his eyes, and they didn't waver. His strong hand slipped behind my neck like he didn't want me to pull away or close up. I was more vulnerable than I'd ever been around the new him. I couldn't remember the last time we were this close. The man I married finally felt like my husband again, and I wanted to hide inside him where I knew I'd be safe and unbroken.

My lips softened into his. My fingers folded around his forearms as we kissed, the muscles tightening under the warmth of my palms. He was stronger than I remembered. Maybe he was right. Maybe he could protect me. I pulled away as I realized something.

"What?" he asked.

"Do you remember how to use your ability, or anything Mac taught you during training?"

His brow sank. "I think I can hold my own. Unless I was some kind of badass who could melt people's brains with my thoughts. I couldn't do that could I?"

I laughed. I'd missed his sense of humor. "No, you couldn't do that, but you could do some pretty amazing things. I figured you and Mac would be up every morning at dawn training..."

He smiled to himself and leaned back against the headboard. "No. Mac was busy counting baby toes and making goo-goo sounds most of the time."

I shoved his shoulder. "Come on. You're messing with me."

"I'm not. Seriously, he's Mr. Mom now."

My cheeks lifted at the thought. "That's cute."

He tapped his chin as if contemplating something important. "So uh...let's get back to these *amazing* things

I could do before. Are we talking special make-out moves or what?"

"Don't worry. You've still got those." I shimmied my shoulder up against his. "No, but really, once you made Sam and Nics stop fighting and they almost kissed."

"No way."

"Yeah, it was hilarious. They both denied it, but it was pretty obvious you had control of them." He raised his eyebrows, impressed with himself. "You could also use your peripheral vision to direct your ability," I answered. I pressed my back against the headboard and looked straight ahead. "You want to try? See if you still can?"

He turned his head too quickly to look at me. "Right now? On you?"

I shrugged, trying to seem indifferent, but I wanted nothing more than to feel his lips again. Why had I ever broken away from them?

"Okay," he nodded, straightening up and focusing on the far wall in front of us.

Nerves tickled the inside of my stomach as I waited for the feeling to take hold of me. When it did, it was better than I remembered. It started in my chest and permeated outward, filling me with a need for him. It had been so long since I'd experienced the pleasure of his power that I couldn't resist. My eyes drifted toward him as he stayed facing forward. They traced his features, stopping at his lips.

"Can I kiss you?" I whispered so quietly I wasn't sure

if the question had been spoken out loud. I didn't know what I'd do if he said no.

He turned to me and laughed, "I guess it worked." I nodded and swallowed as the lingering effects of his ability tested my willpower. He watched me as the sensation faded, a satisfied grin pulling into his cheek. "Still feel like kissing me?"

I smiled, a little embarrassed, but I was glad his ability had lowered my inhibitions. "Yep," I answered.

When I leaned in, he gripped my sides and pulled me closer. This time I vowed not to break away until I'd had enough. And we didn't. Even as we slept, our warm bodies pressed against each other. Skin against skin, like the day's last light as it melts into the horizon.

CHAPTER TEN

WILLIAM LAY NEXT TO ME, AND MORNING LIGHT dappled across his bare shoulders. His hair hung into his sleeping eyes. I stared at him in silence, wanting the peaceful moment to last a little longer.

His eyelids snapped open without warning. "Boo!"

"Ahhh!" I jumped and almost fell off the bed. He caught my wrist and pulled me closer, laughing.

"Just testing your reflexes." He smirked as we sat up. "Apparently I'm not the only one in need of re-training."

"Funny." I shoved his arm. "We'll see."

The warmth lingered where our skin touched, and it distracted me. I stretched my leg out and let my calf graze his knee, wanting to feel it again. The room was quiet as we watched each other, and heat collected under the jumbled white sheets. I could smell him on my skin, like warm freshly cut citrus.

"Give me your hand," he said, reaching for it already.

My eyes followed his fingers as he pressed my palm to his chest.

"What are you doing?" I asked. His heart pulsed with a warm rhythm against my skin.

"I like how it feels," he answered, studying the effect. "How our skin gets warm when we touch." I hadn't realized it was still new to him.

"Did you dream about it last night, the warmth?"

He looked up, surprised. "No. I guess I didn't dream about anything."

I swallowed down the disappointment and withdrew my hand. "Maybe tomorrow." I looked away pretending it didn't bother me. It was more than just warm skin he'd forgotten. He didn't remember loving me before we met.

"Don't worry about it," he said, disarming me with his smile. He put a hand to my cheek and turned my face to look at him. "We can always create a new memory."

No matter how familiar his lips felt against mine, the thrill of his kiss still excited me. His fingers combed my hair to the side, exposing the back of my neck.

"I dreamt about something when I was gone," he said against my skin. "I just want to try it..."

His mouth pressed against the sensitive spot just below my ear. Every hair stood on end as goose bumps ran down my left arm and leg. I sucked in a loud breath, surprised by the feeling.

"Sounds like a good dream," I said with my eyes closed. I was paralyzed by his touch, like if I were standing, my knees might buckle.

His mouth grazed my neck and he guided me back onto my pillow. I slid my hands against his bare waist, but froze as someone knocked. Neither of us moved or spoke. We just stared at the door hoping it would disappear somehow.

"Elyse?" Dr. Nickel's muffled voice sounded concerned on the other side. The knob turned before I could answer.

"Yeah?" I called out, but I was too late. He stepped into the room catching William on top of me.

"Oh! Sorry," he stumbled, torn between looking away and figuring out what was going on. "Son?" William rolled onto his back and I tried to disappear into my pillow. "Why are you back? Is everything all right?"

I don't think I'd ever seen Dr. Nickel look confused. Without his ability, he couldn't read our thoughts.

"Yeah," William answered casually. "Sarah's safe. I just came back to see Ellie."

Dr. Nickel nodded through the awkward moment. "Okay. That's good. That's great..." he said to the floor before leaving.

I threw my hands over my face, mortified.

"How's that for a new memory?" William laughed.

My cheeks were still pink with embarrassment when we emerged from our room. Thankfully the house was empty. I wasn't looking forward to facing Dr. Nickel again any time soon. Continuing our training outdoors seemed like the best way to avoid him entirely.

William followed me to the shed, smiling as I subtly scanned the yard for any sign of his dad. When we reached the door, I ducked inside, half expecting Mac to grunt and pull my stool up beside his. The air still smelled like him, that familiar mix of metal and gunpowder. Instead, swirling dust and creaking floorboards reminded me of his absence.

"Here," I said, handing William a gun from the table. "Bullets are in the bottom drawer of the tool chest."

He looked at the gun. Turned it in his hand like he was trying to figure it out. "Why do I need this?"

I grabbed a gun for myself and tucked it into the back of my pants. "Do you want to practice kissing or do you want to train?"

He shrugged one shoulder. "I was kind of hoping for the kissing thing."

A breathy laugh brushed my lips as I reached for a set of knives. "Work before play, right?"

I led him through the summer pines, secretly looking forward to feeling the effects of his power over me. When we reached the target range set up for my morning runs, I stopped.

"So here's what I was thinking," I started, chambering a bullet. The gun felt comfortable in my hand. Light. Friendly. I took aim and fired casually, hitting an empty can on the right. "I'll shoot right. You shoot left. Whoever gets to the middle first—"

William wasn't listening. He was smiling at me.

I lowered the gun. "Why are you smiling like that?"

"Look at you." He shrugged. "When did you get so... tomb raider?"

I turned the gun over in my hand, as if it was the cause of the change in me. "Um...I don't know." He had that familiar look in his eyes, like he was remembering the way he used to see me. "Why? Scared I'm going to show you up?"

"Kind of."

I rolled my eyes. "Come on. Are we going to do this or what?"

He nodded, taking me seriously. "What's the goal again?"

Nine cans remained on the log in the distance. I waved my gun at them.

"I'll aim for the cans on the right. You shoot from the left. Try and use your ability to mess up my accuracy. Whoever hits the center first wins."

He pointed his toes toward the targets. "Ready?"

"On three."

Our guns went off simultaneously. I hit. He missed. "Again," I said, aiming quickly to compensate for the kick. I aligned the sight with the farthest can on the right. But my eyes drifted. It was subtle, the pull of his ability. His concentration was divided, and I could tell he didn't have full control. My finger tested the pressure of the trigger as I watched him, and soon nothing else mattered. He was focused on something. Head lowered, arms outstretched and tense with muscle. Gentle butterflies made me forget the gun in my hand until I heard the sound of it. I shot. Too late and too far right. I missed.

He flashed a cocky grin as I came down from his high. "I think I'm going to like this game," he said as I ogled.

—

I TRAINED WITH HIM EVERY DAY FOR WEEKS. HE made me shoot targets that weren't mine, practiced using his peripheral vision, made me forget where I was and what I was doing. Every day his ability grew stronger and eventually came back like muscle memory.

Soon my morning run became *our* morning run, and after the pink flush of every sunrise we found ourselves at the target range. It was my favorite part of the day.

"I win," I said, bracing my hands against my legs to catch my breath. The skin on my thighs felt cold from the jog.

"Yeah, yeah. You know I let you win, right?"

I glanced back at him as he slowed to a walk, and something about the look on his face reminded me of Sarah. The ache of loss beat in my chest for the thousandth time.

"What is she doing right now?" I asked, re-tying my ponytail.

"Sarah?" He stared past me as he said her name and rested his hands on his hips. "She's waking up." His chest worked to recover lost breath. "The light wakes her up in the morning. Sometimes I wake up before her and watch her eyelids peek open when the sun comes up. She gets these big round saucer eyes..." He laughed through his heavy breathing.

"Do you miss her?"

I already knew he did, but it was nice having someone around who understood the empty feeling I had without her.

"Every minute of every day," he answered, "but I don't regret coming here."

I tapped the toe of my running shoe against the dirt. What he'd said the night he returned tempted me like the devil on my shoulder: *You could visit.*

"I need to see her." The words spilled out of my mouth unchecked. Only after did I realize how true they were.

"I thought you—"

"I did," I interrupted, still breathing hard. "I keep going back and forth, but I don't know if I can stay away. Being away from her is going against every primal instinct I have. I miss her so much it makes me sick to even think about it."

"You just have to keep focused. When this is all over we'll be together again."

Panic began building in my stomach, turning quickly into sudden hysteria.

"When what is over? How will I even know? *You*

have to lose to win," I said repeating the oracle's words. "I don't even know what that means. Maybe she meant Sarah, but maybe she didn't. I feel like I've already lost her."

William stepped closer, pulling my hands away from my face. I felt so open and fragile, and for a moment embarrassment colored my cheeks.

"It's okay," he said, cupping the back of my head with his hand. He pulled me into his chest. "If you need to see her, then we'll see her, okay?"

I relaxed into him, as if his permission was the key to my stability. "Okay."

I closed my eyes, hoping it wouldn't be a mistake.

William pinched the back of my shirt and fanned it against my body. "I don't know, you might be too sweaty to hold a baby."

"Shut up." I pushed away, secretly self-conscious about how drenched I was.

"You want to go inside?" he asked. "I've been through these drills a thousand times anyway, and Sam and Nics will be up soon to plan the rest of the day."

I didn't like the idea of cutting out the favorite part of my morning. "No, let's finish. We have to keep your skills fresh."

A knowing smile crawled up his cheek. "Uh-huh."

"Okay, so maybe it's more for me than for you," I admitted. I crossed my arms over my chest with feigned sincerity. "I might have a serious problem. I could be addicted."

He tucked golden strands of loose hair behind his ears. "That does sound serious," he played along.

His eyes narrowed with focus, and then I felt it. A subtle flush of heat. The need to be near him. Like thirst. Dry lips that needed to be licked. I couldn't look away. His ability tested my will power. I knew I should resist. It was my job to resist. Part of the training, but all I wanted was to give in. I inched toward him. Leaned toward him. He was the sun and I was every star, every planet, every moon.

His lips moved. I hardly heard what they were saying. He called out targets, and I obeyed, lifting my gun and pulling the trigger. I didn't know why or what I was shooting. Over and over I felt the gun kick back against my cupped palm. It was hard to focus on anything but him. His shoulders. They were broad and strong. I admired him in a daze, forgetting myself, forgetting my gun.

"What are you doing?" Rachel's voice echoed somewhere in the background. "Did you hear what I said?"

"Ellie." Only after William spoke my name did I blink myself out of the trance.

"Yeah?" I asked him, having trouble letting go.

He put a gentle hand to my arm, which was still tense and outstretched ready to shoot. I relaxed it and loosened my grip at his touch. "Adrianna sent Alex. She's ready for you."

CHAPTER ELEVEN

"WE FOUND ANOTHER TESTING FACILITY," ALEX explained as everyone gathered in the living room. "This time in San Francisco. We have a team ready to go, but Adrianna wants Elyse involved. Everyone else can do what they want. Stay or go." He shot a quick glance at William, before addressing me. "You in?"

They were all watching, waiting for the word "yes," but I couldn't bring myself to say it. The vision I had during Sarah's birth was too real, too imminent. Our last attempt to free our people from one of their labs had gotten out of hand. What if this time there were heavier consequences?

"Well?" Alex pushed.

I searched their faces for understanding. "We can't."

"What do you mean we can't?" Nics asked. "Not too long ago we were the ones strapped to tables for testing.

If it was us, would you still say no?"

"No, of course not." I cracked my knuckles, thinking. "What about the vision? We have to be careful."

Something felt wrong about it, like the future was whispering a warning: *Don't do it.*

Alex gave Kara an annoyed look.

"Alex and I are going," Kara said. There was no judgment in her words, only confidence. She was always so strong, sure of every move she made.

I'm not sure, she corrected. *But it's the right thing to do.*

"We're going too," Sam said from the couch.

There will be injuries. We'll need you. Kara slipped her thought into my head.

I looked to William. His fingers tightened around his elbow as he crossed his arms. "I'm with you either way."

"They're prepping now," Alex said, running a finger over his arched eyebrow. "We need to get going. We can go over the plan on site."

—

IT DIDN'T LOOK LIKE WE WERE ON A MISSION. TO THE few around us, we were human. Unmarked. Unregistered. What they were most afraid of, hidden in plain sight.

It was one of those perfect days outside. Blue sky. Warm sun. Quiet. San Francisco streets were rarely empty, but today there was an eerie hush to the rush of traffic. The city I'd left behind so long ago once moved like a

Rubik's cube. Pedestrians walked the streets in perfect rhythm with passing cars and public transportation. They waited their turns as cars obeyed stoplights. Everything flowed effortlessly despite the chaos of so many different people traveling to a thousand different places.

Now the slovenly man walking across the street didn't even have to check for oncoming cars. He adjusted the large white sign hanging from a rope around his neck as he ambled. Written in black were the words GO HOME GREEK FREAKS.

William sat next to me on a bench and I nudged him, nodding at the man. "Subtle," he said, rolling his eyes.

A bus pulled up along the lonely sidewalk, exhaling a sigh as it squeaked to a stop. A few passengers got off, and the bus driver looked at me through the open door. I shook my head, and he slid the glass panel shut. Across the Guess ad on the side someone had etched the words "Praise Aphrodite." I smiled to myself at the clash of public opinion as the bus pulled away. "Looks like you've got a fan club."

We both laughed, but I forced myself to focus. We were here for a purpose. I hugged my shoulder bag closer to my body. It wasn't full of books as most people would assume. It carried weapons.

Edith and Dr. Nickel sat on the bench to my left. We'd been told to wait for the signal. I watched for the side door of the grey building to open. It was hard to believe there were Descendants inside. It was too central.

But maybe that was the point. Not long ago, this was a highly populated Descendant community, a place we had created a network for surviving unnoticed. I wondered how many had remained after registration became required, after we'd spread the word to vacate.

The door opened from the inside and an anonymous foot let down the doorstop, signaling Edith to move us into position.

"Ready?" Edith asked. Her only job was to get us past security using Alex's ability.

I put a hand on her fragile shoulder and hoped I could keep her safe.

Inside, bullets were already being fired. I pulled Edith with me as a spray of gunfire and particleboard ricocheted around us. Dr. Nickel followed, but William was lost in the smoke. My heart quickened, and I moved without thinking, opening my shoulder bag and pushing a gun into Edith's hands. She jolted with every sound, trembling as she placed her finger on the trigger. "Take your dad and go to the meeting spot, okay? If someone you don't know comes, just disappear," I said. She nodded too quickly, and I wondered if she'd even been listening. "You got it?"

She swallowed and clutched the gun to her chest. "Yes." Then they were gone.

I grabbed a weapon for myself and shuffled my feet awkwardly toward the edge of the counter. Before I got a chance to see what was around it, someone darted around the corner and slid into me. "Don't shoot," William said with my gun pointed at his throat. His ability was the only reason I hadn't fired. It stopped me within a fraction of a second, and my mouth hung open in shock. I almost killed him.

"Don't do that—" I stammered.

I didn't hear the man approach from behind me. William grabbed the gun from my hand and pointed it over my shoulder. I jumped as it went off. Things were moving too fast.

William grabbed my hand. "Come on." I looked back as he pulled me along the wall. The man was dead. Blood pooled around his head.

For the first time, I got a sense of what was around me. Nics crouched behind an upturned table, her eyes focused forward causing men to shoot blindly from an open doorway across the room. The bodies of guards stationed here for this very reason were strewn out on the ground like dead fish in a dried sea of blood. Much like the other facility, this place was lined with hallways of clear prison cells, each one containing an unconscious body. Some glass rooms had been shattered, others painted red with death. Alex and Kara worked to pull plugs and set the captives free. I needed to get to them, to help, but waves of black police uniforms started to shadow the doorways.

I fired my gun at them, giving Sam cover as he made his way toward a Descendant who'd been shot. He dragged the body past me, and I switched my bracelet to the right wrist, ready to heal. Before I had time to push the buttons, Sam stopped me. "He's gone, Elyse."

"Sam, I need you," Nics yelled. She and William had been working together to keep the police at bay. She blinded them, while William attempted to stop their advance, and they both fired shots. Two others from Adrianna's team were manning the door on the opposite side of the room. Bodies in black uniforms were thrown against the brick walls by someone or some unseen force. I couldn't tell.

"We need to get out of here," I said to no one and everyone all at once. I searched for Alex, but he was nowhere. Mid-travel maybe. "Alaximandrios."

The team of police pushed closer. They had us beat in the numbers game, and I could see Nics struggling to keep her focus under the gunfire. A break in her concentration and we wouldn't be invisible for long. We were cornered, and they were closing in. William and Sam worked to debilitate the front line, but when those men were down, more came.

My gun clicked with an empty chamber and I reached for my darts.

"We don't have time to wait for Alex," I yelled over the clatter.

"Give me your hand," William said.

I didn't question it. I reached out with my left and he pressed our palms together. "Alaximandrios," I whispered over and over again like a distress signal.

The shuffling of feet and clacking of plastic police shields slowed and then stopped as William stepped forward with me in tow. “Let us through,” he said loudly. Across the room, police still clamored through the door, gunshots shattered glass. Sam and Nics followed us as the men in uniform stepped aside. The heat from William’s palm radiated up to my elbow, it was strong, but I could feel it slipping.

“I can’t hold them long,” he said through his teeth. “There are too many.” Infatuated eyes followed William like he was their messiah, and I gripped William’s hand tighter. If he let go, they’d close in on us.

“Rachel,” I heard Nics yell from behind me. “Paul!” Her voice was lost in the commotion. “We can’t leave them.” She looked at me, and I was at a loss. If we went back, we were all dead.

“Rachel!” I screamed, but William tugged me forward, and my eyes found Sam, desperate for him to do something. He hesitated a moment, then in a decisive second he had Nics over his shoulder, and though she struggled, he moved with quick feet after us.

Police filled the hallway, along with another military unit. As we passed through them, their hands reached out. I didn’t know if it was William’s ability that made them want to touch us, or if his power was fading and they were getting ready to close in. The feel of so many bodies made me claustrophobic. Just as I was about to lose it, we reached an emergency exit. I was drowning, and it was the door to my next breath.

Outside, the quiet city we'd left behind was in complete disarray. People ran from buildings like bugs scattering in the light, searching for cover. They'd switched to survival mode, all other instincts or social obligations went forgotten as they ran down the center of once busy roads screaming. Everything felt like slow motion, like it wasn't really happening. For a second I questioned reality. The adrenaline, the claustrophobia, something was making me see things. This couldn't be real. William urged me forward with a hand on my waist, and I stepped into the street. Before I could see what people were running from, a helicopter lowered too quickly above our heads. It spiraled out of control and sliced its metal wings through the side of the facility. I screamed instinctively as glass rained down on us. The explosion kick-started my awareness, and I heard the scuffle of the police we'd left behind.

"Go," Nics yelled from behind.

William's warm grip pulled me onward, and just like the others, we were running through the streets away from nothing and everything.

The sound of another explosion knocked me in the back, and I flew forward with a wave of heat and pressure. My face hit the blacktop and my ears rang so loudly it nearly silenced the world around me. Everything blurred. I blinked trying to retain at least my sense of sight. William's lips moved in double vision, but his words were muffled and I couldn't hear at first. Slowly my ears adjusted and it all came back like the roar of ocean waves.

"Are you okay?" he shouted, without waiting for me to answer. He scooped me up into his arms and carried me.

"Rachel!" Nics's sobs rose above the shrieks of terror. Behind us, the building we'd just fled collapsed into a heap of rubble. I felt my heart pinch, felt the world spin again. Rachel and Paul were in that building.

The four of us took cover under a cement doorframe to avoid the raining destruction, and all we could do was watch as cars crashed into everything in their way.

Plumes of black smoke billowed up toward the sky from the crumbled wreckage. Sirens and megaphone warnings filled the streets, but it was so loud I couldn't hear what they were saying. Some people ran, others gathered, too stunned to look away. Fire and debris from the helicopter explosion dripped like wet paint onto cars below and a few went up in flames amidst the chaos. It wasn't until the flaming cars began to lift into the air and slam into buildings that I realized we were doing this. Descendants. These people were running from Descendants.

CHAPTER TWELVE

"IT'S US," I SAID TO WILLIAM OVER THE NOISE. "WE have to stop this."

"This way," Sam said, and this time we followed him. Tears streaked Nics's dark cheeks and stung my own, but we didn't have time to stop and mourn. We cut through alleyways. Street after street had taken the same abuse as the one we'd just come from. We followed the sirens until we saw them, an army of rebels working together to tear apart the city. They stayed close together, but something was too robotic about the way they moved. Bullets couldn't penetrate whatever shield was protecting them. As they advanced, their faces were still, their eyes vacant.

The four of us watched from the corner of a distant building as they marched slowly toward us. Everything in me said to turn and run, but I couldn't look away. Glass broke from above as rough waves of wind swept across windows shattering their sleek surfaces. Cars were pushed to the side by nothing and crushed by a force I couldn't see. Those brave enough to approach fell unconscious and slumped to the ground in heaps. The rebel eyes didn't focus on anyone or anything. They worked in a carefully thought out system, crippling the surrounding population and destroying infrastructure. They stared straight ahead and left a wake of destruction behind them as they moved.

I looked closer at the group terrorizing the city and caught sight of a girl on the left. She was younger than me. Light brown hair, sweet pink cheeks, there was nothing evil about her. Something wasn't right. Then I realized where I'd seen that vacant look. In the humans Christoph had at the warehouse. Those blank expressions didn't belong to Descendants. They belonged to humans who'd been mutated with the blood of our kind. This was his army. Who knew how many others there were.

A military-grade tank rolled around the corner closing the gap between us and the rebels.

"We have to go," William said, tugging my hand.

I didn't budge. "We can't! We have to stop..."

The tank bulldozed its way through the wreckage, its steel wheels clawing at the concrete.

Nics headed for the alleyway. "What are we supposed to do? The four of us can't stop it."

I followed her, shaking my head as I looked back. Nothing had gone according to plan. My friends were dead. The city destroyed. We'd prevented none of it. My throat ached until I couldn't hold back. I cried into the air as we ran, my sobs simply another layer of noise that went unheard. I didn't even know where we were going until I saw the address on the building where Nics stopped. Our rendezvous site. The numbers dangled and swung in the breeze like a wind chime. Broken windows and missing walls marred its once pristine façade.

My stomach tightened with fear—Edith.

William looked up hoping to see her. "She'll be okay."

"Alaximandrios," I whispered one last time.

Nothing.

We climbed the stairs, bracing ourselves against loose handrails and pushing debris aside until we reach the second floor. I hoped he was right. She was smart, but was she quick enough with her abilities to keep herself safe?

"Hello?" Nics called.

The apartment sat empty and in pieces. It looked familiar. A yellow kitchen light flickered with life. The windows had been blown out and bookshelves in the living room lay on their side. I'd seen this place. The booming sound of an overhead jet triggered my memory.

"Everybody take cover," I yelled. The blast knocked us all to the floor before we had the chance.

Nics coughed through the dust cloud spilling in through the window. "What's going on?"

I pushed up onto my knees. "They're bombing."

"Who?" Sam yelled.

Drywall dust fell into my eyes, and I blinked it out, desperate to see. "I don't know."

The sound of another plane grew louder overhead.

"Get down. Over here." William put a hand around my waist and pulled me against the wall. Nics and Sam took cover under the breakfast bar amongst upturned stools.

William stood over me as the building shook and pieces of the ceiling crumbled like falling snow.

Every word felt like déjà vu. "It's okay," I echoed what I'd said in my vision. "We survive this. I've seen it." Another blast caused the floor to quake.

He looked down over me. "I'm not taking any chances."

"Hello?" I heard Edith somewhere but couldn't see her.

"We're here," William called out. "Can you get us out?"

She was in front of us almost immediately, searching through the hazy air for the others. Nics and Sam shuffled closer to make contact, and the smoky room became stark white emptiness.

When I opened my eyes we were in our living room, the silence of home almost jarring as we were set free of the breathless upper air of Aether's bloodline.

Somehow, I found myself standing face to face with Kara.

"What was that?" I asked, hoping she'd know something. I could see her searching my thoughts, but that moment of clarity I was expecting never came.

"I don't know," she answered.

The two of us stood stagnant as I battled with the shadow of regret that had followed me to this point. I combed my hair back with my fingers and felt my nails dig into my scalp.

"This isn't our fault," Kara said quietly, to talk me down.

I bit my lip and nodded, catching sight of Alex sitting on the floor against the wall, his face bloody, his arms skinned and burned.

All other thoughts dissipated when I saw him. "What happened to you?"

"We were in the building as it exploded," Kara explained, rushing over to him as I followed. "He shielded me from the blast, and we almost didn't get out."

I knelt down beside him, and his eyes flickered upward. "Can you help him?" Kara asked.

She already knew I could. I switched my bracelet, and my chin began to tremble at the idea of Rachel and Paul in that building. *We left them*, I thought to myself, knowing Kara was listening.

I cleared my throat. "Anything internal?" I asked as I healed the superficial cuts on his arms. He shook his head keeping his eyes down like he was ashamed he needed my help.

"His leg is broken," Kara corrected with her head cocked.

He didn't disagree, but his jaw was set.

"Where?" I asked.

He reached down and pulled at the knee of his tattered jeans revealing an uneven shinbone that protruded through the skin.

"Oh God." Nics turned away.

"I'll have to set it first."

Alex nodded, still a little apprehensive.

"Do you know how?" he asked.

He flinched as I examined the break with my fingers. "Not really, but I can't heal it like this."

"I'll do it," Kara insisted. "I'll hold the bone in place while you heal the wound."

I could see her speak silent thoughts to him as she set her hands on his leg. "Ready, Elyse?"

I nodded and triggered the blades on my bracelet. Alex screamed through his teeth and slammed his fist on the floor. I let the blood spill into the wound until his screams turned to sighs of relief.

I found it hard to sympathize. Did he know that his stubborn refusal to answer my call cost our friends their lives? I wanted to let the curt words slip from my lips, but he looked so vulnerable, I couldn't bring myself to say what I was thinking. Maybe if he would have answered, they'd still be alive.

"We were going back for them, Elyse. That's how it

happened," Kara said with bitterness. "Don't start blaming. People die in war."

"They weren't *people*," Nics snapped, clenching her hands into fists. "They were our friends."

"Do you know where Adrianna is?" I asked, before they had time to tear each other apart. "More innocent people will die if that group of rebels isn't stopped."

Reluctance caused Alex's lips to purse, but he owed me. "Yes," he answered

"Take me there," I said, desperate to blow out the flame before the whole world caught fire. "Now."

CHAPTER THIRTEEN

WHEN ALEX AND I APPEARED, A GROUP OF PEOPLE I assumed was the new Council sat around a table in a small office I'd never seen before.

Adrianna looked up from her seat at the far end, and a wave of relief washed over her. "We weren't sure you made it out of the explosion." She put a hand to her heart and took a breath. "I was hoping you'd show up."

I hadn't met the new Council, but each of their parents was visible in their features. Dimitri's daughter had the tough, hardened look of a girl who'd been raised without a mother's gentleness. Her arms were muscular, and she had her father's eyes. They were a dark grey that held the power to age any living being until its death. Grayson stood beside her, a younger version of Christoph. Antec's son was the oldest, though he'd grown awkward even into his adult years. He scowled at me with crow's eyes, his pointed nose poking through a curtain of black hair. Then amongst them I recognized another face, a girl younger than Edith. Her mother had been imprisoned with me. We'd escaped together. I knew Lilia must have had a child. William said they'd all had children to continue their lines. I just never imagined that child here, with them, planning to overthrow the government and kill the president. Besides she was too young to have a hand in all of this.

"We need to talk," I said, unsure of how to approach the subject without challenging her authority in front of everyone.

She nodded her head, making eye contact with the group, and the new Council filed out. Alex took it upon himself to disappear.

I knew I was here for another reason, but I couldn't help myself. "Lilia's daughter?" I asked once we were alone.

"Yes. Though she happens to be Christoph's daughter as well," she answered. A cold flash of jealousy or disgust caused her lip to curl, and I wondered if his having a child with another woman was what poisoned her against him.

I licked my lips, trying to wipe the shock from my face.

"I'd say she's the most passionate of all of them." Adrianna stood and walked toward me. "Trying to get even for her father's death, I'd imagine. He's the one who raised her." A subtle smile twisted into her cheek, and I wanted to break her head open just to see what she was thinking. I didn't like the idea of Lilia's daughter being manipulated. It made me wonder if I was being manipulated as well.

"What happened in San Francisco?" I asked bluntly.

I gripped the back of a chair, my trust for her wavering. Only a handful of us knew about the experiments Christoph was doing to create his mutated human army. She was one of them.

Her gaze dropped to the floor and she sat against the edge of the table. "It was a mistake," she admitted.

I shook my head not understanding. "So it was you? Why would you...San Francicso is a community city. The Descendant population—"

"I didn't mean for it to get so out of hand," she interrupted. Her lips pursed as she crossed her arms into a defensive stance. "The city has been in a rough state for days. The looting and rioting was making it an unsafe place to be. I thought if I could use Christoph's legion to do some good, get the people under control, it would work in our favor."

She looked up, and I could see genuine regret in her eyes.

"I was wrong," she finished.

I chose to use her moment of weakness to my advantage. "The humans won't trust us now. You've proven to them that we are dangerous. They *should* be afraid. Killing McKinney could backfire. People will just revolt out of fear. Maybe we should call it off."

"No," she scoffed.

We stood in a stale mate facing each other before she felt the need to elaborate.

"For all they know the show of power was intentional, and I plan to play it off that way." She pushed off the table and paced in front of me. "You're right. People could revolt, and they need to know that if they do, there will be consequences." Her long spidery fingers combed the thick brown curls draped over her shoulder. "It may have frightened them to a point where they'll accept our control unchallenged. If people are scared enough they will fold when we have the upper hand. It's us against them, Elyse, and it's our turn to take control of this world. You've seen the facilities. You know what they're doing to our people."

"And what have we done to theirs? You destroyed a city." I could hear my voice starting to rise with indignation. "Who knows how many innocent people you killed in the process?"

"Like I said, it was a mistake. It won't happen again. The legion of crossbreeds has been taken care of."

"So you killed them?" I asked, somehow appalled and relieved at the same time.

She seemed unaffected. "It had to be done."

I wondered if that had changed anything for the future of the rest of the country.

"If you know what I've seen, you know that San Francisco isn't the only city to be destroyed. What if it's you who makes it happen? I can't be a part of it."

She swallowed, frustrated by the validity in my point.

"I can only do what I think is best for this country. Not only for our people, but for theirs. I don't want to hurt them, which is why our plan is to target only one man." She paused, making eye contact. "I can't say the same for humans. They've already hurt us."

She was right. I'd seen it, and part of me did feel the urge to fight back in some way. Maybe it was our right to retaliate against such actions, but another part of me felt sympathy. They didn't trust us. And they shouldn't.

I focused on the grey knit carpet at my feet shaking my head. "It just doesn't feel right to murder a man and forcefully take over."

"And that is why you're not a good leader. Christoph was right about one thing. Peace has a price. This is the cost of integration."

Her words hit me where I was vulnerable. I blamed myself for this.

"Look," I said staring past her. "I can't do this. I don't want a part in it anymore." I couldn't handle making any more mistakes, losing any more friends, watching innocent people die.

"You don't have a choice."

"I do," I said with a nod before turning to leave.

In the hallway the new Council members gawked at me like they were trying to read my mind. I could tell by their uncertain eyes that none of them thought for themselves. They were all pieces in Adrianna's game. Edith had arrived and stood with them near the window with her father.

"Alex sent me to check in on the meeting and bring you home," she said.

"I don't know about the meeting," I answered. "I'm not involved with the council anymore."

Edith stared at me with hesitation, reading my thoughts I imagined.

"Just take me back to the city I guess." I pulled my hair into a ponytail and slid my bracelet up my wrist so it was snug against my skin. "I'm sure there are a lot of injured and—"

"It's not safe," Dr. Nickel interrupted with a shake of his head.

Edith shot a defiant glare at him, and before I knew it her hand was on my arm turning the world around me white. When I opened my eyes I felt sick. I didn't know why I wasn't expecting the reality of the vision I'd experienced during the birth. My throat stung as I took that first step over the mess of debris.

"I'll be back," Edith said from behind me. Her voice made me jump. I'd forgotten she was there. I nodded before she disappeared, leaving me alone.

The street that stretched out in front of me was desolate and in pieces. The destruction was exactly how I saw it would be. Buildings toppled, cars overturned and smashed, glass and metal everywhere. All of it smoky and smoldering. When I noticed the bodies, I couldn't hold back the sick moan in my throat. A man in a suit was on his back staring lifelessly up at the sky. A leg of another stuck out of a car window. Everywhere I looked there were more and more.

I closed my eyes, not wanting to see what I knew was to my right. I took a deep breath and forced myself to turn. I couldn't hide from this. It was there, just as I'd seen it. The twisted wreckage of red metal that used to be the Golden Gate Bridge. Expecting it didn't change my reaction. My knees buckled beneath me. It was us. We did this.

I'd never heard the city so quiet.

A sudden realization made my heart constrict. I knew what else was coming, and I didn't know how to stop any of it. I covered my mouth with my hand, trying to hold in the sobs, but it only muffled them. This was my fault. Adrianna was right. This was the price of integration. The guilt burned in my chest, and every ounce of fear that beat in my heart was for my baby girl. I reached for my stomach, though it was flat and she was gone. I needed to keep her safe. I couldn't let our world be destroyed.

"Are you all right?" Edith asked from behind me. I was still shaking as the sobs faded. I couldn't face her.

Only when I heard another voice did I look up.

"Oh my God," Nics said under her breath. All five of my friends stood behind me. Kara, Alex, Sam, Nics, and William.

"What are you doing here?" I asked.

William helped me to my feet and wiped the tears from my wet cheeks. "We're here to help you with the injured." I brushed debris from my palms, and he pulled me into his strong arms. My eyes closed as I breathed in the familiar smell of his shirt. I needed him, and he came.

"I don't know where—" I began to say.

"Edith does," Kara answered my thought.

"The hospital on Hyde street," Edith added. "It has thousands of patients, but there's also security. We'll have to be careful." Her pink lips and baby face seemed too innocent to witness what I could only imagine we'd encounter.

"Maybe you should go back, Edith," I said to her. I knew her Dad didn't want her here without him.

"It's my ability," she started to whine, and the child in her slipped through. It was easy to forget how young she was with all her power.

"Edie," William gave her a look, and though I was sure it felt strange for him to play the big brother role, it worked. She huffed a little girl sigh and disappeared.

Alex got us to the hospital. There were too many people for the building to hold. The wounded spilled out into the hallways and clustered against the outside entrance. As the sun sank it dragged the light down with it. The city went dark and the sound of human voices trying to stay quiet felt like the scuffle of sewer rats. As I looked around I would have given anything to be someone else, to not have my power. There were too many injured for the hospital to handle, and I wouldn't be able to heal all of them.

The power was out. Battery operated lights were set up along the hallways, and people watched us from the shadows as we passed, trying to gauge whether or not we were a threat. We didn't have the barcodes that marked us as the enemy, but neither did the ones who attacked. Anyone could be one of them. One of us.

My stomach churned as I took it all in. Blood was smeared across the white tile floor in places. People were using shirts and other pieces of ripped clothing to staunch wounds that needed real attention. The black remnants of fire and destruction had followed the victims into the building and everything seemed to be mixed with a layer of soot. It felt like I'd stumbled upon the aftermath of a World War II battle. My brain couldn't make sense of it. I tried to keep the look of shock off of my face and wiped my sweaty hands on my jeans, coaxing myself onward. This was the cost of freedom. *Be stronger. You* need *to fix this. You did this.*

"We need to split up," I said, realizing I wasn't the only one who could ease these people's pain. "Sam, you can help too. If they're really suffering, adjust their blood-alcohol level enough to make them pass out or at least dull the pain."

Sam cleared his throat with a nervous twitch of his lips. "Sure." He nodded, his eager eyes looking for someone to help.

"William and I will take Nics in case we need cover. Sam, you and Kara stay with Alex so he can get you out if you need to."

Sam went left and I went right. We had to be discrete. Making people drink my blood would give us away for sure, and Nics couldn't hide us without it being too obvious.

"I might need you to help me sway these people into letting me help them," I told William. "They'll be scared if I try to give them my blood. They won't understand."

"Got it," William said, and without a second thought he took my hand. I smiled inside, but kept serious.

"Nics, if I say go..."

I didn't need to finish. She nodded, and before I knew it I was searching for someone to help. I stopped in front of a girl who seemed to be our age in human terms, maybe eighteen or twenty. Tangled blonde hair framed her round face, and she hugged her knees close, curling her toes under filthy blood-stained feet. Her eyes were closed, but tears had cut pathways down her ash-covered cheeks. She sat alone and her whole body shuddered. I couldn't see where she'd been hurt, but it had to be bad. Her face was ghost white and she was hardly conscious.

I took a breath and knelt down in front of her. The noise around us muffled any sound I made, and she didn't look up. Body heat had collected in the hallway, and dirty blonde curls stuck to the sides of her sweat-coated forehead. I brushed them back, and her eyes opened so wide it startled me.

"Are you a nurse?" she asked.

I assumed it was obvious I wasn't, but I could see she was desperate. Anyone willing to look past my age, my clothes, the absence of any medical supplies had to be.

"No," I answered, "but I can help you."

Her body shifted, and she became aware of William and Nics standing behind me. She put a hand to her bicep, trying to cover it with her sweater, and recoiled into the wall. "How? Who are you?"

I didn't know how to answer that question. I couldn't lie. We'd all been doing that for too long, and it was time they knew we weren't all bad.

"I'm Ellie. My blood can heal you." The words were out before I realized I should have been more discrete.

Her face twisted with panic, and I could tell she was about to yell for help. Her mouth opened only to soften as William knelt down next to me. "It's okay," he said to her, and she was mesmerized. He smiled at her and reached for the sweater. "Can we help you?"

She nodded as he pulled back the gray cloth that staunched the blood from her arm.

Beneath, three large pieces of metal stuck out of her flesh. William's careful fingers worked them out, and the girl was either so enamored or so in shock she watched without crying out in pain. I watched too, just as taken by his gentle nature as she was. Despite the memory loss, he still had the same kind spirit. The goodness in him couldn't be erased. All the best parts of him were still there, and I loved him for it.

I reached for my bracelet, and glanced at Nics, but she wasn't looking at me. She was eyeing everyone around us. They were staring. Not only because we'd approached the girl, but because I had a dart gun strapped to my thigh and William and Nics had guns tucked into the back of their pants. "Should I hide us?"

I wanted to say yes. I wanted to be anywhere but here, anyone but me, but hiding felt cowardly. "No," I answered. "Just be ready to if..." I wasn't sure what came after the if. If they mob us, kill us, catch us. "Just be ready."

The girl's eyes didn't drift away from William's as the bracelet sliced my wrist and dripped blood into her wounds.

"See?" William said to her, and she smiled.

I didn't watch the skin heal. I waited for the reaction, for the people to call me out as the enemy. Instead they stared in awe, looking at me like I had the last ounce of water on earth and they were all parched. I rose to my feet, exposed and outnumbered, vulnerable, and made my way to the next pair of desperate eyes. A boy with burns. A man with a broken leg. One by one, I made up for this disaster as best I could. Soon there was a line, and I was amazed it was going so well. William kept contact, kept me strong. A hand to my waist, just under my shirt as he sat next to me. His heat spread against my bare skin until felt I it everywhere, nourishing my power. Nics stood guard, waiting for her moment, though I wasn't sure it would come.

"Time to go," Alex said, suddenly in front of us with Kara and Sam. "They're on to us."

I looked down the line at a girl in a dirty pink dress with a gash through her right eye and couldn't bring myself to move.

"I need more time." My vision wavered to black for a moment. Stopping made me aware of how much blood I'd given up already. Still I couldn't leave yet. Not yet.

"You need a break," Kara said with a warning tone.

"Um...guys," Sam hit Nics in the shoulder trying to get her attention.

"Ow," she started, but turned serious and looked at me.

I heard them before I could see them. "Hands up!" Their mistake. Most of us didn't need our hands. Voices echoed down the hallway, a clatter of plastic shields and boots against tile. Soldiers, police, whoever they were seemed to be coming from both sides.

"Can you hold them off? I just need a few more minutes."

Alex rolled his eyes, but Sam answered without a beat. "Hell yeah."

Nics began to focus in an attempt to make us invisible.

I tried not to watch as the soldiers inched closer,

debating open fire in this hospital. I stayed focused on the girl. Everyone in line had backed against the wall, not sure what to expect. I made my way down the hall, heart throbbing, trying to keep steady on my feet. William held me at the waist, and I leaned into him as I tripped toward the girl with the cut face. A hand caught my wrist, a woman with bloody teeth. "I'm sorry," I whispered as I pulled away. Everywhere I looked there were more and more injuries. With each step the burden grew heavier.

A shot rang out and the whole hallway became a nest of screams. Somehow, I made it to the girl. I pulled her to the floor, though she seemed scared to death of me. Her lips shook as she cried, but her mother was there, and I smiled at her. "Thank you," she mouthed. I couldn't hear above the chaos, but her thanks meant everything. She saw me, this woman. She knew we were good. *I* was good.

My breath was labored as I punched the bracelet again, for what seemed like the thousandth time. Everything started to spin together in a blur. Blood dripped into the girl's wound, bodies shoved past us, and William cried out. I tried to look back, but his hand pulled away from my skin and a wave of unconsciousness finally crashed down on me. I couldn't fight the black. It sealed me up in its cocoon, and I was out.

CHAPTER FOURTEEN

AS I REGAINED CONSCIOUSNESS THE HOSPITAL HALLway moved faster than I could process. The linoleum under my back reverberated with the energy of people rushing, guns firing. The ceiling blurred and spun. Screams and panic echoed against the narrow walls. I squinted away from a battery-operated lantern a few feet away. William's hand against my cheek guided my gaze.

"Ellie?" He searched my eyes for recognition. "Here," he said, running a blade over his palm and holding it to my mouth.

It was the first time he'd offered his blood to me like this since he'd forgotten me. It meant more now than it ever did. I drank it in, refreshing and sweet like I remembered.

A man screamed as he passed, "This way! Hurry!"

I looked up, distracted, but William stayed focused, pushing his palm back to my lips. His free hand was in mine, sending warmth up to my elbow, and I started to feel myself come back.

"Ready?" he asked.

I nodded and he tightened his grip. Before he had time to pull me to my feet a soldier stepped beside us. He stood three feet away, dressed in black and holding his gun inches from my face. A million thoughts buried me. This was it. I was dead. My breath caught at first as I lost myself to what I'd be leaving behind. My daughter. The war. William. Then, for the briefest moment my heart settled and waited for the end, as if it knew everything would be okay either way. Like it knew there was more than this life.

"Mark," the soldier barked into his radio, interrupting the peaceful lull I'd given myself over to.

"What?" A voice crackled over the small speaker.

"Excuse me, Sir?" William spoke up. "Do me a favor and forget you saw us."

The man looked past me, at William, then blinked and shook his head. I recognized the infatuation in his eyes.

"Ryan, you there?" the radio voice asked.

He clicked the talk button, dazed. "Never mind."

William gestured with his hand, and the guy handed the rifle over.

"Thaaank you," William said, overly pleased with himself.

His confidence made me smile. I pulled a dart from

my satchel, switched the bracelet to my left wrist and triggered the blades to draw out my poison. The soldier dropped unconscious beside us as soon as the dart hit his neck.

William patted him on his slumped shoulder as we got up. "Good talk."

I caught sight of Nics searching for us against the opposite wall. When she saw me, she nodded for us to move closer. It was like crossing a river to get to her. People stayed huddled on the ground, like rocks fighting the current. Others rushed past, desperate to escape the madness.

"Alex is on his way," Nics said over the noise. "We're getting out of here."

William stood awkwardly next to her like he wasn't sure what to say. He pointed the stolen rifle up at the ceiling, testing its weight. "Free gun."

Nics looked at him for a second, surprised by his comment, before a laugh burst from her lips.

"Ready?" Alex asked, appearing in front of us.

We all reached out and made contact, and in seconds we were home.

Sam and Kara sat on the couch waiting in silence, camouflaged in blood and filth. Their shadowed faces drooped with exhaustion. I had no idea what time it was, but a pale half moon graced the room with her silver light. The still air smelled of pine and lavender, a refreshing contrast to the dank funk of sweaty bodies and festering wounds.

None of us spoke as we took in the peaceful absence of sound, but it was too quiet. I could still hear the screams in my head. It was almost unfair to escape the chaos so easily.

"I'm crashing a suite at the Hyatt tonight," Alex said, wiping his face with his hand. He ran his fingers through his messy black hair, trying to wake himself up a bit.

I didn't say anything. Nothing could beat my own bed.

He looked at Kara. "You coming?"

She pushed herself off the couch and they were gone.

Nics stared at Sam and I stared at her. We were two friends short tonight, and neither of us wanted to be the first to acknowledge that terrible fact out loud. The loss didn't seem real. Talking about it would only worsen the wound.

"Let's go to bed," Nics said, reaching for Sam's hand. He took it, lifting himself to his feet, and wrapped a long strong arm around her as they headed for their room.

William and I did the same, but I couldn't sleep. Rachel's face was etched into the backs of my eyelids, and I was too afraid of what I'd relive when I closed them.

"I'm going to go take a shower," I said, as dawn began to brighten the windows.

"Ellie," William said, catching my hand as I walked away from the bed. "I..." Our eyes connected, and for the first time since we'd returned the both of us recognized yet another thing that had gone unsaid. Both of us had almost died today, twice. "Come here."

He pulled me into his chest, and I buried my face into his neck. I'd never been so grateful to hide myself in that warm secret place I used to always go. For a moment I forgot about the memories lost, the new us, and let myself escape. He winced as I pressed myself tighter against him.

"What?" I asked as I pulled away. He lifted a hand to his shoulder, and I realized he'd been hurt. The blood had kept itself hidden in the black fabric of his shirt. It was frayed and tattered like mine, victim to flying pieces of metal and stone.

"What happened?"

"Just some cuts from the debris," he said moving his hands to my face. "It's nothing."

I let him kiss me before I pulled away again, savoring the silent moment between us. We'd almost lost each other. It could have been us in that building.

"Thank you," I said, sliding my cheek against his, "for getting us out of there."

"I had to. I wasn't going to lose you." His lips brushed mine, so gently they barely touched.

I was hesitant as I thought about pulling his shirt up, but my hands moved on their own. My fingers grazed the skin of his firm sides, and he didn't try to stop me when I peeled it up over his head. He only winced again as the fabric brushed the wounds on his chest and shoulders.

As my eyes passed over his familiar body, the muscles shifted with every breath. I didn't understand how the father of my child, my husband, the love of my life could feel so untouchable to me yet still feel like mine. I traced my fingers below the gash on the right side of his chest and another on his left side. His collarbone was scraped from sliding against asphalt and his shoulder had been punctured by something.

I reached for my bracelet. "Let me—"

"Don't." He grabbed my wrist and stopped me before I could draw the blood. "You've given too much today."

"It's okay I—"

"I'll be fine." His fingers traced the skin beneath the hem of my shirt. "How about you? Any cuts or scrapes?"

"I don't know." I swallowed at the warm feel of his touch. "You should check."

He smiled and our eyes stayed locked as he lifted my tank top over my head. I brushed my limp brown hair aside, and he pulled me closer. Skin on skin. Even after such a day, I could still smell the lingering hint of lime and warmth on his body. As he moved his fingertips up my back, he grazed a sore spot I didn't know was there, making me flinch. "Just a scrape."

His lips tickled my shoulder, and the feel of him so close was too much. My fingers curled into his hair and rested on the back of his neck.

"Shower?" I whispered in an exhale.

Without answering, he took my hand and led me to

the bathroom.

The steam wrapped us in silk sheets of vapor. Warmth soaked into every pore. Clean water dripped from our eyelashes and painted our flushed lips. It washed our wounds and rinsed away all the blood and pain. Breath and skin and bodies so close. A blissful ending to an otherwise unworthy day.

CHAPTER FIFTEEN

I WOKE UP THINKING OF PAUL AND RACHEL. I LISTENED for their voices in the living room, hoping somehow I'd dreamed their death. My stomach clenched with grief in the silence. I'd never hear Rachel's high-pitched laugh again. Never see Paul smile at her overly exuberant explanations of their new and free adventures flying from place to place. They'd never marry.

I turned over in bed to face William, staring across my pillow. He slept peacefully. Lips parted, eyelids soft, chest rising and falling easily. His memory loss seemed so insignificant now. He was alive. I could reach out and touch him if I wanted to. I closed my eyes, hoping I could escape under the warm sheets to a place where I didn't have to remember we'd lost two of our friends.

It didn't matter. Their faces followed me.

I was sure it was well past noon, but I didn't want to wake William. Sliding off the bed, I padded silently across the room, slipping through the door unheard. I wasn't the only one eager to see the latest on the San Francisco attack. Nics sat on the couch, trying to keep her spoon from clinking against the side of her cereal bowl.

"Hey." Her unsmiling face was laden with shadows from a restless night. "I'm sure they'll have constant coverage or a breaking news report," she said, avoiding the loss of our friends. "Something at least..."

As she flipped the channels I realized she wanted to pretend Paul and Rachel were in the other room still asleep like everyone else. I sat next to her and didn't ask if she was okay, if she slept, if she wanted to be alone.

She tucked her feet under her thighs so she was sitting cross-legged on the couch, and I took the remote so she could eat her cereal. I stopped on CNN waiting for commercials to be over. The only sound other than the jubilant chime of advertisements was Nics slurping milk from her bowl. I had to say something, acknowledge the spur in my heart.

"Maybe they're still alive—"

"Don't say that." She went rigid. "They're not, Elyse. Okay?"

"What if—"

Her obsidian eyes held me in my place. "No what-ifs. They're dead. They would've flown back. They would have called Alex. Something. I know it in my bones. They're gone, and I don't want to talk about it."

"Okay," I said, turning back to the T.V. I clenched

my jaw, holding my tongue. *Gone*. Rachel who'd brightened some of my worst moments with her rosy-cheeked smile. Paul who'd accepted me from the beginning, always on my side in his quiet way. Their presence had been a constant light that I'd taken for granted. Now that it was snuffed out, everything around me seemed a little darker.

I focused on the news report, trying to forget my grief for Nics's sake. A brunette behind a news desk greeted us with feigned concern.

President McKinney has declared a state of emergency for the city of San Francisco. The city was completely destroyed in yesterday's firefight with local Descendants. The death toll is in the thousands and rising. Some of the following images may be hard to see. The tangled metal bridge in the water, the toppled buildings, the dead civilians. It was all so fresh in my mind. I could hear the clatter of breaking windows and falling glass, the deafening ring after the explosion ignited the air. My lungs still stung from the smoke. Even after being there in person, none of it seemed real. The sight of the city was otherworldly, like a vicious act of Mother Nature.

Officials won't say what triggered the attack, but the federal government was forced to take extreme measures against a rebel group of Descendants who terrorized the city.

New security footage, however, suggests not all Descendants were a part of the violent attack. Just minutes ago we released the following video recording.

The screen switched from the crystal-clear picture of the newsroom to a grainy slow-framed video feed. It was the hospital. Nics and I shared a glance. A recorded image of the two of us walked into view with William at our side. The cameras captured everything. My ability, my face, the line of humans waiting for my blood. I leaned forward like I was watching a suspense thriller, unable to look away.

The clip ended as we disappeared, and a young male reporter took our place on the TV screen. He stood outside the hospital with a man who seemed healthy, despite his filthy button-up shirt and unwashed hair. I recognized his face. I healed a large gash across his grey whiskery cheek last night. The picture flickered and sound cut in and out.

"We're here with Bob Termil who was witness to the events in the hospital. Tell us what happened, Bob."

"These kids just came out of nowhere, and I mean they appeared out of thin air." His eyes were wide as he remembered. "At first I thought..." he shook his head as he sighed. "I don't know what I thought, that they were going to kill us I guess."

"But they didn't," the reporter urged him to continue. Black lines interrupted the feed, but they stayed live.

"No," his voice climbed with surprise. The sound cut in and out again. "No, they did the opposite. There was this girl who was using her blood to heal people." He touched a hand to his cheek. "Right here. I had a nasty cut that wouldn't stop bleeding. Look at it now." The camera panned in for a close-up of the man's non-existent wound. "See. Nothing. It's *completely* gone!"

"So the people were in line so she could heal them?"

"Oh yeah. There were way too many people for that hospital to handle." He grabbed the camera, with an overly zealous smile. "Thank you, healer!"

The brunette newscaster greeted us once again as the camera went black.

"We need to take a quick commercial break, but we'll be right back with the latest on this developing story."

A smiling teddy bear danced across the screen promoting some sort of floral fabric softener.

Nics threw her hand in the air. "Laundry? Who cares about laundry?"

I muted it and scratched the back of my head, not knowing what to make of being on the news.

"So much for scolding Alex for being famous," Nics added with high eyebrows.

"I'm not going to be famous after one incident." At least I hoped I wouldn't, but even as I denied it, I picked my thumbnail worried about what it would mean.

Nics shifted her feet, pulling them out from under her. "I don't know...that guy was—"

"Shhh," I hushed her. The news cut away to the briefing room, and President McKinney stepped up to the pedestal. I tried to listen, but all I saw was the man Adrianna wanted to murder. His stormy blue eyes exuded bravery and confidence, but the edges wrinkled with concern. Clean cut grey hair complimented his blue pressed suit. I'd seen his picture-perfect wife and two sons next to him many times. He was a man, just like every other man. His title didn't pardon him from pain or death. We locked eyes through the television, and I couldn't make myself believe he was to blame for what the world faced. It was me. I was to blame. My teeth clamped tight trapping in my guilt.

I missed the days when my biggest problem was Alex gracing the cover of People magazine. As if him standing on top of the Golden Gate Bridge was anything compared to this. Those days were gone. The bridge was gone. Our friends, gone.

When I looked up, it was back to commercials and Nics grabbed the remote searching for more news. She flipped past a talk show and I recognized a face.

I waved my hand at her. "Wait, go back."

Alex sat on a plush red sofa adjacent to a blonde woman in makeup and large diamond earrings.

"Oh wow," Nics said with a shake of her head.

"Would you mind demonstrating your ability for us?" The woman asked. "We're all dying to see it."

Alex smirked his sideways smile and answered with a shrug. "Sure."

In seconds he was gone and the cameraman was combing the studio for him. The nervous crowd reacted with applause.

"Are you serious?" I asked Nics, as she pulled her socks off. "He's on a talk show? After last night?"

"This is his third since last week," Sam answered, emerging from the hallway in a t-shirt and boxers. He ran his large hand through his sandy grey hair and yawned.

I got up and headed for the kitchen, too annoyed to watch. The sound of the host speaking my name stopped me in my place.

"So tell us about Elyse." I whirled around in shock. "They're calling her the last healer. Does that have some significance among...your people?"

He laughed.

"What?" she asked.

"She's going to kill me for talking about her."

"Yes. I *am* going to kill you," I said with an edge to my voice, marching back toward the television.

The blonde host scooted closer to him. "So you know her?"

"I live with her," he answered.

Nics and Sam abandoned the screen to stare at me.

"Why are they talking about me?" I asked them.

Nics took the box of cereal from the coffee table and started eating it dry. "You saw the footage. You're the new *it* girl."

"Is it true what they are saying about her?" the host continued with a cross of her legs.

Alex nodded. "Probably." He laughed to himself. "What are they saying?"

"That she can heal people with her blood. That she's the last healer of her kind."

A large video screen behind the plush couches displayed a frozen frame of me in the hospital hallway. I was kneeling in front of a girl with my wrist to her lips. Pieces of hair had fallen from my ponytail, and I was covered in remnants of the day's attack. My sideways glance was enough to tell I wasn't aware I was being recorded. The angle was different from the news, making me think people had taken pictures and maybe even video with their cell phones.

"It appears here she is healing humans injured in the San Francisco attack. Were you there?"

"Yeah, we were there. What can I say, she's got a soft spot for you people," Alex answered.

I grabbed the remote from Nics and flipped the TV off. "I'm not watching this."

William stepped out of our bedroom. "What's going on?" he asked, looking groggy-eyed in his flannel pajama bottoms.

"She's all over the news," Nics explained.

"They're just recapping last night, and Alex is on some talk show." I tried to negate the reality of what had happened. It scared me that what I'd seen in my vision about San Francisco had actually come true, and that I was central to its media coverage. I didn't want any of this. "Ready to go for a run?" I asked William. I wanted as far away from all of it as I could get.

I looked at him, trying to communicate that by "go for a run" I meant "go see Sarah" like we'd talked about. After losing Rachel and Paul it was more important than ever that I saw the ones I loved. Anna and Chloe included.

By the way he smiled I knew he understood. "Sure," he answered, and my heart beat a little faster.

CHAPTER SIXTEEN

I DRESSED IN RUNNING CLOTHES, TRIPPING IN A HURRY to step into my spandex shorts. Hopefully we'd be back before anyone realized we were gone.

When I was ready, I walked with William down our trail and out of sight. He'd told Edith to meet us at the first corner. I waited, quiet and nervous with anticipation. The sun had already started its descent, but it was still high in the sky, fighting its way through the mess of pine and birch below. Everything seemed brighter, clearer, as if an overnight rain had showered the forest with tiny droplets of green. I shouldn't have felt so hopeful, so happy. My friends were dead, the city where I discovered myself had been destroyed, and Adrianna was planning an attack against our nation's president, but I was going to see my baby girl. I inhaled the fresh air, feeling like I could breathe for the first time in months.

Edith waved with excitement as she walked toward

us. I smiled back at her. "Does your dad know you're taking us?" I asked as she approached.

Her eyebrows lifted with adolescent attitude, and she put a hand on her hip. "No. He doesn't get to decide everything I do." The pale freckles on her nose moved with her defiant smirk.

A rush of excitement quickened my pulse as I reached out for her shoulder. I smiled at her before we were plunged into a world of white.

My feet hit the soft grassy ground, and my vision returned. A large yellow ranch house with a barn and a few horses in a corral sat off to the right. Mountains and blue sky painted the backdrop, and rolling fields of sage swayed in the breeze.

Only one word described this place, though I'd never been here before. *Home.*

I could see it. Me, William and Sarah. Hot summer mornings and clear starry nights. One day we'd be a family, living the way we should.

"Come on," William urged with a smile. "She's probably just waking up from her nap." His quick feet gave away his excitement, but the front door opened before I grabbed the knob.

"Ellie?" Anna stopped me where I stood. "What are you doing here? Is everything all right?"

I smiled, choosing to forget all the awful things that had happened since they'd left.

"Fine. I just had to see her."

Anna wrapped me in a quick hug, but my eyes were already searching past a set of golden duvet covered couches into an empty dark walnut kitchen.

"Where is she?" William asked for me as he stepped past us into the house.

Mac emerged from the hallway holding her tiny shape in his oversized arms.

"Look who it is, Sarah," he said in the gruffest baby voice I'd ever heard. "No one followed you did they?"

I couldn't keep my laughter inside. "No."

"Well, get on over here then. This little devil's gaining a pound a minute. My arm's getting tired."

Love melted over my heart as I stepped toward them. I looked up at Mac, saying more with a single glance than I could have managed with words. When he set her in my arms, warmth spread into my chest, thawing the cold emptiness that had been there. I felt her heart beat against my arm, her body wriggle with excitement. Her mouth opened wide and she stared up at me as if truly seeing me for the first time, enamored by my watering eyes.

"Hi," I whispered, feeling a tear track its way down my cheek. The last few months without her had shown me a fierce kind of loneliness. "I missed you."

Her tiny hands were clasped into fists that she kept tucked against her chest. I slipped my finger into her grasp and the corner of her mouth lifted into a smile.

"Did you see that?" I asked, beaming at William who

stood at my side. "She smiled at me."

"Probably gas," Mac added casually from the kitchen as he prepared a bottle.

"Mac!" Anna scolded from the couch.

I'd never been so completely captivated. She was my secret jewel and I wanted to admire every facet. Every blink, every kick, each twitch of her lips kept my attention. I didn't want to miss a single second.

"It's fun, huh?" Anna said as I sank into the couch next to her.

She scooted closer, and smiled. Nothing made people smile the way a baby could.

I shoved her shoulder playfully with mine. "Maybe you and Mac will have a baby one day—"

"Shhh." Her brow squinched into a scowl. "Don't freak him out."

I looked back at Mac who was shaking the bottle a little too vigorously in the kitchen. He was either really focused or pretending he didn't hear me.

"Besides," Anna continued. "Apparently humans and Descendants can't have children."

"Huh." I unfolded Sarah's tiny hand. "Different DNA or something?"

"No clue." Anna shrugged. "Thank goodness I have Chloe."

"Doesn't she remind you of when Chlo bug was little?" I asked, remembering Chloe as a baby. "She had more hair, though. Remember? It was pitch black."

"I know. Can you believe she's such a blondie?" Anna reached out and ran her hand along the golden peach fuzz on Sarah's head.

"Where is Chloe by the way?" I lifted my head to peek out the back window.

"We have horses here," she answered. "She's been out riding—"

"Okay. My turn," William interrupted, squeezing himself between me and the arm rest.

I turned my lips into a pout, but handed her over. William's smile never faded as he watched her, and I realized sitting next to them that this visit wouldn't be enough.

And it wasn't.

I couldn't keep away, and I didn't have to work hard to convince William to go back with me. We went so often it became a secret ritual that always began with getting dressed for a run. She was the perfect distraction, a way to forget all the terrible things that were going on in the world.

According to Nics, the cities were continuing to unravel amidst the looting and chaos of unsettled and fearful citizens. She and Sam had joined Alex and Kara in an effort to help Adrianna police the streets without using violence. I chose not to be involved, telling myself I'd done my part. I'd warned the people, and they had listened. More vehicles flooded our small town and city dwellers continued to leave urban areas for rural life. At first I felt guilty for not doing more, but days with Sarah were a pleasant mirage that promised everything would be fine. Maybe we'd changed the future. Life could be good again.

The sun colored the sky with shades of pink and purple that lightened into grey as we waited for Edith to show. I dug my foot into the dirt path of our running trail with a sigh.

William grabbed my hand and pulled me into his chest.

"I'm really liking this new you," he said, holding me in the cold morning air.

I tucked my arms into his jacket, warming my hands against his back. "What new me?"

He shrugged. "The you who doesn't have to fix the world and lead a war."

I laughed, masking my guilt. I didn't like to think of it that way, of all the things I was abandoning in exchange for my daughter. I looked up as a flock of birds headed for the trees, unable to respond.

"We could stay there you know," he whispered into my ear. "We could be a family."

A smile stretched into my chilled cheeks as I imagined how life could be.

I never should have let myself believe him.

CHAPTER SEVENTEEN

EDITH APPROACHED FROM A DISTANCE AND DROPPED us at the front porch. The sight of that yellow ranch house erased any memory of what felt like my other life. The new me was reckless and selfish. Somehow I knew coming here was wrong, but I didn't care.

As I climbed the steps, anticipation danced in my stomach. The front door opened as usual, but this time two unexpected faces emerged.

"What are you doing here?" I asked Kara. Alex stood at her side.

"Elyse..." Kara's body started forward, but she stopped short. Something in her voice brushed my nerves the wrong way.

"What?" I asked, readying myself.

I saw it in her face before she had the chance to explain. Sad eyes, tight lips—regret. The sound of my name was her last plea for forgiveness. Her shoulders lifted with a heavy breath that changed her posture.

"I did something...horrible." She hardened and softened all at once. "It's too late, and I can't take it back."

Panic crept into my chest until I was sure she could see the worry in my eyes.

"What did you do?"

"You weren't planning on helping us, and we need you. Our people need you."

"What did you do, Kara?" I repeated, feeling my features set into a hard scowl.

"She convinced me it was the only way. I could see her thoughts. They were coming from a place of good intentions. Adrianna's not all bad, Ellie. She said it was the only way to get you on board with us, and she's right. I know what you've been thinking. You were never going to help her, but you need to. *We* need you to. This could all be a part of the prophecy and it will only work if...I just..." Her voice quickened, as the friendship between us dissolved with each word. "I made a mistake."

I shook my head over and over in denial.

"She won't hurt her, Ellie."

"No no no," I repeated the word over and over under my breath, my hands nervously grasping at the back of my neck, covering my eyes, searching for some sort of control, but I had none. I pushed past her through the door.

"They're not here," Kara called after me.

An empty living room. A dark kitchen. Not a familiar

voice or sound to be heard. Was I seconds too late? Minutes?

"Anna, Mac, and Chloe are at the house." She reached out for comfort, then thought better of it and pulled back. "Once you've seen this through, you'll get Sarah back unharmed. She'll be safe and cared for and protected."

I went cold, like being plunged into dark water. My heart couldn't let it in. I couldn't hear it. I paced back and forth, my running shoes echoing against the hard wood floor. "Why?" Tears stung my eyes and I wiped them away, taking the anger out on my cheeks. "Why would you do this to me?" Back and forth. My feet carried me in their aimless pursuit.

"It was a mistake," she answered with her eyes closed.

A cry ripped from my throat. "A mistake?" It wasn't good enough. Before I knew what I was doing I had her pinned to the ground with my hands around her neck. My fingers trembled and breath dragged in and out of my angry lungs.

She didn't fight me. She already knew I could never bring myself to kill her, though my tightening grip challenged that thought.

"I want her back, Kara," I said through clenched teeth. *Get her back for me or I swear I'll kill you.*

The thought made her open her eyes, and with a quick swing of her elbow she had me on my back. She pushed onto her feet, and her features tensed. "Do you think I haven't tried to find her?" Frustration sat heavy on her shoulders. "Adrianna has taken precautions. *She* doesn't even know where Sarah is. She has people moving her around."

I couldn't breathe. *People? What people?* The back of my head rested against the scuffed wood floor as I closed my eyes. I was never raised to believe in anything, but maybe my mother was right. She always told me everyone believes in God one way or another. *Everyone believes in something*, she'd said, *because when they're desperate enough, when they're about to lose everything, lose themselves, they ask for help.* And that's what I did. I closed my eyes and said a silent prayer to whoever was listening. *Please. Let my baby girl be all right. Please help me find her.*

Then, as though determination was all I needed to regain my composure, I sat up and promised myself I'd get her back.

I turned to Alex. "Take me to Adrianna," I said, rising to my feet. "I'm getting her back. Whatever it takes."

He looked at Kara, as if not sure who to be more fearful of, but agreed with a nod. "Sure."

Alex had me there in seconds. I went alone. It was me she wanted. I knew I could get Sarah back, it was just a matter of what Adrianna wanted in return.

I kept my eyes down as I entered what appeared to be her office. If I looked at her, I might not be able to keep calm.

The place had the same feel as the conference room where I'd last seen her. White walls, bright lights, a window with a view of a city I didn't recognize. There were no personal effects, or anything that would give away who or what she was.

I risked a glance. She stood with her hands clasped behind her back, staring out the window. She'd been waiting. Her brown curls were swept up into a conservative bun that complimented her black pantsuit. To anyone else she looked the part of a beautiful leader to be admired and followed. All I saw was a female version of Christoph.

"What do you want?" I asked quietly. Gut hollow. Jaw tight. I could snap.

"Your cooperation." Her tone was even and pleasant. I couldn't match it.

Inside I was crazy with rage, a wild animal whose blood beat with the instinct to kill, but I kept that recklessness trapped in my chest. I couldn't let it sabotage my one chance to negotiate. Instead, the desperate mother in me became I'll-do-anything weak.

"I've given you that." I tried to keep my voice level. "There's no need for this. Give me my daughter back." I forced the word from my lips. "Please."

She cocked her head like I was a child who didn't understand. "You know I can't do that."

I hated myself almost as much as I hated her. I should never have let Sarah out of my sight. *You have to lose to win.* How could I have let it happen? I didn't care about winning. I didn't care about anything but her. I couldn't lose my daughter.

"At least let me see that she's safe," I begged, worry lines betraying my strength.

"Kara knows what I know. Sarah is being well protected and cared for. That's all I can offer."

My subdued insanity slipped out as I grasped fistfuls of my hair. "That isn't enough, I—"

"You don't get to bargain, Elyse." Her words cut me off and turned me to ice.

She was right. I had no leverage. She had pocket aces and I was bluffing.

"So I'll cooperate." I straightened up and forced myself to be still. Could she see me shaking? "What do you want me to do?"

"We're planning on making our move tonight." She stepped around her desk and sat on the edge of it. "We have everything in place to go forward with the assassination, and I want you to be the one to pull the trigger so to speak."

"So you want me to wave the red flag and give your team the go-ahead?"

Somewhere deep down I knew that wasn't what she meant.

She smiled as though the thought was comical. "I want you to be the one to shoot him."

I shook my head, at a loss. "I can't do that." *Yes you can*, the darker side of me whispered. *Whatever it takes.*

I tried with one last-ditch attempt to get some information. "What would you do if I said no?"

She didn't even flinch. "You won't." She crossed her arms, seemingly satisfied with how this was playing out.

A surge of fear and weakness pulsed in my stomach at the thought of some stranger with my baby. What if she was hurt? What if something happened?

"What's to stop me from just killing *you* instead?" I shut my lips, trying to keep any more of the recklessness in me from spilling out.

"Careful," she warned, her features sharpening into a glare. As quickly as the anger flashed across her face, it was gone again and her posture changed. "I know this seems cruel, but it's the life of one man to save thousands. We want the same thing you and I. It has to be your blood that takes his life."

"Why?" I moved closer to the window trying to figure out where I was, as if that would help me bring an end to this. Maybe my vision would come true any moment, and this city would be the first to blow, taking Adrianna with it. Fate's blessing amidst the disaster.

The skyline was simple and foreign. No landmarks or bodies of water. I was lost.

"You know why. The prophecy says you are to free us of oppression. This is how."

"By bringing down the Council, not killing the president," I corrected.

"And you've done that. There is a new Council, but things aren't so simple."

I realized for the first time that I'd never actually heard the exact words of the prophecy. Everyone had their own interpretation of it. Who knew what it ever truly meant? It had been twisted and reinvented so many times. There was no way of knowing how far I was supposed to go, but I wanted it over with. I wanted to be free of its burden.

She tapped her fingers on the desk, waiting for me to respond. I didn't know why. She already knew my answer.

"Are you in or out?" she asked anyway.

Defeated, my gaze fell to the floor. "Just tell me what I have to do."

CHAPTER EIGHTEEN

BACK AT THE COMPOUND, EVERYONE WAS WAITING for me. Alex and I stood in the front yard watching silhouettes gather through the living room window. I looked for William but couldn't make out his face.

"She's been beating herself up, you know," Alex said from behind me. I turned, taken off guard. Oddly enough, blaming Kara wasn't on my mind. All I cared about was doing what I had to do to get Sarah back.

"Good," I said, unwilling to forgive.

"You know it was a mistake," he continued. "She wasn't—"

"Don't," I interrupted. "Just...I don't want to see her here anymore."

He nodded before leaving me alone in the yard.

When I turned back to the house, wondering how I could walk in empty-handed, I saw a familiar face. Anna sat on the porch stairs. The sight of her brought on instant tears. We held each other's gaze from a distance before she stood and walked my way.

As she got closer I broke down.

"You were supposed to watch her," I said, torn between being angry and needing comfort.

She pulled me into her arms. "I'm so sorry." She calmed my frantic sobs hugging my head into her shoulder, but I could hear the devastation in her voice. "I'm so so sorry." Her chest sank under my cheek. "I never thought Kara would...They just took her and disappeared, Ellie."

A red flush brightened her damp cheeks, and she wiped them as I pulled away.

I rubbed my running nose with the hem of my shirt. Fear beat in my chest. Grief drained my strength. "I'm so worried. She's just a baby, Anna."

I turned around and headed for my pine tree.

"It'll be okay," Anna insisted, following behind me. "William told me Adrianna has her, right? That she's safe."

It didn't matter that neither of us were sure of that fact. I needed to hear it. She was safe. I needed to *believe* it. I sat down at the base of the trunk and leaned my back into the uneven bark. It cradled me in its bed of roots, and I pulled my knees to my chest with closed eyes.

"She's going to be fine, Ellie," Anna said sitting next to me. I could feel her eyes on me, see her worried face in my mind.

Her gentle hand rested on my arm. "What happened?" I asked, needing to know the details, to prove to myself I couldn't have prevented it.

"Kara and Alex said the plan had changed," she whispered, as though she'd gone over it in her head countless times. "We didn't think anything of it. You'd been visiting so often...Mac let them in, and Kara asked to hold the baby. I turned around and they were gone." She stared at the grass around our feet. "She just slipped through my fingers, Ellie." A look of horror and regret washed over her face.

My throat ached as I fought another wave of oncoming tears. "I should have been there. She should have been with me."

Anna shook her head. "Don't blame yourself. It wouldn't have changed anything. How could we have known?" Her eyes searched me for something, some way to make it better. "We'll get her back. What did Adrianna say? What does she want?"

I swallowed down the taste of salty tears, trying to accept my task. That's all it was—a task. Not a life. Not a country. Not a sin.

"She wants me to be the one to kill President McKinney."

Her brow sank a little deeper. "She wants you to *kill* the president?"

I'd forgotten she hadn't been around to hear the details of Adrianna's plan. When I came to visit, all we talked about was the baby.

"They want to take the government down. Things have been—"

She nodded. "I've seen. On the news."

"She said it has to be my blood that takes his life." I twisted the bracelet around my wrist, dreading the moment I'd have to use it to kill. "I don't know. I hardly heard a word Adrianna said, I was so desperate to get Sarah. I just agreed to whatever she wanted."

"Well, do you have a plan? I'm sure McKinney will be protected. He's the president. You'll have to be careful." There wasn't a hint of hesitation in her question. It was a simple fact. I had to do what needed to be done to get my daughter back. Any mother would understand. Still, it pulled at my conscience, regardless of the situation.

"I'm sure Adrianna has a plan." I reached up and tied my hair back into a ponytail, feeling the urge to pull myself together and figure things out. "It just...feels wrong. He has a wife and kids. Anna, what if I can't do it?"

"She's your daughter, Ellie." Her lips disappeared into a thin line. "You'll just have to find it in you."

I nodded, not sure I could.

"When does she want you to go through with it?" she asked.

"I'm meeting the team in a few hours." I glanced at the sun, willing it to move slowly. "She wants it done tonight."

Her eyebrows lifted in surprise, but she had no words

of comfort. "Do you want me to go get William?"

"Yeah, could you?"

I watched her walk back toward the house, afraid to be alone with my own thoughts.

Tonight I had to kill the president.

As I imagined myself taking the shot, my innocence abandoned me.

I heard the crunch of dry mountain grass under William's shoes before I had the guts to look up. My chin lifted, quivering with shame.

"You don't have to do this," he whispered as he fell to his knees in front of me. "We'll find another way."

He wrapped his warm hands around my calves, but his green eyes reflected all of my regrets.

"How? I can't gamble with her life, William."

With a brief nod I felt him concede every shred of moral decency he had. He was as desperate as I was. "I just want her back."

Hours passed before I finally got up the nerve to dress for the occasion. My legs were protected by my favorite army green pants and black boots. I wore a black tank to stay cool and kept my dart gun strapped to my thigh so I could be ready at a moment's notice. As soon as I was dressed I settled back into the base of my favorite tree and William sat next to me. We didn't talk. There was nothing to say. The two of us just waited for the minutes to tick by, hoping that as they did, our daughter was safe.

I kept busy carving hollow darts, guessing at which one I'd use to do the job. My stomach clenched with each drag of my knife over the slender wood. The last time I'd used a hollow was on the man who burned me. Like the president, that man had stood between me and my loved ones. His death on my conscience was the price to be paid. But unlike that man, the president hadn't tried to kill me first.

He's tried to kill others like us.

The meek voice was so unexpected I jolted with a start. I searched the trees for little girl eyes.

Edith? I called silently.

She peeked her head out from behind a distant birch.

You should be inside with your parents. Her sweet face pulled me out of my dark cloud for just a moment.

I'm just checking on you. You have to go soon.

It'll be okay. A useless lie she could see through.

I'll come with you if you want. Nobody will know. I won't tell.

William noticed my pause in carving. "What?" he asked as he continued to strip sapling branches for me.

That's very brave of you, Edith, but I have to go alone.

"Keep an eye on your sister for me," I answered William. "Don't let her sneak off, okay?"

He searched the trees for her, knowing she must be out there, but she was already gone.

Alex showed up only minutes later. "They're ready for you."

Nervous energy radiated from my stomach, and I moved too fast picking through the darts I'd carved and checking my gun.

I tucked my loaded weapon into the back of my pants and William caught my trembling arm, slowing me in my frenzy. "Hey."

The two of us sat facing each other as I inhaled quick breaths of courage.

"I love you, okay?" William's free hand held the side of my face, the look in his eyes a mix of desperation and hesitancy. "Follow your gut. You're smart and strong. Do what you have to."

I nodded. I could already feel myself giving over to the harder version I'd learned to be. "I love you, too," I said, pressing my lips into his.

Alex didn't say anything, but I could feel awkward silence emanating from where he stood.

"Let's go," I said, rising to my feet.

"We have to get Nics first," Alex added with a shrug. "Adrianna needs her ability."

"No way," I said matter-of-factly. "Nics doesn't want any part in this."

"It doesn't really matter what she *wants*," Alex countered with crossed arms. "She's in or there's no deal. You want your daughter back, right?"

"Are you serious?" I took a few aggressive steps toward him, and William was on his feet.

"Whose side are you on here?" The muscle in William's

jaw pulsed with restrained anger. "I thought you were a friend?"

"Hey." He threw his hands up defensively. "Don't kill the messenger." He smirked at his clever use of the word.

"You and Kara deserve each other," I sneered.

"One day you're going to look back and realize this was all for the best." He turned without waiting for a response and headed for the house.

I stood dumbfounded for a moment before I followed after him with a renewed sense of urgency. What if Nics refused?

Nics was already on her feet facing Alex when I burst through the door. William's parents stared from the kitchen. Sam looked up from his spot on the couch, sitting tall with alarm.

"Did you know about this?" Nics asked me, still shocked by Alex's request.

I swallowed as fear raised its fists in triumph. "He just told me. I had no idea."

"Elyse I..." she shook her head.

I chewed on my upper lip, unable to speak.

Nics threw her hand over her eyes, thinking to herself. "Damn it!" she shouted. "What do I need? Are we going now?"

I sighed with relief and thanked her with a subtle smile that she didn't return.

"Just your ability," Alex answered. "And yes, we need

to leave now."

"Nics," William said from the doorway. "Take this." He reached into the back of his pants and pulled out a handgun.

Nics stepped forward to take it, but Sam grabbed her wrist. "I…" He shook his head at her, as if to say *don't do this*, but no other words left his mouth. The conflicted look in his eyes only furthered my guilt.

"I'll be fine," she said to him.

William handed her the gun, and turned to Alex. "Any chance I could convince you to take me, too?"

He paused, and I thought for the briefest moment Alex was considering it. "Not part of the plan," he answered. "Sorry."

I smiled a sad smile at William and put my hand on Alex's shoulder. Nics stepped forward to do the same, but Sam stopped her once again.

"Wait." He stood and took Nics by the waist turning her to face him. "I love you," he said. His eyes searched hers before he leaned in, bending his tall frame to kiss her full brown lips.

"I love you, too," she admitted as she pulled away.

With a hand to Alex's arm, we were gone.

CHAPTER NINETEEN

THE LIGHTS OF ADRIANNA'S CONFERENCE ROOM shone bright, making it easy for me to see what and who was around me as Nics and I appeared with Alex. The chairs had been removed and everyone stood facing a diagram displayed on the far wall by a projector. Handguns, rifles, knives, and bullet magazines took up the surface of the table.

Five other people filled the room aside from the three of us. Adrianna, the farthest from me with her son at her side, glowed with pride. She held her hands clasped with excitement like a child waiting to tear into her birthday presents. Kara stood to their right, but she kept her arms crossed and didn't look up. My eyes drifted to the tall black man across from her. His bald head gleamed under the fluorescents. I'd never seen him before.

"Perfect timing, Elyse," Adrianna said from in front

of the display. "We were just about to go over logistics."

Nics stepped a little closer to me, but neither of us uttered a word. We just had to get through this.

"President McKinney plans to make his speech at 5 p.m. from the briefing room," Adrianna began. The straight lines of her grey pantsuit shifted as she paced. Her bun seemed tighter. I wondered if sweeping up her feminine curls and abandoning traditional women's fashion made her feel more powerful. "They've done their best to fortify it, mostly with technology. They call this a smart room." She turned to the diagram where a projected blueprint of the room and its contents rotated and froze in front of us. "The floors have sensors that track the number of people in the room based on weight, so being invisible won't keep you from being detected. On top of that there is a temperature gauge that monitors the number of bodies present." The diagram revolved as a grid of red lines appeared running from wall to wall. "An alarm system protects the space above them, notifying security of any airborne disturbance."

This mission was looking more and more impossible. I peeled the skin around my thumb and stared into the projected fortress of technology. Part of me hoped we wouldn't be successful, until fear reminded me what that would mean.

"How are we supposed to get in there undetected?" I blurted out.

"You aren't," Grayson answered for his mother. His

voice stayed even and non-authoritative, though he looked uncomfortable standing in front of us, like he was on stage. "The system *will* detect you, so you'll have to be careful."

I studied him, trying to decide if he wanted us to be careful so he could become our new leader or if he really cared about us losing our lives.

"Well? Are you going to fill us in on the plan or what?" Nics asked expectantly. Grayson scratched the back of his head, embarrassed by her tone. "I'm assuming you have one."

"Of course we do—" Adrianna cut in defensively.

"It's okay, Mother," Grayson interrupted, but his words were gentle, almost timid. "We do have a plan." The projection changed to a flat map of the room's floor with our names indicating our positions. "Alex will transport the group all at once. The system will immediately notify security of your presence. Jeremiah here," he nodded at the tall black man, "is a descendant of Kydoimos. He'll instill a sense of confusion amongst the guards. They'll know you're there, but they won't know what to do about it. Nics you'll need to keep everyone under your shield, invisible to those in the room—"

"You know I can't guarantee that, right?" Nics cut in. Her high brow complimented her condescending tone. "The more people involved, the more complicated it gets. With guards moving—"

"You'll have to do your best." Grayson shrugged.

"Your main responsibility is to keep Elyse hidden." His blue eyes, soft with subtle sympathy, fell on me. "You won't have a lot of time, Elyse. They'll be sending backup." He shifted his focus to Kara. "Meanwhile, you and Alex are to be the distraction. Take out as many guards as possible, then cover the main entrance. Backup will be coming from there."

"How many guards will there be initially?" Alex asked.

"Ten." Grayson crossed his arms uncomfortably.

Kara nodded like it was doable. "And how many can we expect in reinforcements?"

"As many as it takes, I'm sure," Adrianna answered. "Being quick is essential."

"How much time will I have?" I asked, knowing I would hesitate.

Grayson's sympathy poured from his creased eyebrows and downturned lips. "As long as Jeremiah and your friends can hold off the guards. Probably only a matter of minutes."

It came down to minutes. Minutes that would define me, that would ruin me. Minutes that would win back my heart but sacrifice the better side of me.

"And when do I get her back?" My grasp tightened around the thick hollow dart in my hand. I hadn't realized I'd been clutching it since we'd left. The little piece of wood held the purest part of my soul. Once it left me, it would be gone forever.

"As soon as it's over," Adrianna answered. Grayson

carried the full weight of her conscience. As if when he'd been born, he'd taken hers with him. I could see it in his distant gaze, in his tense shoulders even as he tried to stand tall next to her. It made me uncomfortable. Why did he care? Why didn't he hate me for killing his father?

My stomach flipped with a mix of anticipation and dread. "Where?"

"I'll arrange for her to be here, in this room, when the kill is confirmed."

Kill. That's all I was now. A killer.

"I need to know you won't use her again." I kept my features still, attempting my best poker face.

Adrianna checked her watch. "If things go—"

"We won't," Grayson interrupted. "As part of the Council, I'll make sure of it."

His mother turned to him with a slow cold stare before trying to cover it with a smile. "After this, we'll have what we want. There will be no need for your involvement unless you choose." She looked around. "Any other questions?"

Buried somewhere under my doubt and desperation I had questions, but they were lost. I struggled to come up with something, needing to buy time. "What about these weapons?"

"Choose any you like," she answered. "As long as you use your blood to do the job, I don't care who else you kill or how."

I reached for a handgun, keeping my eyes on the

trigger as I tested its weight.

You could kill her instead. Right now. The devil on my shoulder whispered in my ear. *Hold Grayson for ransom until you have Sarah back.* I licked my lips considering it.

Don't do it, Elyse.

I looked up in response to Kara's voice in my head.

Why? Would you try and stop me? Is she that important to you? Even my thoughts were dripping with resentment.

No. I wouldn't stop you. She glanced at a closed door to the right of Adrianna. *They would. She's protected. We're not alone here.*

She loaded a magazine into her own gun, and I set mine back on the table, readjusting the one I already had tucked into my pants. I had all the weapons I needed.

"The team leaves in fifteen minutes," Adrianna announced before turning to speak with her son.

Nics's arm brushed mine as she stepped closer to me. "Please tell me you have a backup plan or something," she whispered.

I stared at the wall, somehow frantic and numb all at the same time. "No," I answered. "I don't."

Fifteen minutes felt like five. I wasn't ready. My heart beat with panic. I was about to jump from a plane without a parachute. Nothing to hold on to, no plan, no turning back. This was real, and in my mind I was plummeting toward the ground.

I shuffled toward Alex in a daze. Then we were there, a few yards away from President McKinney. Just like that.

At first the room was quiet. No one spoke. A few papers shuffled. The click of the camera as it was adjusted. A throat cleared. A whisper. My head turned at each sound until I could focus. There were few others in the room aside from the guards, but I zeroed in on my target. He spoke to a woman while a pair of older men in suits listened. They poured over white pages, possibly his speech.

Those first few seconds before we were detected stretched on like a slow deep breath.

Kara and Alex moved to the right, seemingly unnoticed. Nics kept us hidden as she stood next to me, concentrating on several things at once, but even she couldn't keep her eyes off of the man in front of us. There was something eerie and solemn about watching a man's last moments of life. Every nonchalant handshake made me wonder if that would be the last person he'd touch.

The moment the smart room detected our presence the secret service erupted into a quiet frenzy. Guards looked up, some moving closer to McKinney while others searched the perimeter. Kara took out the closest agent by ushering him to an exit and shoving him through the doorway. Alex disappeared with another. Hushed voices whispered panicked warnings into invisible earpieces, as if we couldn't hear them, as if they'd be able to stop us. Despite the unease, nobody approached the president.

Nics and I stood too close to him to speak. Instead we traded looks of regret. Half smiles shaped with pity. I never wanted Nics to be involved. I never wanted any of this.

In front of us, the podium stared back, a white canvas ready to be spattered with blood. Large flags dressed the side of the stage, and men in black suits paced along the walls in confused alarm.

I didn't have much time, but my heart wouldn't settle. Neither would the voice in my head that kept reminding me this was wrong. So wrong it was evil, cruel, immoral. Still, the mother who fought for Sarah buried those feelings. I hated who I was. Who I had to be. There was nothing I wouldn't do.

A voice punched through the silence as McKinney stepped in front of me, too focused on his notes to notice the missing guards. *Snap out of it.* With each breath I became more alert. The room was stirring. Secret service agents were searching the space above them, hands on their guns.

"And we're live in five, four..."

I stared at the back of our president's head wondering how long it had been. My throat pinched so tight with nerves I could hardly breathe.

Ready? Kara's voice in my head made me jump.

No. I'm not ready. I'd never be ready to kill an innocent man.

He's not innocent, Elyse. You've seen what he's done to

our people.

McKinney tucked his pen into his pocket and began to speak. Tufts of his grey hair shifted like bird feathers against his neck as he looked down at his notes and up again to address the camera. I kept waiting for someone to stop me, for Kara to tell me there'd been a change of plans. Every muscle in my body ticked with nervousness. Tell me it's over. Tell me I don't have to.

All right. Whenever you're ready, Kara said. My chest ached with panic.

I didn't hear a word he was saying. All I saw was the spot just below his jawline where the dart needed to go. His last words, and I couldn't even focus enough to hear them. Nics touched my hand urging me to make my move.

I did it fast. Punched the buttons on my bracelet. Soaked the hollow dart with my blood. The poison dripped from my fingers, each rivulet carrying the potency of my sins. I filled my lungs with air, and with a simple exhale he fell.

My world would never be the same.

I stood unmoving, dressed in shame as the first bullets were fired. Kara and Alex moved so fast I couldn't tell what was happening. The room erupted into a fury of gunfire as the two of them moved, plucking life from the armed men.

Body after body slumped to the ground, and all I could do was watch.

I never meant it to be like this. I was a fool. A child with the blood of the future on my hands, who didn't know any better until it was too late. I'd done everything right. Everything asked of me. I closed my eyes. Life owed me something in return.

CHAPTER TWENTY

ALEX WAS NEXT TO ME BEFORE REINFORCEMENTS ever showed, carrying us away into the white upper air. I never imagined the breathless space of his ability could seem so infinite. I just wanted to hold my daughter.

The moment my eyes opened I searched for her, but all I found was an empty room. I sighed through my teeth as I waited in vain, hoping they were just late. "Where is she?" I asked to no one in particular. The impatience in my voice was nothing more than naivety.

Kara, Alex, and Nics offered no words of comfort, but I could tell from their faces they were thinking the one thing I couldn't accept—no one was here, and no one was coming.

In the time we were gone the table had been cleared of all weapons and the rooms vacated. I took off for the door across from us, promising myself they were just outside, but it too was empty. I tried the hallway, pacing its length in the dim light. Nothing but more unoccupied offices.

I cracked my knuckles, not sure what to do with my hands, and walked back to the conference room. My thick shield of denial crashed to the ground. They'd used me. Used my daughter.

I glared at Kara. "Was this the plan all along? Get me to do your dirty work—"

"No," she yelled. Her black curls whipped around as she turned to Alex to back her up. "This wasn't the plan. She was supposed to be here."

I covered my face with my hands, sick with anger and hopelessness. How could I have been so stupid? The ache sat in the pit of my stomach and worsened as fear dragged me further into my nightmare.

"We'll get her back," Nics said with a hand to my back, but she was never very good at comforting. The doubt in her voice only made it worse.

As I let my new reality sink in, I became impenetrable. My heart hardened into a thick coat of armor, a barrier against the grief. My hands shook, threatening to push me over the precipice of sanity. Strength was the only way to win. I couldn't crumble into a weepy mess. Time was too important to be wasted on tears.

"Do you know where they went?" I asked, looking at Alex and Kara.

"No idea," Alex answered, but I didn't need him to tell me.

As he spoke, a flat screen hanging on the back wall came to life. Adrianna stared back at us, and for a moment, I thought she had a message for me. Until I saw the American flag at her back and the presidential podium in front of her.

Good evening, citizens. Her features were pleasant as she greeted the camera, like a guest speaker at a public event. *Tonight the country has suffered a tragic loss.* She paused for effect, feigning sympathy. *The death of your president, though unfortunate, served many purposes. We hoped that the death of one man would spare the lives of many. It is not our intention to start a war between humans and Descendants. A war would cost too many lives, yours and ours. Our attack was not against this great country, but against your leadership. After centuries of being forced to hide our true identities out of fear of persecution, your leadership turned our greatest fears into a reality. Unspeakable things have been done to my people.* Adrianna's face was replaced by images of the government testing facilities. A brunette Edith's age, strapped to a table as men in white lab coats drew blood, a young man fighting restraints as he woke from anesthesia, the room full of injured victims after we'd rescued them from the San Francisco location. *We want nothing more than to live in peace amongst you, beside you, as equals. The current leadership has shown they are incapable of coexisting. Until the public can prove they are ready for true change, a council of our people will be replacing the Commander in*

Chief. All government employees, agencies, including Congress shall remain in place. Any opposition will be asked to leave before more extreme measures are taken. President McKinney's death should also act as a reminder that we are *serious—"*

I forced myself to stop listening and turned to Alex. "Take me to her."

He waved me off. "Hang on, I want to hear this."

One of the most important events in our history was taking place, and I didn't care about any of it. I gripped the handle of my gun and pulled it from the waist of my pants. "Take me there now," I demanded, pointing it at Alex.

He rolled his eyes and disappeared, moving closer to the television.

I turned and glared at the back of his head, aiming my gun. He really needed to start taking me seriously.

Nics jumped as I fired.

"Are you kidding me?" Alex yelled. The TV in front of him shattered into a spider web of glass. "I was watching that."

"No, I wasn't kidding," I said, more serious than I'd ever been.

He looked at Kara, but she only shrugged.

"What are you going to do when you get there, huh?" He sauntered over with a dimpled cheeky smile, but his dark hair and blue-eyed charm didn't intimidate me anymore. "Kill her on national television?"

"Maybe," I answered, enjoying the thought.

He shook his head. "Look. She's in the middle of addressing the country. I can't just take you—"

"Alex!" Kara yelled, but she was too late.

Nics pulled her trigger, silencing the conversation with the loud crack of a bullet.

If she hadn't been smiling to herself, I'd have thought it was an accident. Alex let out a cry of pain as blood seeped into his jeans. He grabbed his left thigh, the shock alone stealing his words.

"I've really been wanting to do that for a while now," Nics said, sounding pleased with herself. Her dreads swung as she nodded in approval. "Felt good."

Kara wrapped Alex's arm around her shoulders and helped him to the ground. "So we're just shooting people we're annoyed with now?" She leaned over to examine his leg.

"No," Nics answered. "Of course not. I shot him for a reason."

"Thanks," Alex sneered. "That makes it all better."

"Now he takes her or she won't heal him. That simple," Nics continued. "It's not my fault I enjoyed it."

I smiled at Nics, glad she was with me.

"So, will you take her?" she asked.

"Fine," Alex answered through his teeth.

I healed him in a rush, so eager to track down Sarah I nearly used the wrong wrist to draw blood. When he was on his feet, I grabbed hold of his arm, readying myself for whatever I'd have to do to get my daughter back. If I had to kill Adrianna, so be it.

The breathless silence of the white emptiness ended with me being thrown through raining rubble and chalky air. When I hit solid ground, the wind was knocked out of me. My mouth opened like a fish out of water as I scrambled to my feet, choking on dust. Sweat tickled my right eye as it slid down my face. Only when I wiped it away did I realize it was blood. I rubbed it on my pants and looked around.

"Nics!" I yelled through the deafening sound of planes rocketing overhead.

The ground shook and bombs exploded like claps of thunder.

"Here!" she called out.

I followed the sound of her voice, unable to see over piles of crumbled white walls and chunks of broken marble floor. The chandelier above hung at an angle and pieces of the evening sky shone through the ceiling next to it. I must have been thrown far because I didn't recognize the room. What was left of a presidential portrait lay between tangled legs of fine wooden chairs. Shredded red curtains and coarse stone covered the floor, exposed like the blood and bones of the building. I climbed over the remnants of what used to be a wall and found Nics pinned beneath a doorframe.

"My leg is stuck," she said, trying to pull her shin from below the heavy plank.

I tried lifting it, but rubble had buried the other end and it wouldn't budge. As I scanned the area for something to pry it loose, I caught a glimpse of a face. Grayson's vacant eyes stared back at me from beneath a small mountain of debris. Their sadness held his lifeless promise to me, one he wouldn't be able to keep. I forced myself to look away.

"I can't find anything," I yelled back to Nics. "I'm calling Alex."

Just as I uttered his call name a gunshot echoed from another room. Nics and I made eye contact, and I scrambled back to her.

"Hurry," she pleaded as I tried again to lift the door.

A frustrated sigh rushed past my lips. "Alex should be here—" I wiped at my forehead, still damp with blood.

"Yeah, yeah. I'm here," he said from behind me.

I jumped, and punched him in the face without thinking. "Shoot!" I said, instantly regretting the reflex. "Sorry."

He grabbed his nose, wincing. "No. Really. I love getting punched in the face. It's okay." His eyebrows stretched high as he blinked his watery eyes. "Remind me why I'm helping you guys again?"

"I'm stuck," Nics told him. "Can you get me out?"

"Can I or will I?" he asked, smirking now that the power was in his hands.

"Seriously, Alex. They're bombing the building and we heard gunshots."

"The gun was Kara," he said, shaking his head. "She uh..." His features evened out, losing all their cocky charm. He shuffled his feet, uncomfortable finding his words. "Come on. I'll take you."

He used his ability to move us to the briefing room where Kara crouched in the corner. Her back was to us, and someone lay at her feet. Someone small. With little girl hands and feathery auburn hair.

"Edith!" I yelled, rushing toward them. "What is she doing here?" I knelt down beside Kara and put a hand to Edith's cheek. "Where is she hurt?"

I moved to switch my bracelet, but Kara put her hand on my arm.

"She's dead, Ellie." Her eyes carried every ounce of hurt I felt as she looked at me.

"No, she's not," I insisted. "Just let me try..." I knelt down beside her and forced my bracelet against her lips while everyone waited in uncomfortable silence. "Edith!" I shook her, trembling and desperate.

Kara took hold of my elbow and pulled me away. "She's gone, Elyse. We need to go."

As I stepped back I remembered the gunshot.

Kara, did you...

I covered my mouth with my hands, still too shocked to believe what I was seeing.

"It wasn't me," she said, her expression cold and flat. "The explosions must have done it." Kara placed her arms beneath Edith's limp body and lifted William's sister into her arms.

"Then who did you shoot?" Nics asked, not bothering to be subtle.

"We need to get out of here," Alex said, looking at the sky through a gap in the ceiling. The sound of another strike roared in the distance.

"Adrianna," Kara answered, as we all made contact with Alex. "I killed her."

My heart seized

What about Sarah?

CHAPTER TWENTY-ONE

"YOU KILLED ADRIANNA?" I YELLED AT KARA AS SOON as Alex had us home again.

"Relax," she said with an even voice laced with sadness. "You think I would have killed her if I didn't have information on Sarah? Adrianna played us. We couldn't trust her anymore. I had to kill her."

I stopped listening when she mentioned Sarah. "What information? Do you know where she is?"

Alex and Nics stood awkwardly at the foot of the porch stairs waiting to move into the house.

"No," Kara admitted. "I don't know where she is, but I have a name." She looked down at Edith's closed eyes and my gaze followed. It couldn't be real. She looked like a sleeping child being carried in from the car after a late night.

"A name?" I whispered as I stepped toward Edith without realizing. I brushed her hair back and ran my thumb over her freckled cheek. It felt soft and warm, like she was still here. I shook my head as my thoughts moved deeper into the shadows. What if Sarah had suffered the same fate? My voice hardened. "A name isn't enough, Kara—"

"We'll find her," she insisted, taking a step forward.

My throat stung as I glanced back at the house. How was I going to face William and his family? I didn't have Sarah, and the life I took had only cost Edith hers.

"I'll do it," Kara answered my thought. *I should have put my trust in you and not Adrianna.* "This is my fault."

I walked in before anyone else, hoping to prepare William and his family.

William stared back at me with a thousand questions. "What happened? Did you get Sarah?" He stood, his open palms reaching out for something that wasn't there.

My fingernails bit into my palms as I balled them into fists. "Not yet."

"What do you mean—"

Kara walked through the door with Edith in her arms.

"Are they back?" Mrs. Nickel came down the hallway with a load of laundry. The white plastic basket hit the floor with a loud smack the moment she saw her daughter. As if she knew before any of us said a word.

"I'm sorry," Kara said, tearing up.

I expected gut-wrenching sobs, for Mrs. Nickel to

breakdown and assign blame in an angry outburst, but she stayed calm.

She walked toward us with her arms outstretched. “Give her to me.” Her eyes carried so much sadness my stomach clenched with grief.

Kara placed Edith’s tiny body in her mother’s arms, and Mrs. Nickel headed for the front door. “William, go get your father. He’s in our room.”

I stood by in disbelief as she held herself together with a kind of strength that only comes from having lived so many years, from having already lost a child. Kara followed her, and I did the same, keeping quiet and holding back tears.

We held a funeral almost immediately. Mrs. Nickel was insistent about her spirit needing to rest. Above us, the overcast sky curled and folded into darker shades of grey until it began to drizzle a fine mist into the muggy summer air. I watched with a blank stare as William’s father went through the same Latin ritual Kara did when she buried her family. I tried to listen, but my mind was busy with thoughts of Sarah. She was out there somewhere, without me.

What would happen to her now that Adrianna was dead? Would they still take care of her? Whoever *they* were. Would they abandon her? And the quiet lurking question that I had been afraid to ask, was she still alive? Standing near Edith’s grave made the unthinkable a possibility. As her mother cried silent tears next to me, I pleaded to the universe that Sarah was okay.

I had hope. Kara knew something. My eyes drifted toward where she stood across from me, but her head stayed bowed in Latin prayer. Edith lay on the ground at her feet, her hair laced with flowers, eyes topped with large gold coins. I knew I had to give everyone the chance to grieve, including myself, but I felt a sense of urgency that numbed me to everything. My heart ticked away the seconds making it hard to stand still.

When I glanced up, Kara was looking at me.

The girl who knows where Sarah is, her name is Dehne. That's all I could get out of Adrianna before I killed her. I think that's all she knew.

Why didn't she keep her promise? Is Sarah okay? I had so many questions.

I don't think she ever intended on keeping her promise. Dehne's bloodline is Apate, god of deceit. I think she was keeping me from getting to certain thoughts in Adrianna's head.

Dr. Nickel passed between us to lower Edith into the ground, and both Kara and I paused. This was the last time I would ever see her sweet freckled face. I squeezed William's hand and felt him tighten his grip. Tears had yet to stain his cheeks, but his mouth twisted and his brow stayed tight.

As I watched William's parents pray over their daughter, I refused to accept the same fate. Rachel and Paul were gone forever. Now Edith was too. I couldn't let the same happen to my baby girl.

Do you know how to find Dehne? I asked, turning my gaze back to Kara.

She was Adrianna's assistant, so she was always around the office. I never bothered with her thoughts, because I knew I couldn't decipher what was true and what wasn't, but most of the others lived nearby in an apartment complex. We should start there.

I nodded as Dr. Nickel stepped in front of me and began shoveling dirt into Edith's grave. The clouds thickened, threatening stronger rain, and the smell of wet earth floated up from the ground as if Mother Nature had arrived to welcome her daughter back home. I wiped the moisture from my cheeks and rubbed my chilled arms. Everything in me was begging to start my search for Sarah, but I couldn't stand there and watch him bury his daughter alone. There were shovels in the shed. I ran and grabbed two, one for me and one for William. Dr. Nickel thanked me as I dug the tip into the wet earth, and as he did, I vowed something to myself. This would be the last loved one I'd bury. I couldn't lose anyone else to this war.

After the service I followed William to our tree. It was already dark out, but the stars gleamed like city lights brightening up the night.

He squeezed my hand as we walked.

"You okay?" I asked. It was a stupid question that I wished I could take back.

He sighed but didn't answer. When we reached the

curved roots of the trunk he rested his back against the bark and stared out at the forest.

"I made her promise not to go..."

I sat down next to him and pushed close into his side.

"You couldn't have—"

"I shouldn't have believed her." His voice was rough with anger.

I didn't know what to say.

He rubbed his weary eyes and rested his forehead in his hand. I wasn't the only one carrying the weight of so many lost lives.

"I could have stopped her. I could have done something." He looked at me, his blood-shot eyes wide and open as if confessing his sins. A rogue tear broke free, sliding down his tight jaw.

"None of this is anyone's fault." I'd repeated those silent words to myself trying to convince the guilt to flee hundreds of times. Never once had it worked. "I love you," I offered. The only true form of comfort I had.

His face turned, and I could see him hardening up as I'd done so many times in the past. "I'm not letting that happen to Sarah."

I swallowed, nervous at the thought. "Me either."

"What do you know?" he whispered.

My brow creased. "Huh?"

"You know something." He glanced back at the house. "You and Kara had that look. I know you were talking. Is it about Sarah?"

I nodded.

"Tell me," he said, letting the distraction overshadow his sadness.

"There is a girl named Dehne," I started, eager to share.

Back at the house, grief hung around the living room like a thick smoke. No one knew what to say or how to be. The awkward silence only furthered my need to leave, to find Sarah, to *do* something. I wasn't the only one who was anxious to act.

William pulled his mother aside. I watched her red puffy eyes take in the details of his face, her last child, her only son, as he asked to leave. Her features twisted with conflict knowing what it was like to lose a daughter and not wanting him to share in that pain. She nodded, though I could see in the way she held his hand that she needed him.

Let's go, Kara said to me as she left with Alex out the front door.

I waited for William to kiss his mother's cheek before he nodded for me to follow.

—

THE WHITE LIGHT OF THE UPPER AIR DILATED MY pupils, and everything seemed darker than it was supposed to be. When my eyes adjusted they found the boxy stairwell of an apartment complex. Our feet scuffled against the cement steps and echoed upward toward the top floor as we climbed. Dark grey walls became a canvas for our shadows as our silhouettes danced in the dim yellow light.

"What floor should we—"

Kara cut me off with a quick glance. She nodded her head toward the bottom of the slanted stairway above us. *Don't talk if you can help it. There are a lot of abilities in this place. They're all on edge after what happened. Let's just stay quiet and blend in.*

I wondered for a brief second what so many Descendants were doing in the city in the first place. After our warning, I'd expected most of our people to leave.

The thought was lost as I followed Kara up to the next floor, Alex and William trailing behind us. When we rounded the second flight of stairs I saw the quiet mind Kara had picked up on. It was a man, a little older than we were. His dark brown whiskers were enough to add a gruff edge to his appearance. He sat still on one of the steps keeping his head down and his eyes on his cell phone as we approached, but I felt it the moment he came into view—the urge to run.

It's just his ability. Kara reassured me before I could bolt. *He's here to keep humans out. Come on.*

The man looked up as we passed, but I pretended not to notice, even as the hairs on my arms stood on end. Out of the corner of my eye I caught a glimpse of the barcode tattooed on the soft part of his wrist. He turned it when he saw me, as if ashamed of the mark, and my heart sped up knowing he'd been watching me.

What bloodline is he? I asked, trying to distract myself. My pulse rushed telling me to move faster.

Phobos, she answered. *Fear.*

The feeling faded as we entered the second-floor hallway. It wasn't empty as I expected. People were milling about with their doors left open. Conversations between neighbors created a lofty buzz. A few kids ran from room to room laughing.

The crimson carpet looked almost black in the windowless space, and tiny wall lights were fighting a losing battle. I felt boxed in, like we'd crawled into a tunnel to hide.

Why are there so many families here? I asked, growing more concerned. *It isn't safe.*

Kara answered my thought without a beat. *They're all here with Phoebe. Her bloodline can predict oncoming danger so she sort of has a cult following who feel safe around her. Adrianna was using her as a safety net so she could work from within the city. She was supposed to warn Adrianna if anything you saw in your vision was going to happen.*

I stopped walking and Kara looked back.

Does Phoebe know when *it will happen?*

No, she answered, continuing to walk. *She'll just sense it before it's about to.*

As that brief glimpse of hope faded, I caught sight of

two light-haired boys sitting with their backs against a dark wooden door on the right. I smiled as I knelt down in front of them.

"Do you guys know Dehne?"

The older one puckered his lips to whistle and blew in my direction. A strong gust of wind tousled my hair and pushed me backward. My eyes went wide with shock.

"We're not supposed to talk to strangers," the younger one confessed.

Their eyes searched my wrist for a barcode that wasn't there.

Three doors down, Kara said as I stood, still smiling at the boys.

The four of us headed for the fourth door on the right, but our presence didn't go unnoticed. Concerned mothers watched us, children stopped to stare.

Should we even knock? I asked in my head. *She might not answer if she sees it's us.* The peephole in the center of the door stared back at me.

Yeah, she answered. *There are too many abilities here. We have to be careful how we handle this.*

I knocked. Waited. *Do you hear her in there?*

I don't think so, she answered. *It's hard to tell. There are a lot of thoughts to sort through in this hallway.*

The door opened, and a brunette with a messy bun stood facing us with a big black trash bag. She looked us over for a moment before hoisting the bag over her shoulder.

"Are you looking for Dehne?" she asked. "Because she moved out yesterday. This is all the stuff she left."

I cursed silently in my head and closed my eyes. "Do you know where she moved?" This was my only lead. I needed *something*. "It's really important. She knows where my daughter is."

"No idea," she answered with a shrug. "Sorry."

She pushed past us, not bothering to lock up, and I watched as my only clue made her way down the hall and out of sight.

"Let's just ask around," William suggested with a gentle hand on my shoulder.

"Sure," I whispered, staring at Dehne's door.

Kara turned as if she'd heard something. Her brow creased in the way it always did when she was listening to private thoughts.

"No way," she said aloud as she stared at the hallway exit. "She can change her appearance?"

"What?" William asked.

"I'm such an idiot," she scolded herself. "Her ability is deception. That was *her*. That was Dehne."

CHAPTER TWENTY-TWO

I SPRINTED AFTER HER. THE METAL DOOR SLAMMED against the wall as I barreled down the stairwell, and William's footsteps echoed behind me.

"Dehne!" I yelled, desperate to be heard.

As I passed the Descendant man, a surge of fear hit me like I'd been doused with ice water. I inhaled with shock, and pushed myself toward the exit into the open air of the city. It was a still, dark night, and I realized I had no idea how late it was.

The alleyway I found myself facing reminded me of a movie set, one of those New York crime dramas. All the pieces were there minus the people. An overflowing dumpster with a brick building backdrop and a fire escape. My head whipped back and forth as I searched the street.

"Any sign of her?" William asked, running left. I could see his breath in the moonlight.

"No," I answered, heading to the right. The once

busy intersection had been left abandoned by the familiar rush of traffic. Even the sidewalks were empty. I rubbed my bare arms as I scanned the office buildings. Would I even recognize her face?

I stood there, refusing to believe I'd lost my only lead until I felt William's hand slide into mine.

"Come on," he said softly.

I turned and rested my forehead on his shoulder as his hands wrapped around my waist. He didn't need to say anything. My loss was his loss.

We made our way back in silence, and Kara and Alex met us at the building's entrance.

I couldn't look at them. "We should ask if anyone knew her or if she—"

"You need sleep, Elyse," Kara said, her eyebrows sinking with concern.

I forced my eyelids to open wider. "Don't tell me what I need." Despite my pounding headache, I couldn't care less about sleep.

"Nobody is going anywhere tonight," Alex stepped in as mediator. "Wherever Dehne went, I'm sure that's where she'll stay until tomorrow. We'll come back in the morning."

I turned to William for backup, but his half-smile told me he was in agreement. The moment I conceded, the day took its toll. I felt wafer-thin and shaky, like I could disintegrate into a heap at their feet.

"Okay," I said with a quick nod. "In the morning."

I'm sorry, Kara offered, though her features were still hardened and defensive.

I couldn't bring myself to accept her apology. She'd see through it anyway. Instead, I nodded, my heart bargaining with forgiveness.

Alex had us wrapped in tight white space before I got up the guts to look her in the eye, but both of them left William and I alone in our dark room before I had the chance. I made my way to the bed and sat on the edge, chewing on my lower lip as I untied my boots. Every drop of life had been drained from me, and yet I still couldn't convince my mind to settle. My anxiety thrived on exhaustion. It had me thinking myself in circles.

I snapped on the bedside lamp. "What if this wasn't how it was supposed to go?" I asked William as he stepped out of his own boots.

He pulled his shirt over his head and came around to his side of the bed. "What do you mean?"

"The prophecy." I unclasped my pants and swapped my tight black tee for one of his loose fitting ones. "I was supposed to bring down the council and free our people. Somewhere along the way I made a wrong move. If I'd done something differently maybe we'd still have Sarah."

"There is no wrong move. You did what you were supposed to do." He lifted the covers and slid into bed.

I laughed out my disgust. "How so?" How could anything I'd done be right if it meant we didn't have Edith or Sarah?

"The Council is gone. If one of them dies..." he pressed his lips together. The Council was gone because she was. Of all the Council members to die, why did it have to be her? "If one of them dies," he repeated, "all Council abilities transfer to their heirs. None of them had any children. They were all too young. It's over. The Council is done."

"*I* didn't do that. Whoever bombed the White House did." I climbed in next to him, sitting cross-legged under the cool cotton covers. "Maybe that was my mistake."

"Maybe." He propped himself up on his elbow. "But the Council would still be here if you wouldn't have..."

My throat felt tight as I swallowed. What he really meant was Edith would still be here if I hadn't killed the president. It was all for nothing, and I didn't have my daughter back. The only thing I'd earned for my sin was a black stain on my soul.

"I didn't mean it like that," William said, seeing the guilt in my tortured eyes.

I clicked the lamp off, hoping to hide my shame in the dark, and buried my head into my pillow, turning my back to him. "I know."

"Honestly," William said, inching in behind me. "I don't think the prophecy has anything to do with Sarah."

A haunting thought flooded me with worry. I *had* done everything I was supposed to do, but no one ever guaranteed fulfilling the prophecy would end with my happiness.

You have to lose to win.

"I hope you're right."

I turned and pressed my cheek into his bare chest, letting the rhythm of his breathing quiet my mind.

William's fingers grazed my ear as he combed my hair back and kissed my forehead. "Try and sleep."

Even with most of his memory still gone, we'd never been closer.

"Have you dreamed any memories since you've been back?" I asked, though I knew he would have told me.

His silence was enough of an answer. "I think that only happens when we're apart," he confessed. "Like fate's way of bringing me back to you."

"Maybe," I said with my eyes closed. "Or maybe you'll dream another memory tonight."

His arm pulled me closer and relaxed against my side. "I hope so."

—

Sarah!

Pieces of the city lay scattered in front of me like toppled legos. A graveyard of metal skeletons and broken glass.

I could hear her cry.

The sound made me rabid with the need to find her.

I pulled myself through spaces too tight; jagged metal edges scraped my arms, bruised my shins. She was here somewhere. Under these brick boulders and car doors. I lifted things that were impossible for me to bear, pushed aside streetlights and asphalt. Somewhere under this weight, under this wreckage. I could taste tar and gravel as I stirred up the air and dug deeper.

Sarah! I cried.

Tears blurred my eyes, streaked my cheeks.

Keep digging.

I clawed at rock, getting nowhere, until my fingers bled.

Sarah!

I woke with a gasp and shot out of bed, the cold wood floor shocking my bare feet. My chest heaved up and down.

"What? What is it?" William asked, startled from sleep. He sat up in bed, forcing his eyes to open round and wide.

My pulse slowed as I grounded myself in reality. William was here. We were home. We were safe, but Sarah...

That part was real. The fissure in my heart widened.

"Nothing." I let out a deep sigh. "Just a bad dream."

William ran a hand over his tired face, and I pulled on my combat pants without bothering to shower.

"Come on," I said, tossing his clothes at him. "We have to get back to that apartment."

Mrs. Nickel was up before any of us. Either that or she hadn't slept. Scrambled eggs and sausage were stacked on plates at the small, square kitchen table.

"Thanks, Sophia," I offered with a timid smile.

"No problem, sweetheart," she said without smiling back. She kept her head down as she poured a pitcher of orange juice into four glasses. "You just be careful out there."

I finished tying up my boots and looked down the hall for Kara and Alex. Their light wasn't even on.

"Hey," I said, opening the door without knocking. Two dark shapes clung to each other under the covers. "Breakfast is ready. Come on. Get up."

The blankets rippled with movement and a balled up sock sailed across the room and smacked me in the chest.

"Five more minutes," Alex groaned through his pillow.

"He's kidding," Kara said, popping her head up. Her wild curls stuck out in all directions like Medusa's silhouette. "We're up."

I ate my food so fast I could hardly taste it. If I'd had it my way, we'd have been gone already. We could always eat later. I studied the other plates at the table silently urging everyone to finish. Either William felt the same, or he could tell I was antsy.

"You done?" he asked Kara, scooping up her plate before she could answer.

She let him take it without a word and checked that her gun was fully loaded as she stood.

"Can I finish my coffee?" Alex asked.

My voice shot up an octave. "No."

He rolled his eyes and chugged it down in one last gulp. "Let's do this," he said too loudly before slamming the cup back on the table.

Alex reached his arms toward us, like he was about to bless the group with his touch, and we were there by our next breath.

The air outside was still cold from the early morning. I blew heat into my hands, and it came out in foggy puffs.

"You think we should just go door to door?" I asked as we entered the building.

"Yeah," William answered.

I readied myself for the man we'd seen on the stairs yesterday, tensing for the wave of fear, but he wasn't there. A girl a little younger than me sat in his place. Her hair was a stringy dirty blonde. Grease caused it to separate at the roots, and her tired face didn't seem to care much. I waited for her ability, wondering what it might be, but Kara cut me off mid thought.

It's her. Dehne.

I grew two sizes, ready to tackle her to the floor if I had to.

Wait. Kara put her hand up, stopping me. *She wants to help us.* She bit her lip, unsure. *As far as I can tell.*

What if it's a trick? I pushed past Kara's hand.

"Elyse?" The girl's meek voice seemed too kind, a touch of honey to sweeten a lie. I didn't trust it.

"Yes," I answered, hesitating with uncertainty.

"I'm sorry I ran." She stood and started forward, but stopped herself. Her eyes flickered toward Kara's gun, then my darts. "I was scared you would...I came back to help you."

"Then tell me who has my daughter." I took a few confident steps toward her and saw her tense.

"Do you promise not to kill me?"

I was so close. I could touch the end. Feel it. See myself holding my baby.

"Yes," my answer was breathy and desperate.

"Lilia has her."

My heart blossomed with hope at the name. Lilia. The only original Council member who I could trust. I'd saved her life, rescued her from the chains Christoph had kept her in. Sarah would be safe with her.

William interrupted my peace.

"We can't trust you," he said, crossing his arms over his chest. "Not until we have her back. Tell us where Lilia is, and we'll let you go."

Let her go? Before I could ask, Alex was behind Dehne with a gun to her back.

"I'm a messenger. Just tell me where to go, kiddo."

Dehne whimpered with fear, and the gentler me wanted to stop him, but I stood there waiting for her answer.

"I can't," she squeaked, her eyes glossing over with tears.

"Why not?" I cried out.

"Lilia took off as soon as I handed her over. We thought we could trust her, but we were wrong. Adrianna never had Sarah to bargain with. We don't know where your daughter is."

I wanted to believe her so badly. If she was telling the truth, Lilia was protecting Sarah. She wasn't hiding her *from* me, but *for* me. But it was second nature for this girl to lie, to protect herself. I couldn't be sure.

"Can you tell if she's lying, Kara?" I asked. William turned to her just as desperate for affirmation.

"I can't," she answered, "but William can."

I smiled to myself as I realized she was right. Neither of us had even thought of his ability. He was already in front of her.

Dehne's scrunched brow softened, and her fear melted away as William grabbed her hands. He looked her in the eyes, and she turned beet red with besotted joy.

"Are you telling me the truth?" he asked.

She nodded, squeezing his hands. "No one ever believes me, but I'm a good person. I want to be good. I'd never lie to you."

I tilted my head back and closed my eyes. Finally, something was working in my favor. Lilia had Sarah. I just had to find her.

CHAPTER TWENTY-THREE

WILLIAM TURNED AND HEADED TOWARD ME, LEAVING Dehne alone and embarrassed on the stairs.

"Any idea where Lilia might be?" he asked, the four of us standing in a circle.

Kara's brow creased as she glanced at Dehne, clearly trying to get more information.

I cracked my knuckles, thinking. "We can try—"

Before I could finish my thought, the second-floor doorway crashed against the wall and people of all ages poured into the stairwell. Their faces looked panicked as they rushed for the exit. Adults shoved passed us, not bothering to slow down until I found myself pressed against the railing.

"What's going on?" I yelled above the scuffle of voices and shoes on cement.

A woman grabbed me by the arm, her grey eyes and feathered hair wild with fear. "Are you a messenger?"

Her intensity threw me. “Uh…no. I’m—”

“The last healer,” she said, recognizing me. She looked over her shoulder. “You should leave. Get out of the city.”

She released her hold on my arm and tore down the stairs with the others.

William pushed his way past a family dragging two heavy suitcases. “Should we follow them?” he asked.

No, we should leave, Kara answered silently, but three women stepped between us, and pieces of their conversation trailed as they passed.

“Why, what did she say?” one of them asked.

“Phoebe’s given her warning.”

“How much time…”

“I don’t know!”

The two voices faded into the cacophony as they made their way to the first floor, until little by little, silence returned to the stairwell.

The unsettled air rang in my ears.

“Let’s get out of here,” Kara said, making eye contact with me.

I looked around in vain, realizing Dehne had taken the opportunity to flee.

“Okay,” I agreed, numb with fear. I wasn’t ready for the destruction in my vision. What if Sarah was in the city when it happened? There was nothing I could do to stop it.

—

WE WAITED FOR SOMETHING TO HAPPEN, KEEPING AN eye on national news like the country could explode at any moment.

In a way it did. The government essentially fell the day I killed Mckinney. Though they kept up appearances, violence and rampant crime spread through the cities, poisoning the streets. Law enforcement was outnumbered, most having fled their post, and without Adrianna's task force picking up the slack there was no one left to keep order.

It was easy for me to pretend none of it was happening. I told myself there was nothing I could do. Things had gotten far too out of control. It was the perfect excuse to spend those weeks forcing Alex to take me to all the places Lilia might be, the Beverly Hills estate, the Texas cabin, and for the third time this morning, the Lenaia caves.

"Look, she's not here. We've been here," Alex said, his voice low but harsh.

"I realize that." I faked a smile as I searched past him into the distant corners of the cave with my flashlight. "Hello!"

My voice echoed back to me, accompanied by someone's heavy sigh.

William pointed his light in Alex's eyes. "Oh, sorry," he said casually without lowering it.

Alex threw up his hand to shield his eyes. "Can we go now?" he asked, squinting and annoyed.

Maybe he was right. We were all tired of searching the same places time after time only to come back empty handed, but I couldn't give up. I would never, ever, give up.

"I'm just going to wait here," I answered, unable to let go. "Just in case. Will you come get me when I call?"

"Brilliant plan. Why haven't we been doing this from the beginning?" He grabbed Kara's hand. "You staying, lover boy?"

"Just get out of here already," William answered, shaking his head.

The two of us found a spot against the rock wall, a few feet away from where we used to cook the food for our camp. Those days seemed so far out of my reach. Life was complicated, but we were whole back then. I pushed the dusty red earth around with the bottoms of my black boots. These caves were covered with the footprints of our past, its empty space a memory of who we used to be. I wasn't sure how I felt about it, whether I missed them or resented them for bringing me to where I was now. But the nostalgia dredged up a warm, beautiful kind of melancholy.

I shone my light across the cave and watched as it cut through the darkness as far as it could reach.

"Remember that night in the waterfall?" I asked. It was one of his only memories of us together like that, but it was also one of my favorites.

"How could I forget? I charmed the pants off you."

I cocked my head. "They slid off in the water."

"I pulled them off."

My smile stayed hidden in the dark. "Those moments were nice." The silence around us grew heavy and spoke for me. I felt like I was chasing those moments, trying to find them again instead of taking responsibility for the chaos I'd caused. "I just can't function without her. I can't focus or think about *anything* else. It rules me, this emptiness. I feel like I'm going crazy."

"Ellie, it's—"

I couldn't let him talk. If I did, I might never get this out. "What kind of mother loses her child? Maybe this is supposed to happen. She deserves better than me. I've killed people, William, and no matter what I tell myself, whether I justify it with self-defense or self-preservation, none of it matters. It's changed me. Ruined me." I couldn't stop myself. My deepest most painful secrets needed to be purged. "And I'm supposed to be this leader," I confessed to the dark. "I feel like it's my responsibility to be a leader, but a leader to who and how? Everyone left. It's all just blowing up in my face, and I have no control over any of it. All I want to do is fix it all, make it all okay. Isn't that my job? Isn't that what I'm supposed to do?"

I let out a deep sigh, fidgeting with the button on my flashlight. "Sorry."

He pointed his light my way, tilting his head to check for tears. I wiped them away, feeling small for breaking down. "Hey, we all need a good rant every once in a while.

I've been working on mine, but I'm saving it for the perfect time."

A laugh cracked in my throat. "Well, I'm looking forward to it."

"You should be. I have a lot of issues. It's going to be good."

His shadowed smirk made me smile.

"I miss the way it used to be." I glanced up under the glow of our flashlights, realizing he couldn't remember how things were before this. "Maybe it's good you don't remember. You'd miss it, too."

"I remember some." He traced his index finger along the lines of my palm, leaving a trail of warmth wherever he touched. "I guess it isn't the same. They were dreams, but...why don't you tell me? What was it like?"

I relaxed my head into his shoulder. "It was easy. We were...so young."

He laughed. "We *are* young. It's still our first century."

"That's not what I mean. So much has changed. It hasn't been that long, but I...we used to be innocent, carefree. I would spend all night just worrying about what to say to you or how to act. Our world was so small. Just us."

He laced our fingers into a tight knot and pressed the back of my hand to his lips. "It still is." I could hear his body shift against the ground as he turned to face me. My flashlight fell on its side as William's mouth touched mine, every sensation amplified in the dark. The feel of his warm thumb brushing my ear as he held the side of my face made me shiver. I moved to my knees, chasing his lips as he pulled away.

"Just us," he whispered. Warmth trailed up my sides as his hands found my bare waist and pulled me closer. He was everything I needed in this cold, dark place. My heat. My light. My peace.

His breath warmed my cheeks as our cold noses touched. Then his bare chest on mine, a wall of fire in the rain. My back against rock. I couldn't see, but I could feel. Every inch of me against every inch of him. My hands climbed his arms, his shoulders. His square jaw, rough with stubble, brushed my collar bone. This dark secret place was all that kept me whole. No more thoughts of all that was wrong. Here, with him, just for now, things were right. A glimpse of the freedom we never knew we had.

—

BACK AT THE HOUSE NICS AND SAM WERE SITTING against each other on the floor. They already had the TV turned on, but the news wasn't reporting the devastation we'd all been dreading. The vice president was addressing the nation. His face had turned a pallid white, but he buttoned his suit jacket and cleared his throat as if trying to stay composed.

"What's this about?" I asked.

Dr. Nickel leaned forward from the couch taking in

every word.

"He's attempting to provide some reassurance to the country, but he hasn't really said anything yet."

We're a strong nation, full of strong people. He combed his hair back and took a breath, like someone was instructing him through an earpiece. *Times like these, although meant to tear us down, will only tie us together. This attack will not go unanswered. Harsher measures will need to be taken to ensure we can maintain peace in such a volatile time.*

We all waited in silence for the consequences of our actions, but the acting president never got the chance to finish. A blinding light eliminated the video feed and all that remained was a multi-colored emergency broadcast screen.

"Something's going on," I said as Sam flipped through the channels for more news.

And then we saw it.

The mushroom cloud.

CHAPTER TWENTY-FOUR

FOR THE FIRST MOMENT AFTER WE ALL REALIZED what had happened, I'd never heard a deeper silence. Like the entire world had gone quiet.

"Is that..." Sam's words trailed off as we all stared at the aerial image.

Helicopters circled what was left of the blast from afar as reporters and scientists debated the direction of the wind, where the radiation would go, and what would happen. Over and over they replayed the initial explosion. A blinding light that blotted out the screen followed by a glowing orb that rose from the ground. It turned dark and bled black smoke from its center until it was nothing more than withered flame and ash waiting to poison its next victims. Washington DC had been leveled.

"Who would *do* this?" Nics exploded without really listening to the others. She jumped to her feet, too enraged to keep still. "Adrianna is dead, right?"

All eyes were on Kara. "What? Of course she's dead. You think after all these years I don't know how to kill someone?"

Alex laughed, but he was the only one.

Nics turned to me with genuine fear in her eyes. "What do we do?"

"We take cover," Mac answered with Anna tucked beneath one arm and Chloe snuggled into the other.

War. It strengthened me and ruined me, cleared my mind, gave me focus.

"No, we don't," I said as everything suddenly made sense. "We go in. We help."

"You can't," Anna protested. "The radiation. It'll kill you."

"It would kill *you*," I corrected. "Not me. Not any of us. Descendants don't get sick."

"Yeah. Either way I'm not going anywhere near that," Alex said. "Not my idea of a fun Tuesday afternoon if you know what I mean."

"He's right, Ellie," William said, regret pulling his lips into an apologetic smile.

"We have to," I argued. "This is what the oracle meant. *You have to lose to win*. They need us. It's the only way we'll win their trust."

Dr. Nickel's eyes were red with exhaustion and grief. "She has a point," he added.

His wife looked on from the kitchen, her face twisted with worry. I could tell she didn't approve of putting the last of her children in danger, but she kept her thoughts to herself.

Alex stood to leave. "Good luck getting to D.C., because I'm not taking you." I watched his back as he headed for the door.

"You're just going to walk away?" Kara called after him. The whole group turned to look at her, and suddenly the living room felt too intimate. "I know you believe in making things right. You convinced me of that when we took Sarah. I'm not making that kind of mistake again. If Elyse wants to go, we go."

He stopped, but didn't turn around. "You don't get to tell me what to do," he barked. His shoulders sank in the silence of the room, and his eyes softened as he faced her. "Look. I'm doing her and everyone a favor. Do you have any idea what happens after an atomic bomb?"

I didn't want to have to think about it, but that was even more of a reason to get there as soon as possible. If I needed to save the world one person at a time, I would, as long as it would make me right inside. I'd sift through every city, every pair of eyes until I found Sarah. What if somehow she was there? The thought set me on fire.

"That's why we need to go," I insisted. "Now."

He looked me in the eyes, and before we could discuss any sort of plan he disappeared and materialized inches from my face. "Sooner or later you're going to have to realize you can't save everyone. Even if I did take you, you couldn't heal them all. You'd kill yourself trying, and for what? Why?"

My face became stone. Determination chiseled into every feature. "You know it's the right thing to do."

"There's a difference between doing what's right and self-sacrifice. People are always going to need your help. Protecting yourself doesn't make you a bad person." He turned to Kara with a set jaw. "I'll take her in the morning. The worst will be over by then." Without another word he was gone, and there was nothing I could do.

I headed for my room and sat on the bed, but I couldn't escape what had happened. The television droned through the wall, taunting me. It was torture being trapped in the house when so many people were suffering, but Alex was right. I couldn't save everyone, and that thought ran deeper than the strangers who needed me. My daughter needed me.

I paced by my bedroom window, wrung out and angry. Without Alex, I felt helpless. I couldn't watch the reports on TV, and I couldn't sit still.

All I could do was run.

"Want some company?" William asked as I laced up my running shoes.

Not even he could squelch the ache in my heart. I needed to be alone or away. Somewhere quiet where I could pretend the world was right.

"No, I...I just need to get out." I grabbed a hair tie and pulled my limp brown hair into a ponytail as I headed for the door.

The ground felt familiar under my feet, and that alone focused me. It was so quiet here, so removed from the world's mistakes. My mistakes. The trees knew nothing of my sins. I veered off my normal path, following the scent of sap as a sweat began to break on my forehead. Here I could be open. I could hurt and be cradled by the unknowing pines. With each step the breeze cooled my skin, though my muscles pumped heat into my lungs.

I ran until I couldn't, until a wave of nausea forced me to slow my pace and stop. I braced my hands against my knees in the dappled light. As my chest worked to catch a breath, I let out a cry that only the forest could hear.

A shadow flickered in the distance, and I shot up standing straight. I wasn't alone.

"Edith," I whispered, knowing it couldn't be her. My eyes combed the trees to my right and caught a glimpse of movement behind the thickest trunk.

I reached for my dart gun, not wanting to kill whoever was out there. A small amount of blood would only stun them if necessary. The figure moved again, and I shot without question.

I missed.

"Out of practice, I see," Mac grumbled as he plucked the dart from the bark.

I stepped back and rubbed my neck. "Yeah, well turns out when you train yourself to kill people, killing comes a little too easily. Figured I'd take a break from it for a while."

I imagined McKinney's last handshake, remembered his tight-lipped smile.

"Yeah, a real shame about the president."

He offered nothing more, no words of sympathy.

"So," I said through the silence. Mac wore his guilt like a sheath. He hadn't approached me about losing Sarah, and I could tell just by looking at his weary features that he wasn't ready to talk about it. "Do you have any advice on how I'm supposed to save the world?"

He pushed up the sleeves of his flannel. "One soul at a time, I guess."

I nodded. Nothing seemed more daunting.

His heavy feet shuffled against the dry grass. "I figured you'd need a new weapon, being that you'll be doing more healing than killin' these days." He reached into his back pocket and pulled out a small fold up knife. The handle was a rich dark wood. He handed it to me and let me open the blade. The silver was the thinnest I'd ever seen with patterned olive leaves engraved along both edges.

"I've been working on it a while," he said, rubbing his stubbled chin. "Haven't been able to sleep much. The blade cuts real fine so your wounds will be easy to heal. You'll need more blood for these folks than that bracelet of yours can handle."

I forced a smile through that grim thought. "Thanks, Mac."

"You just be careful, okay?" He waved me off. "Now get back home. They're lookin' for ya."

I nodded as he headed deeper into the woods and tucked the folded knife into my back pocket.

"Elyse!" Nics called through the open screen door when she saw me. She beckoned for me to hurry, and I seized up for a moment before I rushed toward her. "Where have you been?" She threw her arms in the air, but whatever it was had pushed Nics past anger into worry. Her dark brow creased. "They're attacking the cities. It's...it's bad."

In the living room, Dr. Nickel was fumbling with the remote. "We lost the feed," he said, pressing every button.

William's eyes lifted from the scrambled TV screen. "It's not the remote, Dad." He looked at me, shaking his head like he couldn't find his words.

"Tell me what happened," I urged.

Anna sat in the corner of the couch with an arm around her daughter. She combed her black and silver hair away from her tear-filled eyes as she processed the shock. "Washington DC was just the first. As soon as you left it kept coming. New York, San Francisco, LA, Dallas. They must have been planning it, because they took everything out so fast."

"Are we going to be okay?" Chloe's chin dimpled as she cried. "The internet on my phone is out. How do we know what's going to happen? You don't think they'll bomb here, do you?" she asked her mother.

Anna kissed the side of her head. “No honey. We’ll be okay.”

“Who’s *they*?” I asked, in disbelief. I had only been gone an hour at most.

“It cut out,” Sam answered, holding Nics’s hand by the kitchen, “but CNN was saying it was a foreign attack. Something about a treaty among the larger nations.”

“It was foreign?” I wiped at my forehead. “Why? Why would they—”

“They saw us as a threat. We killed the president. If we could get to him, why not the rest of the world?” Nics interrupted, her lips pulled tight into a grimace. Her voice rose. “We should never have gone through with it.”

I stared at the floor in silence.

“I’m sorry,” she said, not really apologizing, “but I feel like I could have done something...”

“You did what any friend would do, Nics,” William answered, taking my hand. “And we’re grateful for that. This isn’t anybody’s fault.”

“No,” Nics sneered. “It’s Adrianna’s fault.”

“And that’s why she’s dead,” Kara’s voice quivered from behind us. Her words were too weak. Something was wrong.

I turned to find two half-charred people behind me. If I hadn’t heard Kara’s voice, I wouldn’t have recognized her. Her hair was melted into a black nest atop her head. What was left of her clothes hung like black ribbon from her limbs.

I let out a startled gasp. "What happened?" I stepped forward just in time to catch her as she fell from Alex's grasp. My arms hooked under her armpits, and her full body weight dragged us both to the floor. Alex sank beside us. His arms were so burnt they looked melted. He shook in violent waves trying not to lay them against his folded knees, which looked equally scorched.

"Who's worse?" I demanded, scanning Kara's injuries. She lay unconscious in front of me, and I was so shaken I didn't know where to start.

"Heal her," Alex groaned. His stiff body rocked back and forth as he hummed a quiet sob of pain to himself.

I fumbled with my bracelet, switching it to the right wrist, and jumping at the feel of the blades cutting into my skin.

William knelt down next to me, resting a hand on my unsteady arm. "What do you need?" he asked. I hadn't realized I'd been shaking until his presence anchored me. I'd never seen a body so mangled, not even after the fire at my parent's old place.

"Um...I—" A circle of faces peered down on us in horror.

"Give her space." William stood with his arms out. He ushered everyone toward the front door. "Wait outside for now."

The absence of an audience helped me focus. Internal injuries first. I let blood drip from my bracelet into Kara's mouth. It was just enough to jerk her awake. She cried out in agony, and her body went rigid from the pain.

"It's coming," I promised as drops of my blood fell onto her left arm, but it was too slow. Healing these types of wounds would take forever at this pace.

"Hey," William said to Kara. His voice was gentle as he knelt down next to her head. "I'm right here." He put a soft hand to her cheek. "See me." She made eye contact with him and her breath steadied, though it was still labored. "We're going to make it all go away, okay?" His gaze intensified, and I remembered how he'd taken away my pain when I'd been burned. She stared lovingly into his eyes, and he smiled back at her.

My heart pulled in two directions as I used my new knife to cut my palm. The secret, darker part of me didn't like to share William, and I knew the stab of jealously was so selfish I would never admit it to anyone. Still, I was thankful for her relief. As much as she'd done to me, betrayal and all, I couldn't deny our friendship.

I ran my palm up both her bare legs, painting her with sheets of blood.

"Thank you," she whispered to William, though I wondered if her words were meant for me.

Alex was the living dead next to me. His burns resembled decay against his pale complexion. They reached up his neck onto his cheeks. I hardly noticed him blink.

"Alex," I said, scooting closer to him. He didn't acknowledge me, and I was afraid I'd lose him to shock.

"Hey, stay with me." I snapped my fingers in front of his face and his eyes closed like his light had finally gone out.

CHAPTER TWENTY-FIVE

"HELP ME CUT HIS CLOTHES OFF," I SAID AS I MOVED to cradle Alex's head in my lap.

William listened without question, breaking away from Kara to look for scissors in the kitchen. She moaned and rolled onto her side, watching me as I pulled open Alex's slack jaw. I clenched my fist over his mouth forcing the blood from my veins. The sting of the cut worsened, but I didn't stop.

"Is he going to be okay?" Kara whispered with her eyes closed.

"Yes," I answered, though I wasn't sure. I glanced at his chest, which struggled to rise and fall. The fabric of his white shirt had fused with his skin. Bile rose into my throat at the sight of it.

William knelt at Alex's feet and began cutting tattered pants away from burned flesh. I moved to heal Alex's torso, but hesitated, not knowing how to handle the places where skin and fabric melded together. "How do I heal this?"

"Where's your knife?" William asked, wrinkling his nose at the smell.

I handed it to him as he attempted to make work of the shirt and caught sight of Kara's open eyes. Silent tears streaked her soot-covered face.

"He's out," I reassured her as she watched William cut skin that wasn't salvageable. "He can't feel anything."

Alex's breathing faltered, and I checked for a pulse before continuing to heal.

"He'll be okay," I promised. "His pulse is strong."

She nodded, but I'd never seen such a horrified look on her face. Her eyes were wide, like she was afraid to close them.

Alex stayed unconscious throughout the healing process. We did our best to clean him up as Kara pulled herself together. She managed to stand, and I helped her to the shower, carrying most of her weight.

"Will you stay?" she asked as I started the water.

I adjusted the temperature and looked back at her. "Sure," I answered.

I sat in silence on the toilet seat as she washed herself clean. Steam changed the air into a warm fog that coated the mirror and beaded the white tile walls with droplets of water. The faucet squeaked when she shut it off, and I handed her a towel.

"I can still feel it," she said as she wrapped the towel around herself and pulled back the shower curtain. The skin on her arms and legs was bright pink and new. Her hard layers had been shed, inside and out. The girl in front of me was fragile and shaken, reduced by trauma to the weakness of a child.

"Yeah, that happens," I answered, glancing at her hair. The shower had cleaned her body, but it couldn't repair the melted mess atop her head. I cleared my throat. "Sometimes the brain registers the pain even though the wounds are healed. Like phantom pain."

She turned to the mirror, noticing my eyes avoiding her hair. "That bad, huh?"

I waited for her to wipe the fog away so she could see herself, but she didn't. She stared into the opaque glass, her towel tightening around her chest as she breathed.

"They nuked Chicago," she said, as if trying to convince herself that it had really happened. "I thought I died, Ellie. I thought we were in hell..."

"You don't have to tell—"

She continued as if I'd said nothing, as if she needed to purge the horror she'd seen.

"It happened so fast. One second we were walking into a café in the city, the next..." I couldn't tell if it was hard for her to remember or just hard for her to face what came after that, but she paused. "Everything was on fire. Buildings, cars...people. I couldn't figure out what had happened. It was like I just blinked and the world exploded. Alex and I were separated, and I was trying to find him, but...the people. They were...Ellie, I couldn't tell who was who. They didn't look alive."

Her shoulders started to shake, and I stood, reaching out to comfort her. As soon as my hand touched her bare arm, she jumped.

"Sorry," I said immediately.

"No, it's okay." She whirled around disoriented and embarrassed, like she had been miles away. Her hand shot up to her melted black hair, as if to cover it. "Can you go check on Alex?" she asked.

I nodded vigorously. Anything to make up for what she'd gone through. "Sure. Yeah." I smiled a sad smile and opened the door to leave.

Alex was still resting on the living room couch where I'd left him. His eyes were closed in a peaceful sleep. I looked for William, but found Nics in his place, settled into the armchair.

"You know this is their karma, right?" she said, pushing herself back until the chair reclined.

"For what?"

"For playing against you. For Sarah." She snorted with disgust. "You're so quick to forget she gave your daughter away."

Her words stung. They were an unwelcome reminder of Sarah's absence, but I didn't expect Nics to understand. Forgiveness wasn't her strong suit. "Nobody deserves this, Nics."

"She's just wound tight because of all that's going on," Sam spoke up from the kitchen. I hadn't seen him there. He bit into a turkey sandwich. "Don't take it personally, El—"

"Oh shut it, Sam," she snapped. "You were saying the same..."

Kara stepped out of the bathroom, and the two of them went quiet. I didn't blame them. I didn't know what to say either.

Her head was shaved down to the root.

She ran her fingers over the stubble on her scalp, a little uncomfortable with us staring. "I never was very girly anyway," she said.

"No, it looks good," Sam responded too quickly.

But he was right. It suited her.

"Very GI Jane." I nodded. "In a good way."

She caught sight of Alex and headed for the couch without acknowledging us.

"Have you seen William?" I asked Sam.

"Outside," he answered through a full mouth.

I ducked out the front door, leaving the four of them to stew in the tension Nics had created. Voices came from the shed, and I assumed Mac, Chloe, and Anna were huddled inside watching the news. News I'd have to face eventually.

I scanned the yard and found William alone. He sat cross-legged at the foot of Edith's grave on the left side of the house. I hadn't been to visit yet, and the sight of the raised earth made my throat pinch. She was really gone. I bit my tongue trying to hold myself together.

He looked up at the sound of my footsteps. “Hey.” His unoccupied fingers picked at the grass.

I sat down beside him. “Hey.”

The cool dusky air gave me a chill as I pulled my knees up and wrapped my arms around them. I didn’t speak. We both needed to breathe through a moment of silence.

“I miss her,” he said, tucking a golden piece of hair behind his ear.

Miss. The word didn’t even come close. You miss someone when they go out of town for a week. There was no word big enough, deep enough, painful enough to encompass the emptiness of loss. All the what-ifs and how-comes never go away, but they get quieter. I’d lost so many of my friends and family I’d learned to live with the pain as if it were my own chronic illness.

“It gets easier,” I told him, before letting out a sigh.

“I wish I could remember when we were kids. I feel like I can’t do justice to her memory.”

“You can’t blame yourself for that.”

A gust of wind shook the pines that towered a few yards in front of us.

“She deserves better.” He looked at me. “A better brother would have kept her home.”

I folded my fingers between his and leaned into his arm. “We can’t save everyone.” It still amazed me how profound Alex’s words had been.

“Yeah, but we can be smart. We can stay out of this

war so no one else has to die." His jaw muscle pulsed, and guilt tightened its grasp on my heart. "I just want to find Sarah. I don't care about anything else."

I ran my thumb along the edge of our clasped hands, willing myself not to get lost in thoughts of Sarah. Whether it was true or not, I had to tell myself she was safe with Lilia, wherever they were. Any other scenario ended with me curled into a heap on my bed, and I couldn't imagine ever getting up. That alone was enough of a reason to keep myself distracted until Lilia reached out to us, and I had to hope she would. We didn't have a lead. We'd looked everywhere.

"I want to find her, too," I said, letting go of his hand to fidget with my cuticles, "and I wish I didn't have to take part in this, but I don't think I have a choice."

He shook his head, but kept his gaze forward. "You do have a choice."

"You just want me to let half the country suffer like Alex and Kara?" I crossed my arms, readying myself for his resistance.

"You can't save everyone. Right?" His voice was calm and steady, but he clutched his hands together until his knuckles were white.

"But I can save *some*. I *need* to save them. It's how this ends. I can feel it. I finally understand that now. I did this. I have to fix it. We have to help them rebuild. It's the only way we can live together peacefully. They need us."

He fixed his eyes on Edith's grave. "And if you're wrong?"

"I'm not."

As the sun went down, my anxiety shot up. I went to bed early hoping to sleep it off, but every breath seemed too shallow, every position uncomfortable. I ended up studying the inside of my eyelids until William slipped in beside me.

"Alex is doing better," he whispered, noticing me stir. "He said he'll still take you in the morning."

I picked up on the word *you* and lifted my head.

"Aren't you coming?"

Silence answered me back.

"Only because I have to," he answered finally.

I let my head drop back into my pillow as William's warm body pressed against my back. His arm curled under mine, the weight of it heavy on my chest.

"You know I love you, Ellie," he spoke softly into the back of my neck. "I just want you to stay safe."

"I will," I promised, finding his hand with mine.

William's touch was a comfort, but even he couldn't settle my subconscious. I tried to stay still as his breathing slowed into a gentle rhythm, adjusting my arm slowly beneath my pillow.

Waking up was the only thing that convinced me I'd slept at all. My fingers reached across the bed expecting William's body to warm beneath them, but the sheets were cold. I opened my eyes to see him fully dressed and sitting at my feet. I was afraid to ask, afraid the knot in my throat would choke me if I opened my mouth.

"Where are you going?"

"Just ready to leave when you are." The fact that he was ready, but hadn't bothered to wake me said more than the hesitancy in his voice.

There was a specific kind of tension in his words. Not anger or even resentment, but a defeated resolve like this war would always come first.

When you rely on someone else to hold you together for so long, it's only a matter of time before they fold under the pressure. I could feel him letting go, feel pieces of me start to slip out of place.

I pushed off the covers and found my thickest pair of cargo pants, determined not to let the silence between us bother me.

He grabbed my boots and set them beside me as I sat on the bed. Our eyes connected. Mine sorry, his burdened.

Once I'd tied the laces I couldn't bring myself to stand. Instead I clasped and unclasped my bracelet. "Tell me it's okay. Tell me I can do this." I stared up at him for a silent moment. "I need to know you're with me on this."

He crossed his arms and licked his lips. "I'm always with you." His words didn't match his body language. The muscles in his shoulders were tense.

His arms dropped when I nodded, defeated and

terrified.

"Hey," he said, sitting next to me on the bed. I turned to face him and he took my hand. "Just because I don't want you to go, doesn't mean I won't help you." Warmth grew where our skin touched, both of us absentmindedly linking and unlinking our fingers. "I understand why you have to do this. I just wish it didn't have to be you." He kissed my cheek, and I wrapped my arms around his back.

"Thank you," I whispered, tucking my face into the warm pocket between his neck and collarbone.

"Just promise me the next time the world explodes we can stay home and watch Jeopardy."

I laughed and pulled away. "Deal."

Kara peeked her shaved head through the door just as William and I stood to leave.

"You ready?"

"Yeah," I answered, slipping Mac's knife into my back pocket.

In the living room, Alex wasn't the only one waiting. Everyone was there, dressed and ready to go.

"We all want to help," Nics said, looking at Sam who nodded in agreement.

Even William's parents were prepared. Both held buckets filled with rags and other first aid items.

Though I knew Anna had no intention of risking the radiation, she still stood with the group to see us off.

"You know we'd come with you if we could," she

said, hugging Chloe close.

I nodded as Sam handed me a two-way radio and held up his own. "The cell phone towers will be out, so these will help us communicate."

A subtle smile lifted my cheeks, and I clipped the radio to my pants. "Okay."

"All right, brace yourselves, people." Alex said, gesturing for us to make contact. "Where to first?"

He looked at me to answer, though I noticed he could only hold my gaze for a second or two.

"New York," I answered, picking a city at random.

And the blinding light carried us away.

CHAPTER TWENTY-SIX

A SINGLE IMAGE GRACED MY EYES—HELL.

What was once the Hudson River was now a place for lost souls. Its water ran black, carrying the dead out to sea. The injured collected at its shores, seeking refuge from fire and pain. Their blood stained the cement ground, and their cries were a constant song of sorrow. Smoke added a gloomy haze that carried a stench so putrid I covered my mouth with my hand, not wanting to breathe it in.

In the distance, the skyline stood out as nothing more than a garbage heap of scrap metal. I couldn't imagine it any worse.

"I think we should—" My voice was silenced as I felt myself being plunged back into white airless space.

"I can't." Alex stared at me seconds later from across our living room. His eyes wide with unsuppressed trauma. He let out a heavy breath and began pacing. "I'm sorry.

It's too much. Just...just give me a second."

Nobody spoke. I wasn't the only one who'd seen what I'd seen. The once hopeful hearts who'd stood before me minutes ago hung their defeated heads.

"Can I say somethin'?" Mac piped up, scratching the side of his head. "I'm not so sure this is the way to go about things." His eyebrows inched up as he recalled the scene. "Did you get a look at the numbers you're dealing with there, kid? Once they see what you can do, it won't be safe. Not for any of us."

I saw his point, but not helping wasn't an option for me. Not after what I'd just witnessed.

"I'm assuming you have a better idea?" I asked, hoping I'd agree with his plan.

"We bring them here," he said as if it were the only way.

"No," Mrs. Nickel insisted with a pleading edge to her voice. "This is our home, Mac. It's our only safe place. We can't give that up."

Anna and Chloe stared on with confused faces.

"What about hospitals?" William suggested. "The ones on the outskirts of the city that are still standing. They'll be overrun. You could heal in a private room. We could keep things under control if we had a system."

"What about the people we saw?" Sam asked. No one answered. "So we just leave them?"

I opened my mouth to answer, but all that came out was silence and guilt. People were going to die. I had to face that. We all did.

"Yes," Kara said for me. "We leave them. It's not safe to go back."

"Can you get us to a hospital?" I asked Alex, anxious to get moving.

He was still pacing, chewing on his thumb knuckle. "Uh, yeah. Okay. I think so."

I'd only been witness to the horror of the aftermath for a matter of seconds, but it had left a dark stain on my heart. I couldn't imagine walking around amongst it the moment it happened. After what Alex had been through, I was grateful he was still willing to help us.

"Thanks," I said, reaching for his shoulder.

The hospital hallway reeked of filthy bodies and untreated wounds. I pulled the collar of my shirt up over my nose and gagged. A few pairs of apathetic eyes stared up at me through the chaos of a woman screaming for a nurse. Of coughing and sobbing. Cries of pain. A man pacing in front of a boy asleep or unconscious against the wall. William grabbed my hand as I took in the shrill sounds and rancid smells of catastrophe.

I thought I was prepared. I'd helped at a hospital before. I knew what to expect, but this was so much worse than the bombing in San Francisco. There, people were mostly scared with minor injuries. Here, people had come to die.

Alex appeared in front of me. "This way."

I snapped out of my shock and followed him down

the hallway, past rooms of more people and shared hospital beds.

"This isn't sanitary," I said over my shoulder, but my voice was lost.

A woman wearing jeans and a green shirt stained brown with old blood balanced a bag of saline on the windowsill above a young man. Her eyes followed us as we passed, and I wondered if she was a nurse or someone taking matters into her own hands.

Alex turned into an almost empty room with three walls full of empty shelves. It was small, but two families had claimed the space, the mother of one laying unconscious on the floor. Next to her a child of four or five clung to her arm. Burns blackened her young fair face.

Against the opposite wall a father hugged a pale teen boy into his side. The boy shivered uncontrollably.

"This room is taken," the man spoke up. Sweat darkened the edges of his grey hair and dripped down the sides of his flushed face. Even the underarms of his grey polo shirt were stained with damp circles.

"We need the space," Alex said, waving him off. His nerves were getting the best of him and the explanation came off aggressive.

The teenager's father rose to his feet, ready to fight for the right to stay. His nostrils flared as he bit his lips. "Look, you little punk—"

"We're here to help," I said, stepping forward. "What happened to him?"

The man's dark eyebrows relaxed and his stance changed, though he still seemed unsure. His shoulders curled in as he looked at his son and knelt down at his side. He ran a restless hand over his face as if he could wipe away the worry in his eyes.

"He uh..." The man shook his head, and removed the leather jacket covering what used to be his son's right arm.

I tried not to react, breathing out a slow shaky breath.

"I can heal him," I said, looking up.

"How?" the other father asked. "They're out of supplies."

"My blood," I answered. "It has healing qualities."

Confused faces made the connection, but the four-year-old was the only one who spoke.

"You're her? The last healer?" Her bright green baby girl eyes widened with fascination. She peered through blonde untrimmed bangs.

I forced a smile, kneeling in front of her. "Yep." Her dimpled grin was missing a few baby teeth, and I wondered whether or not she'd lost them in the blast.

"Are you going to make us better?" she asked, unburdened by the city's devastation.

I glanced at the boy's father, whose deep brown eyes danced with uncertainty.

"If you'll let me."

"Yeah!" she said in a high-pitched squeal that made me laugh. Her eyebrows rose as she remembered something, and her voice dropped to a whisper. "But be quiet, 'kay? My mom is sleeping."

I looked to her father. Disheveled brown hair, red watery eyes heavy with loss. They connected with mine, and he shrugged as if to apologize for his lie. His wife lay too still. Too pale.

My heart reached out of my chest and ached for the little girl in front of me. The emptiness I felt for my own child throbbed at the reminder of that severed bond. No child should be without a mother.

"Okay," I promised, holding her tiny hand. "I'll be really, really quiet."

The injured boy was close to unconscious, but I waited as his father paced and grabbed a handful of his hair.

"Sir—" I prompted.

"Just do it," he said, choking on a sob. "Please. Anything you can do. Whatever it is. If it will save him."

I rushed forward to get to work, forgetting about the others who'd come to help me. As I turned back, William was the only one left in the room. He held a bucket of water and a stack of white rags.

"Alex and Kara are guarding the door," he reassured me, "and the others are helping where they can. Don't worry about them. Do what you have to do."

I nodded. "Okay. Help me lay him on his back."

The shift woke the boy from his catatonic state, and his screams began.

"Help him! Do something," his father shouted.

I opened my new knife, initiating the first cut. A cut that would bleed all of my good intentions until they made up for my wrongs. As I mended his wounds, my heart lightened under the weight of all the guilt. For a moment at least.

William and I stayed in that room all morning as countless people entered injured and left healed. I didn't stop to rest or take time to process the horrors I'd seen. Any time I took for myself might mean a life lost. One I could have saved.

"Here," William said, handing me a turkey sandwich loaded with all the fixings. "You need a break."

I took it and wiped my forehead with the back of my hand, pushing the sweat into my hair. "Where did you get this?" I asked, trying my best not to complain about the heat.

"I went rummaging through people's bags," he answered with a straight face. My brow must have wrinkled with disapproval because he laughed. "Oh come on. Alex took Mom home to make lunch. What did you think?"

His lightheartedness drew out a smile in me, and I sat with him on the floor against the back wall.

"Maybe I could heal while I eat. Just a minor injury or something," I thought aloud.

William stopped chewing and stared at me. "That's disgusting."

"Really?" I said, seeing his point. He took a drink

from our shared water bottle and handed it to me.

"Really."

I gulped down as much as I could and shoved another bite in with it. "Then eat faster," I said through my food.

He nodded and stuffed half his sandwich in his mouth.

As soon as I was finished, I wished I had saved some for someone else. So many people weren't only injured, they were starving. Vending machines had been cleaned out and the cafeteria had nothing left.

You're doing enough, Kara spoke silently in my head as she opened the door. A young woman holding her new baby stepped in behind her. *Don't make feeding everyone your burden, too.*

Kara smiled and closed the door again, leaving the mother alone with William and me.

I stared, my eyes refusing to blink. Something about seeing this girl and her baby felt like falling off a cliff. I'd been balanced, right on the edge, but this...she'd made me lose my footing.

Her dark hair was the same color and length as mine. She was taller, but thin framed. We were the same her and me. If I were human, maybe I'd be exactly in her shoes.

"Um," she said, breaking the silence that seemed to take a hold of William, too. "Should I...They didn't say what I was supposed to do next." She stepped forward, unsure.

"Nothing," I said, my voice cracking into a whisper. I cleared my throat. "I mean, you don't have to do anything."

"Where are you hurt?" William asked, leading her to the chair against the right wall.

"Oh." Her eyes fell to the face of her child. "I have a few minor scrapes, nothing terrible. We were protected from the blast, thank God." She sighed a grateful breath. "But she's just been sleeping so much. I can't get her to wake up."

I smiled, stepping closer to get a look at the sleeping baby. She was different than my Sarah, with rounder eyes and a pointed chin instead of the full face I had in my memory. Still, precious and peaceful all the same.

"They do that," I said, cocking my head as I watched her. "How old is she?"

"A little over a week," the mother said, moving the swaddling blanket away from the baby's face so I could see. "It's been so hard...and then this happened." She sniffled and her voice wavered as tears puddled in the corners of her eyes. She dabbed at them, trying to stay strong. "Do you have kids?"

I paused, unsure how to answer. No, I didn't *have* my baby. I couldn't stare at her while she slept or hold her warm body close to my chest. My heart stammered.

"We have a baby girl," William answered for me, peeking at the pink bundle. "She's pretty new, too."

"Do you want to hold her?" The mother pushed her

tiny daughter into my arms before I could answer.

I'd forgotten how it felt. All the familiarity of motherhood had faded in my daughter's absence, but somehow my arms remembered. I cradled the baby's delicate head with the crook of my elbow and curled my other arm around her bundled body.

"She's beautiful," I said quietly. Holding someone else's child didn't bring back fond memories or fill the hole I had in me. It made it worse, widening the ache until it was everywhere. "You're very lucky." I reached out, handing her back.

"Thank you," the mother said, biting her lip with concern. "But do you think you could just check if something is wrong? I'm worried about the radiation. What if she's sick? What if I'm sick?"

I looked at William, who took it upon himself to answer.

"We don't have any way of knowing that," he said, rubbing the back of his neck.

The idea of the two of them being beyond my help was an uncomfortable thought. I could only do so much. William had brought up the point earlier in the day, and I'd been giving each patient a portion of my blood by mouth in hopes it could counteract any radiation poisoning, but only time would tell. Once the body was past a certain point, it would be beyond my help. I only hoped I could stop it before it started.

"But we can try something," I said, unwilling to accept

the worst-case scenario. "Do you have a bottle?"

I worked through the days, moving from city to city in hospital rooms that had been set up for me. Nurses began to get on board, helping facilitate the lines that formed down crowded hallways, but none of them could do what I could.

"Can't we help administer blood to those who are waiting?" one woman asked, desperate to do more. But it didn't work that way. Once the blood was out of my system for any length of time it lost its effect.

The world outside could have been as black and infinite as the universe, broken into millions of stars, and I wouldn't have known. I ate, breathed, and lived those rooms. New York –white tile, white walls. San Francisco – grey floors, green walls. Los Angeles – yellow light, peach doors. They became my world. Each night I pushed myself past my breaking point, always hoping to heal just one more, and each night only William could convince me to leave the untreated for another day.

"Let's sleep," he said, holding my weary face with his warm palm. "You need a break. We both do."

His green eyes threatened to harness his power, and I couldn't argue.

"Okay."

At home in our room the image of the worried mother wouldn't leave me. It had been days since I'd treated them, but I still wondered where she was, if she had enough food and water. Was she by herself tonight?

Had I done enough to help them? At least they were together. Something I would never take for granted again. If there ever was an again.

"Do you think I'm naïve for still hoping we'll get Sarah back?"

I stared at the dried drops of blood on my boots as I sat on the bed and untied them. William sat with his back to me on the other edge of the mattress and looked over his shoulder.

"No." He stayed still too long and then turned away to kick off his own shoes. "I'm still hoping."

I pushed the blankets aside, tucking my feet under my legs.

"What if she's not okay?" My throat began to sting and suddenly I was drowning in panic. "You've seen what it's like. So many cities." I could feel the tears coming. "What if—"

"Hey." William's hand gripped my shoulder then slid up my neck to my cheek. "She's okay. I know it."

I nodded too many times. "I would know right? I would feel it. Mother's intuition or something. I would know."

"Yes," he said, rubbing my thigh with a comforting caress. "You would know."

He hugged me into his chest and kissed my forehead. I sank into him and didn't pull away. Hope had been my saving grace. It had kept the darkness at bay. Without it I would have to grieve.

"How long are we allowed to hope?"

His fingers ran in and out of my hair as I breathed in the smell of his shirt.

"Forever."

CHAPTER TWENTY-SEVEN

WE WAITED FOR AIDE. FOR WEEKS WE WAITED. AS far as I could tell, the US government was non-existent. I expected someone, some foreign country, to send troops. At least I had hoped that they would. When no one came, I had to accept that we were alone in this.

There was never any report on a foreign response. We were nothing but a problem that had been swept under the rug. The rest of the world, seemingly united against us, wanted to forget. Overnight, the country we'd known had evaporated in a gigantic puff of toxic smoke.

We were lucky we had The Compound.

In the days following the bombings, Mac combed television channels for all the information he could get, but soon the networks went dark. International flights stopped within hours of the attacks, even out of cities that still had airports and buildings standing. No one wanted in, and nobody was allowed out.

As the weeks passed, the lack of structure transformed cities into nests of crime. Looting and violence became a way of survival for most. We did our best with the hospital systems we had in place and word spread quickly about our presence. Though it seemed we were the only Descendants who were openly offering help to those in need. Our kind were good at hiding, and fear kept them quiet.

At the very least we had our own abilities to make things easier. Sam and Mrs. Nickel calmed those in shock and managed their pain. Kara sought out the more serious injuries and used Alex to transport them to the front of the line. Dr. Nickel and Nics did what they could, distributing food to patients. Mac kept the facility we were using protected with his safe haven, at least until we left for the night. He also drew up a map, pinpointing ground zero cities to help us get a better idea of how widespread the damage was, but a map was just a map. Only time would determine what we were left with.

"Any idea what's going on out there?" I asked Kara as we strapped our boots on and shared a plate of precious hard-to-come-by eggs at the kitchen counter. "I'm in these hospital rooms all day."

"We've been with you mostly. Working the halls." She shrugged, and took another bite of her omelet. "But the things we're hearing aren't good. People are hungry."

I slowed my chewing, realizing the value of my mouthful. "Alex said it's getting harder to find grocery stores that haven't been ransacked. Even our local store is empty. Nothing on the shelves. It's abandoned."

"Are there still people camped out?"

"For now," she answered. "They'll probably run out of food too eventually."

My stomach wrapped itself into a knot as I tried to ignore the impulse to help everyone. Some things were out of my hands. I had to focus on what I could control.

"We're running out of supplies at the hospital, too." I began doing a mental rundown of yesterday's cases trying to think of things I needed to bring with me today. There were clean sheets in the dryer for the hospital beds. I needed to grab those.

"...we need to think about the next phase of our plan," Kara said, finishing a thought I hadn't really been paying attention to.

I was only half listening. Radiation was a bigger problem for me now. People had been coming back sick, and I didn't have enough blood to heal such widespread disease of that magnitude. William and I were going to figure something out, some kind of system. Whatever it took.

"Hello?" Kara flicked me in the forehead. "Elyse?"

"Ouch. Jeez." I rubbed the point of pain. "What?" I snapped.

She rolled her eyes. "You're not even listening."

"I know. I know. Next phase of the plan. Let me think about it."

This new place wasn't the world we knew. It was survival of the fittest. Cities had no power, no lights at night, nothing worked in the day. People found ways to make it, but nothing was the same. Our radios with batteries searched the static airwaves for news. Sometimes we found it, most times we didn't. Kara was right. We couldn't wait forever. We needed to do something.

I wasn't the only one who expected help to come. Most humans still did. Those who suffered from radiation poisoning asked when it would be. I told them soon. I knew it was a lie, but I couldn't bear to break their spirits. Ironically, Descendants were built differently. Our bodies didn't get disease. Those of us who survived the strikes didn't get sick the way humans did. Foreign efforts to kill us were in vain. They ended up killing their own.

Three hours later, behind the peach door of the Los Angeles hospital room, I hadn't given much thought to the next phase of the plan. The smell of vomit and feces seeped in through the walls. No matter how clean we tried to keep things, most patients couldn't control their sickness as they made their way through the halls. Most of my morning visits had been level one cases—severe.

"I bet you're just loving this aren't you?" An old man with wiry white hair licked his yellow teeth as he stared into a cup of my blood.

"Dad!" The willowy brunette next to him was his adult daughter. She nudged his shoulder. "Sorry. He's just not taking it well," she apologized.

"The gods get to swoop in and save the day." His faded blue eyes challenged me as he looked up. "None of this would have happened if not for you." He wiped a streak of vomit from his pallid cheek and tilted the cup, downing the blood.

I watched him swallow, numb to his blame. Guilt had already been planted in me. Its roots were a tangled mess in my heart that grew far deeper than he could ever know.

"That should cause the symptoms to subside," I said, calmly wiping my wrist with a towel. "We're not sure how long it will last, but we'll be back on Thursday if you need another dose."

"If we can get in," the man huffed. "The line's a mile long."

I tried to ignore the disdain in his voice and kept talking. "We're still not sure if repeated doses will cure you of the radiation, but we're hopeful—"

The old man's eyebrows raised in fury as he turned the empty cup in his hand. "So, you're saying I just drank blood for nothing?"

"We're grateful." His daughter interrupted. "Really. Thank you."

She ushered his hunched body out the peach door.

I watched it close and wondered how doctors did this every day. I'd only been at it a month and already I felt used up and thin. I was a disposable dishrag soaking up the mess, keeping it locked up in the fibers of my skin. It was only a matter of time before I had nothing left. I shut my eyes and rubbed my fingertips against my eyelids.

"Nothing to top off a morning of vomit like the world's grumpiest man." William faked a smile before taking a swig of water from our water bottle.

"He's sick," I defended the man.

William walked toward the door anticipating our next patient. "Yeah, well, he had about five seconds before I hypnotized him into thinking he was the Lucky Charms leprechaun."

I laughed, despite myself and bit my cheek as two young women walked in. The injured one limped, holding her left foot slightly off the floor. Her jeans and UCLA sweatshirt had seen better days, but aside from the obvious pain she was in, she looked healthy.

The other was shorter, but still attempted to help her friend walk. She had a thicker frame and tan skin that matched her coppery brown ponytail.

"Her foot is broken," the tan girl said, as the slimmer one winced with each step.

William scooped his shoulder under the patient's other arm. "Let's get her on the hospital bed."

I watched the three of them make their way across the room, silently dreading what had to come next. Broken bones were hard. Although I was grateful these girls didn't seem to have any signs of radiation poisoning. Her injury wouldn't be as easy to treat. Broken bones had to be set before they were healed. I hated causing more pain before taking it away.

William helped the girl onto the bed and propped her leg up with a pillow.

"Hi," I said, visibly examining her foot. I glanced up before touching her. "Can I…"

She nodded, taking a deep breath as I lifted the torn hem of her jeans.

"So you're Elyse?" the short tan girl asked, tapping on to the rail of the bed. "The last healer?" She nodded her head, bobbing to her own drumbeat.

"That's me," I answered.

"I'm Rylan and this is Jena."

I glanced up with a smile, remembering I needed to work on my bedside manner. Being shy and tired meant I had to work at it. But I had gotten good at being who people needed me to be.

"Nice to meet you," I said, returning to my work.

Her foot was swollen down to her toes and purple in places, but the break was higher up, just above the ankle. I could see the bone pressing against her skin.

"I think I need Bonnie for this," I told William as I opened the cooler to grab an icepack.

"On it," he said, jogging across the room. His voice carried down the hall before the door had time to close behind him. "Hey, where's Bonnie?"

As we waited in silence, I made my way to the table in the corner, covering my mouth to stifle a yawn. I grabbed a clean paper towel and two spray bottles. One with soapy water and another with clean water to rinse the injured area.

"Tired?" Rylan asked as she started to pace a little. Her big brown eyes followed my every move. Like an unabashed child, she stared with curious intensity that had me feeling self-conscious.

"Yeah," I nodded. "Sorry, it's been a long—"

"No. No. I wasn't..." she stuttered. Her speech was quick and her body jumpy. "I can just help if you need." She pulled back the long sleeve of her blue and grey striped shirt, and thrust the barcode tattoo toward me as though it were proof. "I'm of Ponos. I can give you a little energy boost if you want."

"Oh," I said, my eyebrows lifting in surprise. "Yeah. Okay." I stood still, not knowing what to expect.

Rylan walked toward me wiggling with excitement. "I can't believe I'm helping *you*, the last healer." She took my hands gently in hers, and I could almost feel a buzz in her touch. "I can remember my parents talking about you when I was in my thirties. We've been waiting a long time."

I met her smile with pursed lips and a wrinkled brow. "I'm sorry. I'm sure this wasn't what you were expecting. This mess..."

She held my hands a little tighter, her face bright with a joy I didn't understand. "*You* didn't make any of this mess. All you did was set us free."

Our eyes connected for a moment before I recognized the refreshing surge of energy lightening my whole body. It felt like waking up mid-day, like a deep breath after a run.

"Wow." I laughed a little, my mouth open in shock. "I feel like I could sprint down the hall right now."

"Go ahead. Plenty more where that came from." Rylan shimmied a little dance as Bonnie, an experienced ER nurse, peeked her head in. The hairspray in her brittle blonde hair kept the teased beehive atop her head in place.

"Did you need me?" she asked, drying her hands on her sky blue scrubs.

I glanced back at Jena, feeling guilty for not paying more attention to my patient. She looked up with a quiet smile, and I realized I hadn't heard her speak a word since she'd stepped in the room.

"Yeah," I answered Bonnie. "Can you help me set her ankle? I want to make sure there isn't another break in her foot. See if you can tell."

Bonnie leaned over the foot of the bed. "Hi, honey," she said, her hoarse voice harsh and comforting at the same time. "What's your name again?"

"Oh," Rylan cut in. "She doesn't talk usually. She's a descendant of Echo. Their bloodline doesn't speak."

"Why?" I asked as Bonnie listened with curiosity.

Rylan shrugged. "That's how it's always been."

"That's how it's always been," Jena mimicked, rolling

her green eyes at her friend.

I shot Rylan a look as she opened her mouth to explain. "Well, she can echo, obviously."

"Doesn't sound like much of an ability," Bonnie's aged hands slid along the girl's shin.

"Actually, it's a *really* good ability," Rylan countered. "She can duplicate things. It's how the four of us have been living off of the same jar of peanut butter and jelly for a week."

"Four of you?" I asked.

She nodded. "My mom and little sister are waiting outside for us. We're going to find a smaller town after you get her all fixed up. Unless you have some place we can stay..." she trailed off, embarrassed for asking. "It's just pretty bad out there, so..."

Rylan wasn't the first to ask. I wanted to say yes to everyone, but I was under Mrs. Nickel's strict orders to deny anyone access to The Compound. It hurt to say no.

I glanced at the floor and shook my head. "Sorry. If we said yes to every—"

"I understand," she answered too quickly.

"Are you ready?" Bonnie asked as Jena braced herself against the edge of the hospital bed.

She nodded, biting her lips, and I wondered where William was. He could at least help with the pain. I raised my hand to delay the inevitable but was too late. Bonnie jerked the bone into place and Jena's mouth stretched wide, her face twisting in agony. Her silent cry was almost worse than the real thing. I fumbled for the Dixie cups as she rolled back and forth on the white sheet.

"Here," I said, sliding Mac's knife along the same incision I'd used over and over again these past weeks. "Forget the cup." I pressed my cut palm to her mouth, and she blinked, startled by the taste of blood in her mouth.

Soon, sweet relief relaxed the tight lines around her eyes, and she pulled away.

Thank you, she mouthed.

The door swung open, interrupting us. I turned, expecting an emergency or some other tragedy that would require blood, more borrowed beats from my heart.

"Ellie..." Kara stepped in, the sound of my name spoken through a smile.

A woman shuffled behind her, the hem of her dull and dirty grey dress dragging along the linoleum. Then a face followed, fair and meek but familiar. I blinked hard, questioning my mental state, my level of fatigue. I'd spent every day imagining this moment. Maybe it wasn't real. Lilia's smile only widened.

My eyes fell to the bundle in her arms. A dark grey shawl with fringe had been used to swaddle a baby. *My* baby. She lifted her toward me.

"Sarah?"

As I breathed her name the heavy knot in my chest unraveled.

CHAPTER TWENTY-EIGHT

IT DIDN'T SEEM REAL. I'D WAITED SO LONG. TEARS OF gratitude slipped down my cheeks as I stepped forward toward her. My shoulders shook with suppressed sobs. Everyone was watching. Bonnie the nurse. My patients. Kara and Alex. But all I saw was my daughter.

As I reached for her, I split wide open with love. She parted her tiny lips to yawn, keeping her paper-thin eyelids closed in peaceful sleep, and all of the hard angry walls I'd built around me with bricks of self-blame and indignity collapsed. I was pure and new. Whole again.

I slid my arm under her head, so it rested in the crook of my elbow, and cradled the rest of her with my other.

"Where is she? Is she okay?" William searched the room as he rushed through the door. When he saw me holding her, he wrapped his arms around us, and I couldn't keep my sobs quiet any longer. He pressed his forehead to mine and smiled at me with the whole world in his eyes. *Our* world. Our family.

Tears of relief blurred my vision, but I let them come. It felt good to cry happy tears. She was here. In my arms. I did everything in my power to keep from clutching her too tightly.

It was impossible, but she'd changed, grown somehow, despite the fact it would take her a decade to become a toddler. Her eyelashes seemed longer, her face rounder. The peach fuzz on her head had darkened, but her features were still the perfect combination of William's and mine. I could stare at her forever.

"Should I let the next patient know you need some time?" Bonnie asked, clearly uncomfortable in the moment.

I looked up, coming back to the world. "Oh," I said, trying to decide how I was going to heal without ever letting her go.

William pulled the shawl away from the baby's chin. "I don't think it's a good idea to keep her here. I want her home."

"Me too," I answered, but I wasn't about to let her out of my sight.

"So are we done for the day?" Kara's eyebrows rose with doubt as she read my thought. "The line is around the building."

I held Sarah a little closer. To me it was the only option.

"Yeah." I thanked Lilia with a silent smile, eager to

hear her side of things. "We're going home."

—

AT HOME, I HELD SARAH ON THE COUCH, CLINGING to her like she was my beating heart. I'd never felt so tense and so comfortable all at once. Her puckered lips sucked at the air even as she slept, and I smiled as I watched. Aside from William and Lilia, everyone else was still at the hospital. The house was empty, which meant Anna and Chloe were out on a walk. I wasn't sure who knew I had Sarah back, but I was grateful I didn't have to share this moment with a living room full of prying eyes.

"Has she been doing this a lot?" I asked Lilia, who sat next to me on the couch. Sarah continued to suckle.

"Oh yes." Lilia's small lips spread into a smile, lifting her high cheekbones and deepening the lines around her grey eyes. "Whenever she's asleep." Age had been good to her. Now that she wasn't chained to a dungeon wall, her vanilla grey hair was curled at the bottoms, reminding me of a fifty-year-old Marilyn Monroe.

William leaned in over my shoulder, running his hand through my hair as he watched our baby's belly rise and fall. "She's gotten cuter."

Lilia placed a gentle hand on my forearm, her skin noticeably softer than mine. "I'm so glad you're not angry with me."

"No, not at all." I breathed out all of my relief.

She clasped her hands together, her eyebrows downturned as she explained. "It ate away at me every day thinking of you and how you must have felt. Not knowing where she was or who had her."

I shook the memory out of my head, not wanting to relive that feeling. "We tracked down Dehne and she gave us your name. Once I knew she was with you, I felt a lot better about it." The emptiness was too fresh. I took a breath, ready but unable to forget. "Being without your child is...I wouldn't wish it on anyone. I didn't know when or if I'd ever find you..."

"You know why I did it, right?" Her face was pleading. She looked back and forth between William and I, needing to be absolved. "To protect her. I couldn't leave her with Adrianna. I didn't know what she had planned, but it didn't matter. I had to keep her safe."

"Lilia," William spoke for us. "Without you we wouldn't have our daughter right now. We're so grateful. You don't have to explain yourself."

"I did the right thing, didn't I?"

"If you hadn't taken her, Lilia..." I paused, unable to imagine that reality. "I don't know where she would be or how I would have ever found her."

"I'm glad you feel that way. I couldn't risk making contact with you, so we hid on the outskirts of a small town in northern Nevada while I figured out what to do. Then the bombings...I was so worried I wouldn't find *you*. But people know you, Elyse. Humans and Descendants are flocking to you from all over the country, hoping you'll save their lives. The oracle was right. You're fulfilling the prophecy and bringing us all together. You're changing the world."

It had been a long time since I'd thought of the prophecy. The weight of it felt like bench-pressing a mountain. I had hoped all of it was over. Maybe it would never be. William cleared his throat, noticing my silence.

"My turn," he said, scooping Sarah into his arms without asking.

"Hey!" I reached out for her, terrified by the feel of my empty arms.

He readjusted, cradling her closer. "What? You're being a baby hog. Why don't you go take a shower and let me stare at her for a while?"

I glared at him. "I don't need a shower."

"Yes, you do." He shrugged, apologizing with his high shoulders. "You smell like hospital and have blood all over your pants." He nestled into the corner of the couch, holding Sarah against his chest. "Don't worry. I'll be watching her."

I smelled my shirt and glanced toward the bathroom. "Try to keep her asleep," I said, wishing I didn't have to do things like shower or eat. "I want to be here when she wakes up."

Steam rose around the mirror and snaked along the white tile walls as I stripped down. For the first time in months I wasn't in a hurry. The uncertainty of not knowing how she was at that very moment was still a nagging concern, but the urgency that had been pushing me forward, always forcing me to move faster, had vanished as soon as I held my baby girl. She was safe. Home. We were together.

I turned to face my reflection, finally acknowledging the struggle I'd been through. I couldn't remember the last time I'd actually looked at myself. My eyes had changed. They were shadowed and sunken from blood loss and lack of sleep, but there was intensity in them that outshone any weakness. The hard line between my lips softened into a smile as I dragged my hands through my dark hair. I was a survivor.

I pulled back the shower curtain and stepped under the rushing water, my sore muscles releasing their ache under the heat of the stream. Hours of hunching over injured bodies had done a number on my back. My knees were bruised and swollen from kneeling on linoleum each day, but getting Sarah back had lifted the weight off of my heart. I rolled my fingers over the knots in my neck, breathing in the warm moist air. Things would be different. I would be different.

My pulse rushed with excitement at the thought of creating a new world for my daughter, and suddenly I was moving faster again. I needed to get back to her. What if she was hungry? Maybe she was sleeping too much because something was wrong. I tore the lid off of the shampoo and slathered it into my hair, using the excess as soap. I'd been away from her long enough.

I shuffled to my room with a towel around me, my hair dripping as my wet feet slapped the wood floor. William hushed me as I entered. Sarah was sprawled out like a frog in the center of our bed, her arms out to the side. He held his hand up, checking her face for movement.

He waved me forward. "Come here, she's waking up."

I hurried toward them, clutching my towel to my chest. She wrinkled up her face and opened her eyes with a few slow blinks.

"Hi," I said, drawing out the word. I laid my head on the bed next to hers, disregarding my sopping wet hair. We stared at each other for a minute or two before her little legs began to kick. Her breathing picked up as her limbs flailed in different directions.

"I don't remember her doing this before." I stood up, my eyebrows sinking with concern. "She's getting all worked up. You think she's not feeling good or something? Did you check her for injuries or ask Lilia?"

"Relax," William chuckled. "She just wants you to pick her up. She's excited."

"Oh." I grabbed a white T-shirt and some yoga pants from the dresser and threw them on. "Are you sure?" I asked, as I dried my hair with the towel.

William lifted her up, placing her head on his shoulder. "Yeah. She started doing it when we were with Mac and Anna."

I sighed. "I thought once I had her back all of this anxiety would go away, but I feel like I'm *constantly* thinking about her and worrying about every little thing even though she's right here."

William cradled the back of her head and slid her into the crook of his elbow. I watched her bright eyes gaze up at him in wonder. "It'll never go away," he said. "We'll always worry. Even when she's a hundred."

I threw my wet towel over the bedframe and watched as he shushed her with a subtle bounce. The smile in my heart reached my lips.

"What?" he asked.

I shrugged. "You're just good at that. It's cute."

"Yeah well, I'm sure you're better. Here," he said, handing her to me. "Want to try?"

I nodded, tearing up as he placed her in my arms. My throat stung as I held her squirmy body close to me, the warmth filling me up.

"I just can't believe we have her," I choked, letting my emotions out of their prison cell.

William wrapped his arm around my shoulders and pressed his forehead to my temple, kissing my cheek. He didn't have to say anything.

"Now that we do have her," he said after a moment, "we need to think really seriously about the best way to care for her." He pulled away to look at me. "I don't want her anywhere near those hospitals."

"I agree," I said instantly. "It's too dangerous."

"Not only that. We need to make sure *you're* safe, and one of us is going to need to stay here to watch her. I can't protect you if I'm here—"

I shook my head. "I'm not leaving her side."

"So you're done with healing?"

I didn't know how to answer his question. Healing wasn't something I chose to do. It was something I *had* to do.

"I can't be done..."

CHAPTER TWENTY-NINE

I WATCHED SARAH'S FEATURES SCRUNCH INTO A number of different cute baby faces as I weighed my options. William sat on the bed staring up at me as I walked back and forth with a subtle bounce.

"Well, what do you want to do then?" he asked.

"I want both. I want to be home, *and* I want to help people."

He shook his head. "Bringing patients here isn't a good idea. You know that. We're lucky to have a home that is safe. Not a lot of people have that anymore."

I thought of Jena and Rylan. Homeless. Maybe all of this was happening for a reason.

"So we give it to them." I bounced more vigorously, settling Sarah's squirmy limbs. Excitement brewed in my blood, and I began to put the baby back to sleep without realizing it. "What if we create a refuge? Descendants have all sorts of abilities. We could use them to build a safe place. Like The Compound but bigger. Nobody in or out without screening." I was talking fast, so fast I didn't even know if William was listening. He rubbed his chin with his hand when I stopped to look at him. "Am I crazy?"

A knock at the bedroom door interrupted our conversation.

"Ellie?" Anna peeked her head in. "Oh my God." She pushed the door open and rushed toward me, covering her mouth with both hands. Tears glistened in the lamplight. "How did you find her?" she sniffled, tucking the straight curtain of black and silver hair behind her ears. "Where was she?"

I smiled so wide my cheeks started to cramp. "Lilia showed up at the hospital." My voice rang with a joy I hadn't felt in months.

She reached out. "Can I?"

I nodded and transferred the little bundle into my best friend's arms. Anna wiped her flushed cheeks, and I knew exactly how she felt. Her daughter was my family, just as Sarah was hers.

Within the hour, everyone was home, each taking their turn to fawn over the baby. As Sarah was passed back and forth I tracked her every move, trying to let go. Trying not to resent every minute she was more than inches away from me.

It didn't take long for the excitement to fade, for the rest of the house to disperse and enjoy an excuse to take a day away from the devastation and suffering.

Mr. and Mrs. Nickel settled on the porch coming up with reasons Sarah made the world's cutest granddaughter. I could hear their jubilant voices hum through the wall as I poured myself a glass of water. White clouds rose like smoke above the evergreens in our back yard, and the blue sky hovered above it all, the atmosphere of our haven seemingly untouched by the poison air that floated around the cities. I peered out the window, looking for some sign of Mac, Anna, or Chloe who were tinkering in the shed. A few blue birds took cover in the trees, but that was it. Sam and Nics had shut themselves in their room to quietly bicker beneath the sheets. For the most part, the house was quiet. Lilia was taking a much-needed nap, and William had fallen asleep on the couch with Sarah on his chest.

I took a sip of my water, hoping to remember this feeling. Everyone home. Safe. Happy. This was what life used to be like. On the day the bombings began I imagined people were living like this. Enjoying a nap on the couch, kissing in a quiet room, sipping a glass of water. Then it was over.

I had to give this back. Somehow, life had to be good again. For everyone.

"Can I show you something?" Alex's voice behind me made me jump, and I spilled half of my water on the kitchen tile. Thankfully my gasp hadn't woken the baby.

"What the hell?" I whispered my harshest tone, turning around to glare at him.

"Oh get over it." He rolled his eyes. "Come on."

Without my permission, Alex grabbed my forearm and plunged me into the upper air. The white space choked me. I hadn't had time to take a breath.

I sucked in a lung full when I could. "If you're trying to piss me off, it's working." I looked around, the shock of the scene dissolving my anger. "Where are we?"

The two of us stood in the middle of a multilane freeway. Cars as far as I could see in both directions sat bumper to bumper, completely abandoned. On my right, the ocean stretched out, touching the horizon. On my left, rolling hills that had yet to be scarred by the presence of man.

"Camp Pendleton," Alex answered with his hands on his hips. He vanished for a split second and appeared again on the roof of a silver Dodge Caravan, gazing into the hills. The metal bent beneath him as he shifted his feet.

"Where did the people go?" I asked, unsettled by the eerie parade of empty cars. Each windshield stood for a family or a couple, even if just one person per car, the number was astounding.

"No clue," Alex said, jumping down. The rubber soles of his converse smacked the pavement. "I think this is as good a spot as any. I've been looking for hours. There is a lot of abandoned military equipment since this used to be a base. It might come in handy if we need it."

"Military equipment?" I looked at him like he was

nuts, shielding my eyes from the sun. "What are you talking about?"

He turned his palms up as if I was the one missing something. "For the refuge. Kara said..." Something clicked, and he scratched the back of his head.

His scoff surprised me. "What?"

"Apparently, Kara has been picking through *everyone's* brain, not just mine. She told me about your idea for a safe place for people to be. I was supposed to find a good location, but I'm assuming she hasn't told *you* that has she?" He turned away from me and mumbled under his breath. "She has no respect for privacy."

"What? Are you guys fighting or something?"

I waited for his smart alec remark, wondering why I had even asked. Instead, he lifted himself onto the hood of a dirty white Toyota and stared at his shoes. "I'm not a very open person, I know that." He looked up and pressed his lips together. "But it doesn't give her the right to go digging through my subconscious." His words were clipped and raw. "Yeah, I lost my family. Yeah, my dad is gone. What does she want me to do about it? I've looked for my sister. You know I've looked. She's gone, too."

My eyebrows rose in shock, but I didn't say anything. His emotional outburst seemed to come out of nowhere. Venting to me must have meant he was desperate for someone to listen. His eyes, pained and angry, dared me to offer him sympathy, but it was a trap. A way for him to turn my sympathy into resentment or his weakness into aggression. The two of us stayed in the moment. Him unsheathed and vulnerable. Me unwilling to turn away.

The silence between us amplified the distant sound of crashing waves. Wind blew a cool breeze, tickling the ends of tall grass that grew on the sides of the road.

Alex put his hands behind his head and tilted his bright blue eyes toward the matching sky.

"Maybe if we create this refuge my sister will come, you know?" He cleared his throat, uncomfortable with his emotional wounds exposed. "Maybe this is the only way to find her."

I leaned my back against the driver side door of the Toyota, watching the water glisten. "Maybe."

"Why do I even torture myself with thoughts like that?" he asked.

I shrugged, enjoying the feel of the warm sun against my dark hair. "You have hope."

"I shouldn't. It's been too long. She would have found me by now. Fame hasn't been all for fun. I had my reasons for getting attention." He sighed, letting his gaze drop. "She knows my call name. She would have used it by now. I know it in my heart. I'll never see her again."

I turned to face him. "It's okay to hope. It's the only thing that kept me going."

His black hair had gotten longer over the months and it hung forward as he studied his shoes. "Yeah, but how long is it okay to hope for something that isn't possible?"

I thought of Sarah. Of how I would have never given up. I liked William's answer to that question.

"Forever."

He nodded, and I could feel him hardening up again.

"So, we're going to have to find some way to move these cars," I said, breaking the awkward silence.

"I can move them," Alex answered. "I've actually got my eye on that Mercedes over there. A lot of these still have gas in them and keys in the ignition. They could be useful."

I stared into the open window of a BMW wondering how long people had held out before abandoning their vehicles.

"If we build here..." I lost my words to a different train of thought. I didn't know where to start. So much had to be done to create a livable home for so many. If we had help it could work. "Okay here's the plan. You and Kara find every Descendant you can. We need abilities. We need wood to build, fresh water, crops—"

Alex laughed, interrupting me.

"What?" I asked.

"What do you think Kara has been doing all day?" His demeanor changed as he jumped onto the pavement, and I could hear the excitement in his voice. "Come on. I'll show you," he said, grabbing my forearm.

"No, I need to go—"

I thought of nothing but Sarah as I traveled in Alex's white void. Home. I needed to go home. William would be worried, and more than anything, I wanted to hold my baby. I knew it was selfish of me to abandon the hospitals in the middle of it all, but sometimes a mother's job is to be selfish if it means doing what is right for her child.

When we appeared, chaos erupted in front of us. What used to be the line of patients had turned into an angry mob of desperation. I stood in shock as three young women stuffed their jackets full of anything they could find, tissue boxes, antiseptic towelettes, tongue depressors. A balding man in his fifties ripped the sheets from one of the beds, screaming at someone in the corner to stay back. Sound ricocheted off of the slick hallway floor, blending into a cacophony that was hard to sift through. A few feet in front of us, a teenage boy lay on the floor as people stepped on and over him. Two parentless kids dug into his pockets and began untying his shoes.

"Hey!" I yelled, realizing what they were doing.

I lunged forward, and the two kids scurried like rats along the wall.

"Kara!" Alex yelled from behind me, and before I could turn to look he was gone.

A few doors down I could see a scuffle. A crowd closing in. I looked back at the teenage boy on the floor, my conscience divided, and in that split second, the barrel of a handgun silenced my internal conflict.

I held my hands up, my heart leaping in frantic patterns. "Don't shoot."

CHAPTER THIRTY

THE MAN'S HAND SHOOK AS HE HELD THE GUN AT me. Sweat dripped from his mess of curly brown hair. He looked like a lawyer, not someone who knew how to use a firearm.

"Get up," he said, pushing his wire-rimmed glasses up with his free hand.

I stumbled to my feet, backing up.

"What do you want?" I asked, my pulse racing with nerves. "Whatever it is, you can have it."

"What do you think I want?" he yelled, wiping the sweat from his forehead. His complexion was sallow and his breathing heavy. "I want your blood." He waved his gun toward another hallway with fewer people. "Uh. Th-that way."

I did as he said, glancing behind me as I walked.

"D-don't try anything," he stuttered, pointing the gun

at my back. "I-I mean it."

When I reached the end of the hallway, he backed me into the empty corner. He blinked his eyes like he was trying to see clearly, and I whispered Alex's call name under my breath. I didn't mind healing this man, but I couldn't take any chances with his gun.

"What the hell?" Alex said, startling the lawyer as he appeared out of nowhere.

The gun went off and my back hit the wall. Pain cut me in two, but I was used to pain. It was the shock that paralyzed me. I watched a deep scarlet seep into my white cotton shirt.

"Oh God!" The lawyer man dropped the gun as I slunk to the floor clutching my stomach. He lunged at me, pushing me onto my side, and I gasped, trying to breathe. "I'm so sorry," he said. "I need it. I need the blood."

"Get off of her!" Alex yelled, as the man licked the crimson puddle on the floor.

Then white air stole me away.

When our living room came into view it spun, blurring the ceiling, walls, and whoever was standing in front of me. I closed my eyes, unable to process anything but pain.

"Sarah," I whispered through ragged breath.

I blinked, forcing myself to stay conscious and caught a glimpse of William's face. His hand touched my cold cheek, but I couldn't keep my eyes open long enough for him to ease my pain with his stare.

"Hey," he said with force, shaking my shoulder. "Stay with me, Ellie. You don't get to die today."

I bit my tongue trying to focus, but my chest stuttered with the rhythm of my weak pulse, and I couldn't get a breath.

"The bullet," I heard Alex add.

"Squeeze my hand." William's calm steady voice comforted me, but I could tell he was rushing.

My clammy fingers fumbled for his. Then searing pressure made me scream. My eyes flew open in shock, and the room faded to black for a minute before rushing back.

William's warm skin pressed against my lips, and his blood worked like a tonic as it healed me from the inside.

My lungs filled with glorious air, and my pulse gathered strength. In minutes I felt the pain begin to fade into a faint ache, until my body let go of the memory of the wound.

"You okay?" William asked, steadying me as I leaned forward. His cheek muscle pulsed, and he let out a heavy sigh.

I nodded, holding my bloody fingers out in front of me. "Where's Sarah?"

Nics, Sam, Alex, and Dr. Nickel crowded me, looks of concern paining their faces.

"She's with my mom and Anna," William answered, helping me to my feet. "Come on. I'll help you get cleaned up."

I followed him in a trance to the bathroom, still stunned by the quick turn of events that felt more like a dream than reality. It had happened so fast. I touched my stomach as William closed the door behind us. His face was still laden with worry, but I was actually glad it happened. I needed to see what I did. Those people needed help. More help than I could give, but if we all worked together, it might make a difference.

William stepped closer as I sat on the toilet.

"What happened?" The sleeves of his t-shirt tightened as he crossed his arms over his chest, a mix of worry and disapproval in his eyes.

I held my red hands between my knees. "The hospital is out of hand. We can't go back there, but—"

He exhaled through his nose, trying to hold back his frustration. "Why were you even there, Ellie? I thought we agreed."

"Alex...he just. You know how he is. He didn't ask..." I stared at the white tile floor, reliving the moment as William wet a towel in the sink. If Alex hadn't taken me, I would never have seen how bad things had gotten.

William knelt in front of me, and ran the wet rag over my palms. It absorbed the color of my blood, leaving my hands flushed but clean.

"Do I finally have your permission to kill him?"

I smiled, taking his sharp tone for sarcasm, but he didn't smile back.

"Yeah. Maybe I'll help you." I forced a laugh, letting

him clean the grooves of my fingernails.

His green eyes flipped up with concern.

"How's your stomach?" He found the hem of my shirt and rolled it up. "Does this hurt?" he asked as he ran his fingers over the place the bullet had been.

It didn't, but I liked the feel of his hands on my skin. "I don't know. Maybe."

His eyebrows lowered. "It shouldn't." He pushed up to his feet. "Stand up. Let me see your back. Did it go all the way through?"

I pulled my shirt over my head, hoping to dilute the seriousness of what had just happened. If he was afraid I would get hurt, I was sure he'd fight the refuge idea.

"How about this?" he asked, sliding his warm hands down my back. "Any pain?"

"Hmmm. Try it again."

His thumb traced the sides of my spine, and a wave of goosebumps triggered other sensations. "Nope. Good as new," I said, turning to face him.

He still looked too serious. "I think maybe you should take a shower. There's a lot of blood on your back."

I tucked my hands under his shirt, and pulled it over his head. "Okay, but you're going to have to help me scrub. I can't reach back there."

—

I USED WHAT WAS LEFT OF THE DAY TO REST, sleeping when Sarah slept. The bassinet beside the bed lay empty. Even that few feet of distance between us seemed too far. Instead, I kept her nestled beside me in my bed, cradling her as we both drifted off.

When I woke up from my nap I snuck out of the bedroom leaving Sarah asleep in the center of the mattress. Kara surprised me in the hallway. Her arms were crossed and her brow furrowed in thought. Seeing her reminded me of the scuffle in the hospital hallway before I was shot.

My eyes combed her body for any injuries. "You okay?" I asked, keeping my voice low.

She shrugged, refusing to address what had happened. "Are you?"

I nodded, glancing at her shaved head.

"Look," she said, tucking phantom hair behind her ear. "I know you got shot and I'm glad you got your rest, but I have a lot of Descendants waiting around for you to tell them what to do. The hospitals aren't the safest places anymore. They're going to leave if—"

"Wait," I said, still waking up a bit, "start over."

"We need help with the refuge." Her hand gestures were quick and impatient. "You said to find all the Descendants we could. We're ready and waiting for you."

Things were moving faster than I'd expected. Kara had taken things into her own hands before my thoughts on the refuge had ever formed into an idea to be discussed or planned, but I liked fast. I didn't want to make time for critics.

"Why didn't you wake me up?" I asked, charged by the idea.

"I was going to," she said too loudly.

"Shhh." I paused to listen for the baby before she continued.

William wouldn't let me, she said silently, adding a subtle eye roll.

Her fingers shifted on her bicep revealing a purple bruise that ran up her sleeve, and my eyes lingered.

Things got a little out of hand at the hospital. I was searching the lines for more of us, she said, keeping our conversation between us. Her hands slid into her pockets.

I thought of her alone at the hospital before Alex and I had arrived. Humans could get violent.

So if we hadn't shown up—

I can take care of myself. It was fine. She glanced down the hall. *So what's the plan? Can we move forward with this thing or what?*

I could feel the urgency in the tense way she stood and the way her hands couldn't find the right place to be. I'd never seen her fixated on something.

I leaned my back against the hallway wall. *Why are you doing this?*

What? she asked, but Kara never needed to ask that question. She knew.

Why are you putting yourself in harm's way to see this

through? You could have waited. We could have helped you.

You know why, Ellie. Her eyes drifted to my bedroom door where the baby slept. *It's my fault you can't leave her side to help people. It's my fault you killed McKinney.* She swallowed down her self-hatred and looked past me. *All of this is my fault. I just need to fix it.*

She leaned against the opposite wall and slid to the floor, resting her elbows on her knees.

Welcome to the club, I thought, moving to sit next to her.

No matter how hard I try I always end up being the bad guy. She rested her head against the wood paneling. *I make the wrong choices. I can't protect the people I love. Maybe I'm just not...good.*

No. You're good, I disagreed.

How so?

Because you try to be.

"Oooh. Super secret hallway conversation," Sam said as he stumbled past us toward the bathroom. The both of us stared at him, waiting for him to shut the door. "What? No boys allowed?"

I shooed him away with my hand, and he locked the door.

"So what should I do?" Kara asked in a low voice. "What should I tell the groups I have waiting?"

I thought of Sarah. Of how I couldn't leave her. I wasn't ready to take on both roles, mother and leader.

But nothing was more important than her. That simple fact changed everything.

"I don't know," I answered with ease. "Ask them how they want to start. Get them involved."

There was no choice, no other path. Sarah was my future. She was my freedom. Not spearheading our recovery or leading our new community. My life was being a mother. Not only to Sarah but to those who needed to be cared for. The simplicity of that realization made me smile to myself. By giving up control, I wasn't only setting myself free. I was setting them all free.

Kara cracked her knuckles as she studied the wall. "Shouldn't you come with me?"

I shook my head. "I can't. I'm staying with Sarah."

CHAPTER THIRTY-ONE

IT ONLY TOOK THEM A MATTER OF DAYS TO SET UP a working refuge. Kara had already instructed everyone in the house to pack their bags. She paced around my room as I attempted to shove my entire wardrobe into a green canvas duffle.

"So what about *this* house?" I asked, a little reluctant to let go of our newest home.

She grabbed a pile of socks from the bed and tucked them into the tight corners of the bag, her eager energy making me move faster than I needed to.

"It'll be here if we need it." She smiled as she spoke. "We're starting anew."

I laughed at her cheery disposition. "You're really excited."

"What? Bitter cynical Kara isn't allowed to be happy?" She crossed her arms but couldn't force the joy out of her eyes. "Just shut up and pack."

"I'm packing. I'm packing."

Kara's rushing ensured I was ready before anyone else. She insisted William and I get settled because the baby would need a place to rest, but I was sure she was just excited to show us her progress.

William carried our bags, and I wore Sarah in a sling snuggled against my chest. Alex met us in the front of the house. I wasn't sure how the baby would react to the breathless white space of his ability, so I made him promise to make it a quick trip. She hardly noticed.

Rows of mature fruit trees with trunks thicker than my waist reached toward the open sky. The smell of rich wet earth and orange blossom reminded me of summer days when I was a kid. I peered through the leaves at glimmers of sunlight, wondering what lay beyond.

"We have several growers with us," Kara explained. "They can grow any crop, flower, tree, you name it."

As we reached the edge of the orchard, rows of vegetation covered the acres in front of us. Fields of green ran from the hillside to the highway, and just beyond that the ocean shimmered with golden light. It seemed strange to be growing crops near the beach, but climate didn't matter to Descendants who could grow trees with nothing but their thoughts.

"You got rid of the cars," I said, noticing the open road in the distance.

"Not all of them," Alex smiled. "I saved you a Bentley."

I laughed, knowing he was probably serious. "Perfect.

I'm sure I'll be needing it for long road trips and things."

He shrugged. "Hey. You never know. With the amount of people lined up at those hospitals, we could build ten of these places."

A rustle in the trees made me look back. I squinted, all my senses heightened, and saw a pair of dirty pink sneakers a few rows away. They dragged a ladder behind them and hiked up the rungs.

"Who's here?" I asked, finding myself heading toward the stranger.

"Growers," Kara answered as she followed. "They're harvesting the fruit."

As I ducked under branches I caught sight of another set of shoes. A man in tan and brown work boots.

I held my left hand to Sarah's back and brushed the leaves with my right as I ducked again. "How many are there?"

Kara caught up to lead the way leaving William and Alex walking at a slower pace. "Maybe ten."

I raised my eyebrows at her. "Wow."

Both workers stayed focused on a single tree as I stepped into view. The pink sneakers belonged to a girl who looked Chloe's age in human terms. Her dark hair formed perfect spirals around her tan face. Atop the ladder she wrapped her hands around two branches and closed her eyes. The man below her pressed his palms to the trunk. He was older but with the same curly dark hair and tan skin. I waited in anticipation for something to happen. My eyes widened as it did.

The tree swelled with life. It sprouted leaves and buds until it was lush and thriving. The buds grew thick and green until each one burst open with a gasp and bloomed into hundreds of glorious white flowers. The smell overwhelmed me, and I shook my head in amazement. In seconds the orange blossoms withered and rained to the ground, pattering the soft earth below.

I felt William step beside me and set down the bags. "Did you see it?" I asked in a whisper, not wanting to interrupt them.

He nodded and ran his hand along my lower back.

Within the cocoon of each flower a tiny seedling remained. The small green orbs grew into full sized fruit and began to lighten as they matured. With one final thrust of energy each gleamed such a brilliant shiny orange I had to resist the urge to run up and pick one.

"Go ahead," Kara urged.

"Huh?" William asked.

She gestured forward. "Elyse wants to pick one. Go ahead."

Our voices caught the attention of the two growers. They looked at each other before the girl climbed down her ladder and both headed toward us.

"That was amazing," I said as they approached. Sarah's eyes opened at the sound of my voice. She blinked slowly and looked around, fascinated by the vibrant greens around us.

"Thanks," the girl spoke with a smile. "We were—" She stopped speaking mid-sentence and her large lips parted. "Are you?" She looked to Kara. "Is she the last healer?"

Kara presented me with her hands as if she had just completed a magic trick. "The one and only," she said, her voice thick with sarcasm.

The girl's curls bounced as she patted the pockets of her jeans. "Oh wow. I've been waiting. I mean, I...can you sign my...does anyone have a pen?"

Alex snorted and I shook my head, trying to hide my embarrassment. I couldn't imagine why she'd want my name on anything of hers.

"I'm Daniel." The other grower reached his hand out to shake mine. I squeezed his firm grasp tightly. "And this is Amy, my sister." He nodded toward her. "Please excuse her forward nature. She's just excited to meet you. We both are."

I furrowed my brow. "No, it's fine. I'm just as excited to meet you. I glanced up at the tree behind them, its branches sagging under the weight of so much ripe fruit. "I've never seen anything like that. Really. Incredible."

"Do you want to taste it?" Amy asked, her large dark eyes widening at the idea. She rushed off to pick an armful of oranges before I could answer.

"Can you do any fruit or just oranges?" William asked, taking note of the trees around us.

"Anything that grows its roots into the earth. Our

bloodline is of Auxo—"

Alex sighed as if bored. "Are we going to spend *all* day watching plants grow?"

Amy approached with more oranges than she could carry, and I reached out to take one.

"Thanks," I said, marveling at the color. My nails bit into the warm dimpled skin and the pungent juice dripped down the side.

"Just take a bite already," Alex urged as I continued to peel.

I ignored him, breaking off a pulpy wedge and biting into it. I smiled at the sweet tangy taste. "It's delicious," I said as I took another bite. The prospect of good, healthy food had me hopeful and excited. This refuge could actually work. "Really. Thank you." I glanced at Alex. "I guess we should probably go, though, before Mr. Impatience over here loses it, but it was nice meeting you."

"But you're not leaving for good, right?" Amy asked with concern as she rubbed the heel of her hand with her thumb. "You'll be close by?"

"Amy," her brother scolded. "Sorry." He took a breath, feeling the need to explain. "We lost our parents in the attack. You're the reason we're here. She feels safer knowing you can heal."

Amy scratched the back of her head and avoided eye contact.

"I'm so sorry." An awkward silence made all of us fidget. "Well, I'm here to stay," I said, trying to reassure her. "I promise."

She nodded casually but didn't look up. "Okay. Good."

"Nice talking to you," Alex cut in with an abrasive voice. He nudged me into William's side and grabbed Kara's hand, taking us to a new place and leaving the grove behind.

"That was rude," I said as soon as I could move again.

Alex ignored my glare and started forward through a cement courtyard lined with palm trees.

"Are we still in the refuge?" I asked, taking in my surroundings.

The building in front of us stood four stories high and ran along the edge of the courtyard. Its façade was a sandy colored stone enhanced by a brick red roof and matching window coverings. At the entrance a sign read Bachelor Enlisted Quarters.

"Yep. Still in the refuge." Kara's smile grew. "These are the barracks. We need to fix them up, but they will be perfect for housing everyone."

"Will be?" William questioned. "I thought everything was done."

She rolled her eyes. "Relax. We're working on it."

"They should be working on water and electricity now," Alex yelled from up ahead. "I brought a team here this morning."

Kara and I shared a smile. Despite his snippy tongue, Alex was excited. It was fun to watch him suffer through the slow pace of walking one step at a time.

He waited for us at the front door tapping his fingers on the glass pane.

"Thanks for helping with the bags, by the way," William said to Alex as he passed.

"What?" Alex shot back with a laugh. "Wishing you didn't have such a pansy-ass ability?"

I ignored them and looked around the lobby. It had a modern feel with industrial black carpet floors and sleek hanging lamps that would look nice once they could function. Block pattern glass partitions separated the larger room from a few smaller ones that may have been offices. In some places the glass was missing but the shattered pieces had been swept up and discarded. A few chairs were stacked against the far wall along with several circular red tables.

"So it was just empty?" I asked, trying to picture what it would be like with people enjoying the space.

"Should be," Kara answered. "Mac set up the safe haven right away. No outsiders can get in without going through him."

I cracked my knuckles, feeling the excitement flutter in my chest. I could see it coming together. We were going to help people. We could build a community together and start fresh.

"How many rooms are there?" I asked.

"Well, if you count the other buildings..." Kara paused to do the math in her head. "About fifteen hundred."

I gasped. "Are you serious?"

"What about a dining hall?" William asked, stepping beside me.

Kara nodded with her hands on her hips. "Of course."

It was nice to see her taking charge of things. She was good at it.

"Where's Alex?" I asked, looking around.

William glanced over his shoulder. "He's making out with the lamp post outside." His sideways smirk was all I needed to connect the dots.

I opened my mouth to insist William set him free of his ability, but something made me stop. Kara shrugged when I looked at her with raised eyebrows.

"Fine with me," she answered. "He's driving me nuts."

I bit my tongue trying not to smile too wide as she led us to the stairs.

"Each room has two beds," she said as we entered the first bunk. "Some have microwaves and fridges, but most were ripped off by looters." She pushed a chair out of her way and sat on the edge of the empty wooden desk. "No idea why someone would want microwaves when there is no electricity."

I lifted the mattress of one of the twin beds and found a storage space beneath it along with two drawers for clothing.

"They all have that," Kara added.

"This is great," I said lowering the mattress. Kara shrugged with a satisfied smirk. "You were right. It's perfect."

After visiting a few of the identical rooms we headed back downstairs.

"Yeah, and there are basketball and volleyball courts outside. Even places to barbecue," Kara kept on as we reentered the lobby. "I'll show you later where I'm thinking we could set up a school."

"So when do you think we can get electricity going?" William asked. "I don't see anyone working on anything—"

Kara stopped and put an arm out in front of us. "Shhh!"

What? I asked, keeping my words silent.

Kara's eyes narrowed at a long partition that had once served as a workspace with multiple desk chairs and computer hookups.

We waited in silence.

Someone's here.

Whoever it was must have realized we were onto them. A man stood, his gun drawn in our direction. His biceps shifted under his army green t-shirt and I could see sweat glisten through his blond shaved hair.

"Turn around and face that wall," he yelled, squatting behind the partition for cover.

I looked at William. None of us were prepared to fight. I wasn't even sure Kara had a weapon. He was all we had.

His eyes focused, but our hesitancy caused the man to fire warning shots into the ground. I panicked. Without thinking I shoved William behind a tipped foosball table to our right and I scrambled after him.

Sarah's cry fueled the quick pace of my heart. I had to find a way out, and I wasn't above begging.

"Please," I yelled. "I have a baby."

CHAPTER THIRTY-TWO

WILLIAM AND I STAYED HUNCHED BEHIND THE foosball table. I couldn't see Kara, but I didn't imagine she was standing there in front of his gun any longer.

"Shhh," I whispered, hushing Sarah's worried cry. Her bottom lip folded under and trembled as she wailed. "It's okay, baby girl."

The man spoke up. "We have two of your kind. Cooperate or—"

"Or what?" I heard Kara say before the sound of a bullet being chambered. I silently hoped the weapon was hers, but there was no way to tell.

Then someone made a move. William and I listened to the two of them scuffle.

It took everything in me not to peek my head up and look, but William held my hand firmly to his side.

When he let go, I reached for him. "Wait—"

I began to rise to my feet, but William's eyes connected with mine and I felt the impact of his ability almost instantly.

"Stay down," he demanded, and I was happy to obey.

The sounds of the scuffle faded, the outcome no longer my concern. I stared up at William lost in the feeling of being near him. It was all that mattered.

His hold broke the moment a gun slid under the foosball table and hit my feet. I picked it up.

"You okay?" William asked, reaching down for my hand.

I nodded, and he lifted me to my feet.

Kara had the man on his knees with his hands behind his head. She held his own gun at him, and licked the cut on her lower lip.

"All I wanted to do was show you something," she said to him with the edge of annoyance in her voice.

"You said *we*." I tucked the gun into the back of my pants as Sarah's cries quieted. "How many of you are there?"

He smirked, pleased he had secrets to use to his advantage. Only secrets didn't work with us.

"Around a hundred," Kara answered. "Most of them injured. They're camped out in the hills waiting for aid that still hasn't come. He's highest in command. Name is Jeremy."

The man's lips tightened, and he stared at the floor in front of him, seeming afraid for the first time.

"So they were already here when Mac put up the safe

haven," William said, thinking aloud.

"Hey." I lowered myself to the shooter's level, resentment finding its way to the tip of my tongue. I didn't like people shooting at me or my daughter. "We're on the same team. *We're* not here to hurt anyone."

He didn't look at me, but I could see him listening in the way he shifted his focus in my direction.

"Like I said," Kara added. "I just wanted to show you something."

She knelt down next to me so that she was directly in front of Jeremy and reached for the sides of his head. He pulled away with force, his chest rising and falling with more intensity.

"What are you doing?" he demanded with fearful eyes.

"Relax." Kara heaved a sigh. "I'm not going to fry your brain. How many times do I have to say it? I just want to *show you something.*"

His muscles stayed tense as she pushed her fingers against his temples, but he didn't fight.

He gasped as the shock of her ability took hold. At first, Jeremy's olive eyes blinked and shifted too quickly. I imagined the images spilling through his consciousness and how disorienting it was the first time I experienced her memories through my own eyes. When his eyes closed, I could see the tension slip from his arms and shoulders. His head turned and his eyebrows twitched in surprise or curiosity as he explored the experiences she was sharing with him.

When Kara stepped back, he brushed a hand over the top of his short hair seemingly surprised by his own change of heart.

"I'm sorry for shooting at you," he said to me.

He rose to his feet, making him a foot taller than me, and put his hand out to shake mine.

I looked down at Sarah, who was still squirming uncomfortably. The old me would have found it easy to forgive. With my daughter put at risk I had to work for it.

"Just glad no one was hurt," William said, stepping in to take Jeremy's hand.

"Who the hell is this guy?" Alex sauntered in with a bag of potato chips. He popped one in his mouth with a loud crunch. All of our heads turned his way and he stopped mid-chip. "What? Am I interrupting something?"

"Nice of you to show up," I said, my eyebrows climbing up my forehead.

"Oh yeah," he scoffed. "After what lover boy pulled back there? You guys deserved to climb the stairs."

"Hey, I'm sorry," William said in an apologetic tone. "If I had known we were going to be shot at, I would have made sure you were front and center."

Alex's eyebrows pinched tight as he looked at Kara. "Shot at?"

"Never mind." I shook my head, still a little amused by the thought of him making out with a street light. I turned back to our new soldier friend. "*This* is Jeremy.

He's been helping a group of injured soldiers—"

"Not all soldiers," Jeremy interrupted. "Once people began abandoning their vehicles they had nowhere else to go but here. Most are civilians."

"Why not use the facility?" William asked.

"We weren't sure when or where the next attack would be. The base could have been a target." He looked around at the cold and empty space as if mourning the loss of a friend. And maybe he had lost friends. Hadn't we all? "It was too hard to move the injured once we were settled."

I twisted the bracelet on my wrist knowing I couldn't sit back and do nothing. "What's the nature of most of their injuries?"

"What do you mean? A few broken bones, a guy scraped his head up pretty bad..."

"Anyone sick?"

He nodded, saddened by the thought. "Thought it was the flu at first. Almost everyone sick didn't make it. We're doing our best to make them comfortable, but—"

"Fill the rooms," I said to Alex. "I'll treat the worst cases first." I faced the soldier. "Jeremy, you know who needs the most help. Go with him."

"Sure." Jeremy headed for the door. "Come on. It's this way."

Alex didn't move. Instead he looked at me. "Somebody want to get the new guy up to speed?"

"Go for it," I answered, feeling my stomach grumble

with hunger.

Within a matter of seconds Alex vanished and reappeared in front of Jeremy. "Walking is for humans," he said before the two of them disappeared.

Our new life seemed to fall into place by nightfall. William watched Sarah in our room while I treated patients in their own beds, running back and forth down barracks halls to check on our daughter between heals. Once Jeremy released the two members of our group that had been recruited to generate electricity and water, the barracks came alive. In less than a week our new home was nearly full. Kara vouched for every member, insisting none would threaten our safety.

Each day I could feel the positive energy grow as children ran down the halls and laughed from open doors. Over time the stark and sterile building blossomed with the chaos of hope.

As new patients poured in, I treated them first, checking with Kara each morning to get a patient priority list. For the first time all week I finally felt adjusted to my routine. After I brushed my teeth, I kissed Sarah's cheeks and stepped out the door on my way to Kara's room.

"Hey," I said, catching sight of her in the hallway.

Her face was grave as she headed my way.

"What?" I asked, almost dropping my supply box.

"It's someone we know," she said with a sigh. "William should come, too."

CHAPTER THIRTY-THREE

WE DIDN'T HAVE TIME TO DROP SARAH WITH ANNA, so Alex had her meet us there.

"Everything all right?" Anna asked as she took Sarah into her arms.

"I don't know," I answered.

"I'll wait here. Right outside the door, okay?" she reassured me.

William stepped inside our newest patient's room and I followed, Alex and Kara leaving the two of us alone. A girl lay on the bed. Her eyes were closed, but I would recognize those high ebony cheeks and perfect spiral curls anywhere. She'd taken William's memories.

"Hannah," I whispered, lowering to my knees beside her. Her eyes were swollen shut and bruised, one side of her face scraped and scabbed. I waited for her still form to move, for her chest to rise and fall. It didn't. "What did Kara say? Is she..."

"No, she's alive," William answered kneeling beside me. He took her hand. "Barely."

When I looked at him, his jaw tensed and I could see him struggling with his thoughts. He knew something I didn't. I wasn't sure why her condition affected him so much. Maybe because after his memory loss he and Hannah were in the same boat, new to our community and alone. I hadn't realized they'd bonded over that.

A thousand questions wanted to slip past my tongue, but I held them back.

"Kara said..." He dropped his gaze and shook his head.

I tugged at his hand. "What?"

He sighed. "It doesn't matter. I can't let it happen. Neither can you." He took my wrist and lifted it toward her. "Hurry. Before it's too late."

I let my hand rest on the bed beside her and stared at William. "Not until you tell me what you know."

"It won't change my decision."

My eyes didn't waver.

His hand brushed Hannah's as he continued. "If she dies, I'll get my memories back." He cleared his throat. "All of them. The old me."

He was right. It didn't change anything. I couldn't let her die. Still, the possibility of it, the answer we'd been waiting for, it felt like a knife in my heart. Everything we wanted was right here in front of us, and I couldn't give it to him.

"I'm sorry," I said.

He turned to me and held my cheek with his warm palm. "Don't be." His lips pressed against my forehead. "We're both different people now. We're closer because of it. It's supposed to be this way, and I love the you that's here in front of me. I love the way we are and what we have."

I nodded, hoping it was true.

"I love you," I said, pressing the buttons on my bracelet.

He ran a warm hand against the back of my neck and through my hair.

"I love you, too."

—

HANNAH HEALED UP JUST FINE AND WAS OFF exploring the groves with Chloe by mid afternoon. By dinner William seemed to have forgotten the whole thing. He stretched out belly down on his bed and tickled Sarah's feet. I hung up the damp towel from my shower and threw my hairbrush on the side table.

"You ready?" I asked, wringing out the excess water from my wet hair. "I'm starving."

"Me too," he answered, scooping Sarah into his arms.

I reached for the door and jumped when I opened it. Kara stood in the frame blocking my way.

"Jeez," I sighed, my hand still on my chest.

"Hey." She stepped in without really looking at me.

"We need you guys to pack up. Got to change rooms."

"No way." I shook my head and glanced back at William. "We just got here."

I tried pushing past her, but she stepped in front of me.

"Come on," William groaned. "My stomach is eating itself."

"Seriously," Kara said with hands on her hips. "I need the room."

"Well, you need me more," I argued.

"Aren't you tired of sleeping in separate beds?" she asked, eyeing the two of us.

William cocked his head. "She has a point."

"Please," she pushed. "Don't make me ruin the surprise."

My eyes narrowed. "What surprise?"

—

"WE'RE CALLING IT ORCHARD HILL," KARA YELLED from up ahead as we walked through an avocado grove and around the tree line.

The view from the hillside was spectacular. Orchards surrounded us, and just beyond the green fields the span of ocean looked like deep blue silk rippling in the wind.

"Hurry up!" Kara called, breaking me away from the scene.

As I turned the corner around the edge of the grove, I could see the side of a structure—a house. My eyes widened when I realized which house. I picked up speed, holding Sarah tight in my sling to keep her from bouncing.

"How did you do it?" I asked, unable to believe I was staring at our old home, The Compound. "Did you rebuild it or—"

"Rebuild it?" Alex scoffed, coming out the front door. "I just about melted my face off transporting this thing. I'm taking all of the credit."

He sauntered toward us with a proud smile, his timid sister in tow. It had only been two days since he found her eating alone in the dining hall.

Not even Alex had been able to get her to say what had happened while she was missing, but the trauma of it had left her with no memory. She didn't recognize him or know his name. She hardly knew her own. But she was alive.

"Hi Jen," I said, trying to make her feel welcome.

She twisted her straight rope of black hair and used it to cover the flock of ravens tattooed on the front of her shoulder. "Hi."

"Well, are you going to come in or what?" Anna yelled from the porch. "We're having dinner here tonight."

"I'm in," William said, heading for the house.

Anna came down the porch stairs and met him. "Everyone's in back."

I could hear voices as I followed the two of them to

the back yard, Mac's booming laugh the loudest of all. Smoke rose from a barbecue, and Tivoli lights were strung from the roof edge to a line of sycamore trees. They dipped over a grassy back patio with a long black wrought iron table surrounded by matching chairs.

"Hungry?" Mac bellowed as he turned what looked like chicken legs on the grill.

"Starving," William yelled back.

Sam and Nics were playing a game of horseshoes, but threw them down when they saw us. Nics took Sam's hand and yanked him toward us. "Took you long enough."

"Can I hold her? Please. Please. Please." Chloe jumped a little next to me as I headed for the table.

"Okay. Okay. Hang on a second." I unclipped Sarah from my sling and settled her gently into Chloe's arms.

"You made it!" William's mom beamed as she came out the back door holding a steaming casserole dish. "Isn't it wonderful?" She set down the food and hugged him.

William's father followed close behind with a bowl of salad. "Hey, kids."

Mac carried over a plate of freshly grilled chicken and everyone found a place at the table. A cool ocean breeze found its way through the trees, rustling the leaves and sending the smell of cooked food my way.

As I settled into one of the black outdoor chairs, I listened quietly to the handful of conversations happening around me. Nics and Sam bantered about their horseshoe game, William's parents talked quietly about the future, and Chloe's high-pitched baby talk accompanied the twitter of the birds. Their smiles were genuine, and I knew without a doubt that these people were my family.

William handed me a plate and I caught a glimpse of understanding in his loving eyes.

We were home.

EPILOGUE

MOTHER NATURE AMAZES ME. HER WATERS STRETCH toward the horizon and lap at the sand as though nothing has changed. The sun sets her stage with a backdrop of brilliant color each morning, blessing the infected earth below with warmth. She's known all along that things would go on. And they have.

I finally understand what the oracle meant. *You need to lose to win.* We've lost in more ways than words, but somehow life has found a balance. Losing it all was the only way to get where we are, the painful price for perfect days like these.

We aren't the only family at the beach today. Colored towels and umbrella's litter the designated area protected by our safe haven. The weather is always beautiful here. A salty breeze sweeps the heat from my shoulders, and I dig my toes into the soft grainy sand with each step. William has Sarah in his arms up ahead of me. His rolled-up jeans are wet at the bottoms from walking in the water. He squats down and puts Sarah's feet in the frothy tide, and I can hear him talking to her in a sweet voice, though I can't quite make out the secrets he's imparting.

William laughs over the sound of the waves and smiles at me, shaking his head at her cuteness. She's still just a bundle in his arms. As I smile back at him I realize I finally feel happy to be who I am. It's hard to believe I ever cursed myself for having such a long life ahead of me. These days I feel nothing but gratitude for the hundreds of years I have left to watch my daughter grow.

To my right, a child with black hair and a bare chest growls like a lion and pounces through the shallow waves toward his friend. His name is Elan. I know because he arrived alone two days ago. I don't know how he got here, he won't say, but he is one of us.

He isn't the only child I recognize. The blonde girl he's chasing is Jezebel. I treated her and her mother for radiation in the beginning, and it hasn't returned since our last session. She squeals and runs kicking up the water in her pink bathing suit. She looks back over her shoulder with a toothy grin, and I know she's healthy and happy here.

Elan catches up and whispers something in Jezebel's ear. They take hands and duck their heads under the water. My heart catches. They're too young to swim alone. I scan the sand for an adult and find Jezebel's mom. She waves back at me with reassurance as though the two of them have been doing this for hours. I nod, but keep watching, the mother in me overly protective.

They stay under far longer than anyone could hold their breath, and I have to see what they're doing.

Up close I can see their blurred shapes surrounded by a pocket of air. One of them sees me and Jezebel pops her head out of the water. Elan follows.

"Hi, Miss Ellie." Jezebel's eyes light up, her wet hair plastered to the sides of her face. "We were being fishes. Fishes can breathe under water."

Elan sucks his cheeks in and puckers his lips. "Yeah. We're fishes."

"Wow." I hold back a laugh and attempt to take them seriously. "Show me again."

They join hands, human and Descendant, and duck under the water together.

And there it is.

My redemption.

CHILDREN OF THE GODS

DESCENDANTS LIST

OLD COUNCIL

Adrianna

Bloodline: Hera

Ability control for female Descendants

Antec

Bloodline: Hades

The ability to confine Descendants to the "Underworld"

*The Underworld is a void of nothingness where Descendants are trapped in a semi-conscious limbo.

Christoph

Bloodline: Zeus

Ability control for male Descendants

Dimitri

Bloodline: Demeter

The ability to age or grow living things

Dr. Nickel

Bloodline: Ares

The ability to mimic Descendant powers

Lilia

Bloodline: Hestia

Ability control for Council Members

*Must be in the presence of two Council members for Council abilities to work

NEW COUNCIL

Grayson

Bloodline: Zeus/Hera

Ability control for Descendants

Antec's Son

Bloodline: Hades

The ability to confine Descendants to the "Underworld"

*The Underworld is a void of nothingness where Descendants are trapped in a semi-conscious limbo.

Dimitri's Daughter

Bloodline: Demeter

The ability to age or grow living things

Edith

Bloodline: Ares

The ability to mimic Descendant powers

Lilia's Daughter

Bloodline: Hestia

Ability control for Council Members

*Must be in the presence of two Council members for Council abilities to work

ELYSE & FRIENDS

Alex

Bloodline: Aether

Messenger—The ability to move from place to place using teleportation

Call Name: Alaximandrios

Elyse

Bloodline: Asclepius

The ability to heal or poison with her blood

Kara

Bloodline: Prometheus

The ability to access to the mind

Mac

Bloodline: Soteria

The ability to create safe havens

Nics

Bloodline: Nix

The ability to manipulate light and create darkness or invisibility

Paul

Bloodline: Hermes

Messenger—Flight

Rachel

Bloodline: Iris

Messenger—Flight (changes form)

Sam

Bloodline: Dionysus

The ability to change liquid to wine

William

Bloodline: Aphrodite

The ability to persuade by infatuation

OTHER DESCENDANTS

Aaron

Bloodline: Clotho

The ability to revive the dead before the spirit transcends

Amy

Bloodline: Auxesia

The ability to grow plants and trees

Daniel

Bloodline: Auxesia

The ability to grow plants and trees

Dehne

Bloodline: Apate

The ability to deceive

Dr. Nickel

Bloodline: Ares

Old Council member – Could mimic Descendant powers. Abilities have been passed down.

Elan

Bloodline: Amphitrite

The ability to breathe under water

Eva

Bloodline: Bia

The ability to repel objects with force

Florence (Oracle)

Bloodline: Delphic Oracle – Pythia

The ability to see the future

Hannah

Bloodline: Mnemosyne

The ability to erase memories with her blood

Jena

Bloodline: Echo

The ability to duplicate objects

Jeremiah

Bloodline: Kydoimos

The ability to cause confusion

Phoebe

Bloodline: Phoebe

The ability to sense danger

Richard Adler (Elyse's Father)

Bloodline: Hephaestus

The ability to manipulate metals, woods, and stone

Robert

Bloodline: Boreas

The ability to generate winter weather

Rylan

Bloodline: Ponos

The ability to generate energy

Sarah Adler (Elyse's Mother)

Bloodline: Asclepius

The ability to heal or poison with her blood

Sofia (Mrs. Nickel)

Bloodline: Aphrodite

The ability to persuade by infatuation

Unnamed

Bloodline: Harpocrates

The ability to eliminate sound

Unnamed

Bloodline: Tethys

The ability to draw water from the ground

Unnamed

Bloodline: Astraeus

The ability to create the illusion of stars

Unnamed

Bloodline: Lelantos

The ability to stay hidden in plain sight

Unnamed

Bloodline: Phobos

The ability to cause fear

Unnamed (Young Boy)

Bloodline: Zephyrus

The ability to create wind

ACKNOWLEDGMENTS

This book series was life-changing for me. It brought me into the publishing world and opened so many doors that led me to where I am today. And it wouldn't have happened without the love and support of so many amazing people.

First, thank you to God for always directing my path. Thank you to my friends and family, especially my mom and sister who were always there to talk book ideas. Lots and love and thanks to my husband and children for inspiring me and for always weaving their way into my stories. Thank you to my in-laws for always reading my books and offering feedback. Huge hugs and massive thanks to my writing partner, business partner, and best friend, Holly Kammier. You are irreplaceable.

To Molly Lewis, your support, guidance, and edits throughout the process of publishing was invaluable, and I will never forget what you did for me. To Matt Pizzo and Daniel Silva, thank you for giving my series a shot.

Thank you to my foreign rights agent, Whitney Lee Fielding, for selling my books to international publishers and for your continuous support.

Thank you to all the Acorn Publishing authors out there for being such a wonderful community. You're the best.

Thank you, readers, for loving my characters just as much as I do. I'm so grateful for you.

ABOUT THE AUTHOR

JESSICA THERRIEN spent her youth in the small town of Chilcoot, California, high up in the Sierra Nevada Mountains. In this town of nearly 100 residents, with no street lights or grocery stores, there was little to do but find ways to be creative. Her mother, the local English teacher, inspired her to do all things artistic, and ultimately instilled in her a love for language.

Her Children of the Gods trilogy has been translated and sold through major publishers around the world, such as Editions AdA (Canada), EditionsMilan (France), Dunwich Edizioni (Italy), and SharpPoint Press (China).

Aside from her Children of the Gods series, Jessica is also the author of Carry Me Home, The Mercenary's Daughter, and a kid's picture book called, The Loneliest Whale.

Jessica currently lives in Southern California with her husband and their three children.

You can visit her online at

WWW.JESSICATHERRIENBOOKS.COM

ALSO BY JESSICA THERRIEN

THE MERCENARY'S DAUGHTER

"A hugely entertaining novel. It pulls you in and doesn't let you go."
—**TOM O'CONNOR**, SCREENWRITER *of*
THE HITMAN'S BODYGUARD and IRONBARK

"One of the coolest and downright fun books I've read in a while."
—**TOMMY WIRKOLA**, WRITER/DIRECTOR *of*
HANSEL & GRETEL: WITCH HUNTERS and DEAD SNOW

"Completely compelling. The pages might rip from turning them so fast."
—**NEIL TOLKIN**, SCREENWRITER *of* LICENSE TO DRIVE
and THE EMPEROR'S CLUB

When Special Ops recruit, Tara Kafee is dishonorably discharged, there's only one place to go—Home.

But there's more waiting for her there than she's ready for.

It's been four years since she's been back and ten since her mother walked out on the family never to be heard of again. She's determined to rekindle things with her father and keep him close. That is, until he goes missing.

Soon after stumbling upon a safe room full of weapons, fake passports, and a mission's dossier marking a target in Cuba, she reluctantly accepts the help of her angsty teenage brother. He's the only one she can trust, so together, the two set out for Havana.

Tara is determined to get her father back, whatever it takes, but things are never easy when you're the mercenary's daughter.

"A riveting page-turner. Jessica Therrien broke my heart into a million pieces—and then put it back together again. This book will haunt and uplift readers long after they turn the last page."

—KAT ROSS, best-selling author of The Midnight Sea

CARRY ME HOME is a work of fiction inspired by the true story of a teenage girl's involvement in several Mexican gangs in San Jose and Los Angeles. The members of her crew call her, Guera, Spanish for "white girl" and it doesn't take long for her to get lost in their world of guns and drugs.

* * *

Lucy and Ruth are country girls from a broken home. When they move to the city with their mother, leaving behind their family ranch and dead-beat father, Lucy unravels.

They run to their grandparents' place, a trailer park mobile home in the barrio of San Jose. Lucy's barrio friends have changed since her last visit. They've joined a gang called VC. They teach her to fight, to shank, to beat a person unconscious and play with guns. When things get too heavy, and lives are at stake, the three girls head for LA, seeking a better life.

But trouble always follows Lucy. She befriends the wrong people, members of another gang, and every bad choice she makes drags the family into her dangerous world.

Told from three points of view, the story follows Lucy down the rabbit hole, along with her mother and sister as they sacrifice dreams and happiness, friendships and futures. Love is waiting for all of them in LA, but pursuing a life without Lucy could mean losing her forever.

www.ingramcontent.com/pod-product-compliance
Lightning Source LLC
Chambersburg PA
CBHW020555310726
48979CB00008B/1226/J

* 9 7 8 1 9 5 2 1 1 2 4 7 8 *